SHOULD THERE BE A NEW CAST OF ACTORS FOR STAR TREK?

IS CHRISTINE CHAPEL TOO GOOD FOR SPOCK *AND* KIRK?

WILL STAR TREK IV OPEN WITH THE BIGGEST COURT-MARTIAL IN FEDERATION HISTORY?

These are just a few of the conundrums debated in this all-new collection of articles from *Trek®*. You'll explore the complex relationships that keep the crew of the *Enterprise* working together as a brilliant unit, learn the origins of Star Trek from ancient mythology to the turbulent 60s, play the game of "what's next?" with movie experts, and travel through the ever-expanding Star Trek Universe on a voyage of discovery to keep the dream alive.

THE BEST OF TREK® 9

W9-AOT-601

More Science Fiction from SIGNET

(0451)

☐ THE BEST OF TREK edited by Walter Irwin & G.B. Love. (116828—$2.50)
☐ THE BEST OF TREK #2 edited by Walter Irwin & G.B. Love.
(123689—$2.75)
☐ THE BEST OF TREK #3 edited by Walter Irwin & G.B. Love.
(130928—$2.95)*
☐ THE BEST OF TREK #4 edited by Walter Irwin & G.B. Love.
(123565—$2.75)*
☐ THE BEST OF TREK #5 edited by Walter Irwin & G.B. Love.
(129474—$2.95)*
☐ THE BEST OF TREK #6 edited by Walter Irwin & G.B. Love.
(124936—$2.75)*
☐ THE BEST OF TREK #7 edited by Walter Irwin & G.B. Love.
(129776—$2.75)*
☐ THE BEST OF TREK #8 edited by Walter Irwin & G.B. Love.
(134885—$2.95)*

*Prices slightly higher in Canada

Buy them at your local bookstore or use this convenient coupon for ordering.

NEW AMERICAN LIBRARY,
P.O. Box 999, Bergenfield, New Jersey 07621

Please send me the books I have checked above. I am enclosing $_____
(please add. $1.00 to this order to cover postage and handling). Send check
or money order—no cash or C.O.D.'s. Prices and numbers are subject to change
without notice.

Name _____

Address _____

City _____ State _____ Zip Code _____
Allow 4-6 weeks for delivery.
This offer is subject to withdrawal without notice.

THE BEST OF TREK® #9

FROM THE MAGAZINE FOR STAR TREK FANS

EDITED BY WALTER IRWIN AND G. B. LOVE

A SIGNET BOOK

NEW AMERICAN LIBRARY

NAL BOOKS ARE AVAILABLE AT QUANTITY DISCOUNTS WHEN USED
TO PROMOTE PRODUCTS OR SERVICES. FOR INFORMATION PLEASE
WRITE TO PREMIUM MARKETING DIVISION, NEW AMERICAN LIBRARY,
1633 BROADWAY, NEW YORK, NEW YORK 10019.

Copyright © 1985 by TREK®
Copyright © 1985 by Walter Irwin and G. B. Love

"In Search of Spock: A Psychoanalytic Inquiry" was previously published
in *The Journal of Popular Film and Television*, Volume 12, No. 2, Summer
1984; reprinted here by permission of Heldref Publications, Washington, D.C.

All rights reserved

TREK® is a registered trademark of G. B. Love and Walter Irwin

SIGNET TRADEMARK REG. U.S. PAT. OFF. AND FOREIGN COUNTRIES
REGISTERED TRADEMARK—MARCA REGISTRADA
HECHO EN CHICAGO, U.S.A.

SIGNET, SIGNET CLASSIC, MENTOR, PLUME, MERIDIAN AND NAL BOOKS
are published by New American Library,
1633 Broadway, New York, New York 10019

First Printing, September, 1985

1 2 3 4 5 6 7 8 9

PRINTED IN THE UNITED STATES OF AMERICA

ACKNOWLEDGMENTS

Grateful thanks are due, as always, to the many, many people who have helped to make this ninth collection possible:

Sheila Gilbert of NAL, our stalwart editor. Leslie Thompson, Bill and Pat Mooney, Elaine Hauptman, Chris Myers, Texas Al Davis, and the rest of our friends and fans.

Our contributors and our faithful readers. Without them there would be no *Trek*.

Special appreciation this time around to Joyce Tullock, Ingrid Cross, and the rest of the fans in Baton Rouge for their hospitality and kindness during a visit and also during *Deltacon I*. We had a great time!

Thanks again, everyone!

CONTENTS

INTRODUCTION

Thank you for buying this ninth edition of articles and features from our magazine, *Trek*. We know that you'll enjoy this collection just as much as you did the previous eight.

We think we have an unusually fine mix of subjects this time around; a mix which we feel reflects the continuing growth and ever-expanding diversity of Star Trek fans and fandom. You'll learn about the trials and travails of publishing a fanzine; a doctor of psychiatry will take an intensive look at Mr. Spock and how and why we relate to him; a teacher will tell you about his college class devoted to Star Trek; Nurse Christine Chapel is profiled; and you'll read speculations on forthcoming movies and readers' thoughts about *Star Trek III: The Search for Spock*. And much, much more. As always, we've tried to choose articles and features which will be interesting, exciting, educational, and maybe just a tad controversial.

If you enjoy the articles in this collection and would like to see more, please turn to the full-page ad elsewhere in this volume for information on how you can order and subscribe to *Trek*. (And, please, if you have borrowed a copy of this volume from a library, copy the information in the ad, and leave the ad intact in the book for others to use. Thanks!)

And if you have been stirred to write an article or two yourself, please send it along to us. We would be most happy to see it, as we are always on the lookout for fresh and exciting new contributions. You may be encouraged to know that *all* of the contributors featured in this volume sent us material after buying and reading one of our earlier collections. If you feel your skills are not up to writing a *Trek* article, but you have a good idea for one, please let us know about it. If we like it, we'll assign it to one of our regular contributors and give you credit when it's published.

We *want* to hear from you in any event. We carefully read every piece of mail that we receive; we welcome (and heed!) your comments, suggestions, and ideas. (For example, many fans indicated they'd like to have us comment upon or answer letters in our *Trek Roundtable* section. So now we do. The updating of the Star Trek comic book article and the Christine Chapel article included in this volume are also both in response to reader requests.) Let us know what you're thinking about Star Trek, the films, science fiction, even the world in general. (Please, however, remember that we can't give you the addresses of Star Trek actors or forward mail to them. We also can't help anyone get a Star Trek novel published; nor do *we* publish Star Trek fiction. If you send us a story or novel, it's just a waste of time and postage.) We really look forward to hearing from you, however. Mail from our readers is the only way we have of knowing if we are doing a good job, and presenting the kind of Star Trek articles and features you want to see.

If you'd like to submit an article, obtain information about back issues, or just write to say hello, our address is:

TREK
2405 Dewberry
Pasadena, TX 77502

Again, many thanks, and we hope you'll enjoy *Best of Trek #9*!

WALTER IRWIN
G. B. LOVE

A SPECULATION ON STAR TREK IV

by Tom Lalli

As much as those of us who were privileged to watch the original series loved our weekly doses of Star Trek, there was one pleasure which was largely denied us: We were given very little in the way of episode-to-episode continuity, and therefore did not have the fun of wondering what was to happen to our heroes next. In short: no cliffhangers. The advent of the films (especially Wrath of Khan) *changed all that; now the game of "What Next?" is just about the major preoccupation of fans. You'll find lots of that throughout this collection (and those to come), but it's nice, once in a while to present an article devoted to such speculating, like this one by Tom Lalli.*

"Curiously, though the Star Trek world appears in disarray because of this film, the opposite is intended. Spock is back. The only thing now missing from the matrix is a ship and exoneration. That's an easily solvable dilemma. I'm sure you can guess the directions for *Star Trek IV*."

The man speaking is Harve Bennett, the driving force behind *Star Trek II: The Wrath of Khan* and *Star Trek III: The Search for Spock*. And he's right—the dilemma is easily solvable. The question is, if the problem is resolved in, say, the first half hour of the film, then what will *Star Trek IV* be *about*? And is it possible that these problems, of a ship and exoneration, might not be solved at all?

We will deal with the latter possibility first. Could *Star Trek IV* be about the court-martial of Admiral Kirk and his crew, and their subsequent escape and flight to the stars? *Star Trek IV* would then be doing just what *The Search for Spock*

11

did, which was to pick up the pieces of the previous film (*Wrath of Khan*) and rearrange them (which prompted a *Mad* magazine spoof entitled "Star Trek III: In Search of Plot"). It is not only the comments of Mr. Bennett which make this unlikely. For one thing, Admiral Kirk and his fellow conspirators will almost certainly not be jailed, even if a court-martial is held and they are found to be guilty. Given their past records, and the fact that they have saved the galaxy countless times, the public would be wholly on the side of our heroes. Unless the Federation, which has always been a just government, has changed radically, a court-martial is unlikely. Kirk had a similar problem in "Amok Time," another episode in which he disobeyed direct Starfleet orders to get Spock to Vulcan for a ritual which would save his life. As we know, it took all of thirty seconds to escape that predicament, with the helpful intervention of the Vulcan matriarch T'Pau Star Trek IV could begin in similar fashion, with an influential Vulcan, perhaps the Priestess T'Lar, intervening on behalf of Kirk and his friends. Starfleet surely realizes that a court-martial, after the success of the mission to save Spock, would be highly insulting to the Vulcans, and possibly damaging to relations. No one wants this to happen. It is not even out of the question that the crew might receive a hero's welcome, after resurrecting the famous Vulcan and stealing a Klingon ship to boot. Despite this, many fans are speculating about what would once have been sacrilege—suppose Kirk and company become outlaws, with their own ship and their own mission?

One thing is clear . . . such a scenario would change Star Trek drastically. Which is not to say that the Star Trek movies have not already altered Gene Roddenberry's original version, for they certainly have. The original Star Trek was about the exploration of outer (and inner) space. In the three Star Trek films, there has been *no* space exploration to speak of. In the television series, we were constantly visiting alien planets and meeting their inhabitants, and we never saw twenty-third century Earth. In the movies, *most* of the planetside activity occurs on Earth, and the only new aliens we see are usually in the background (token aliens, as it were). But still, the format of Star Trek has not yet been altered beyond repair. If Kirk and his crew are welcomed back into the Starfleet fold in *Star Trek IV*, as Mr. Bennett suggests, they could be granted a new ship and a new mission. Star Trek could then return to its roots, and get on with the mission of "boldly going where no man has gone before." If the characters are to be made fugitives from Federation justice, however, this would entail a serious revision of our view of the Star Trek world. The focus would shift totally onto the characters, and the hopeful vision of the Federation and its Starfleet, which is so important to Star Trek, would be destroyed. So, although the crew may not ever return to the "mainstream" of Starfleet, it is unlikely that they will be outlaws, either.

Further evidence that *Star Trek IV* will not linger on the loose ends of *The Search for Spock* comes from an interview with DeForest Kelley in which he said that the new film will probably "get right into an exciting story." In other words, the film will not feature a drawn-out court-martial. It will also not linger on Spock's condition, though there will probably be some minor aftereffects of the mind meld between Spock and McCoy. As Mr. Bennett says, "Spock is back." After all, the last two films have been surrounded by speculation and controversy concerning Spock's condition, and another round of that would be simple overkill. We saw in "Return to Tomorrow" that Spock could share consciousness with another (in this case Nurse Chapel) without either party suffering any side effects. On the other hand, he pointed out in "Is There in Truth No Beauty?" that such melds may result in "loss of separate identity." Nevertheless, most of the evidence indicates that Dr. McCoy and Mr. Spock will be back to their old selves.

It is not as easy to dismiss the possibility of serious consequences to the crew for stealing the *Enterprise*. Why, one might ask, should they get a hero's welcome when one was so conspicuously absent after the encounter with Khan? It is very possible that Starfleet has been keeping the exploits of the crew *secret*—either for security reasons, or to prevent Admiral Kirk from gaining too much power, or both. James Kirk has not had the full approval of Starfleet Command for his action in *any* of the three Star Trek films, and it may be that the bill is finally coming due for his unauthorized escapades. If it is true that the public does not know of Kirk's successes with V'Ger, Khan, the Klingons, and Spock, then it is up to Starfleet to decide how to handle the renegades. And Starfleet has changed since the days of the television series. The security guards on starships are now equipped with armor. Dr. McCoy was immediately arrested and committed to an insane asylum when he tried to buy passage to Genesis. And, most important, it appears that Starfleet is no longer interested in exploration, only defense. Perhaps the fleet no longer has need of these middle-aged explorers; perhaps the leave which the crew was put on in *The Search for Spock* was meant to be a permanent one. In this case, *Star Trek IV* would probably contain one of Jim Kirk's impassioned speeches in favor of exploration and the quest for knowledge. We may get to see a confrontation between Kirk and a Starfleet high official, like the one that was supposed to occur in *Star Trek: The Motion Picture*. And he will have the help of the Vulcans in his fight, for they will surely not go along with any Starfleet plan to hush up Kirk's most recent adventure. With that kind of influence on his side, Kirk should find it fairly easy to at least avoid punishment, and one would hope that the crew will finally get the hero's welcome they so richly deserve.

Whether or not they will be given another ship is another matter. As *Starlog's* David Gerrold has pointed out, there have been indications that Headquarters wants to break up the old gang "once and for all." Just what is the crew's status with Starfleet? How many missions are they allowed? One element of *The Search for Spock* which may give us a clue is the ease with which the *Enterprise* was stolen. It may be that Starfleet decided to allow Kirk to take the ship, on the off chance that he really could revive Spock. It is also possible that the Federation knew of Klingon activities near Genesis, and was using the *Enterprise* as bait to get information. As is documented in Richard Mangus's article "The Secrets of Star Trek" (*Best of Trek #7*), there are several instances in the television episodes when Starfleet may have sent the *Enterprise* crew on a mission without informing them of all the dangers. This may have been the case in "Where No Man Has Gone Before" and "The Ultimate Computer." If Starfleet Command was allowing Kirk, CIA-fashion, to engage in a mission for which he was responsible, his success would make any disciplinary action unlikely. Perhaps Starfleet actually knew that Commander Kruge was the Klingon agent in the area, and figured that Kirk could whip him even with half a ship. *Star Trek IV* may see Kirk and his crew continuing in this role of secret agents for the Federation, which would be an acceptable compromise between returning to the original mission and becoming outlaws.

All this talk of a new ship raises another question: Does the crew want a new ship? The supporting characters are not yet "over the hill," and they most likely will want to be reassigned. The only possible exception is the fatherly Mr. Scott, who has nothing to keep him from his tech manuals now that his beloved *Enterprise* is gone. Nothing, that is, but his intense loyalty to Admiral Kirk. If Kirk goes on another mission, Scotty, Uhura, Sulu, and Chekov will join him. The same, of course, goes for Mr. Spock (if he *is* back). Although he may eventually have plans to finally follow Sarek's wishes and join the Vulcan Science Academy, or perhaps follow in his footsteps and become an ambassador, Spock's devotion to Jim Kirk comes first. Leonard McCoy's situation raises another question—age. He is the oldest of the gentlemen, and a reminder that the issue must soon be addressed, and some new blood brought in. Of more immediate concern is the question of whether or not Dr. McCoy can still function as a starship's chief surgeon. The answer is a definite yes. He is as vital and as full of life as ever, and is fully capable of taking up his old duties as a Starfleet officer. And though he may be tempted to retire to a life as an "old country doctor," McCoy would not let Jim Kirk go on a mission without him. As a dying McCoy says in "For the World Is Hollow and I Have Touched the Sky," "Without me, Jim? You'd never find your way back!" Thus, Admiral Kirk will have his old crew at his disposal.

But does Jim Kirk want to go back into space? This may seem like a silly question, since it was not long ago that McCoy and Spock were urging him to get back his command for his own good. But that was before *The Search for Spock*, before the destruction of the *Enterprise* and the death of Kirk's son. Jim may want to rethink his position, and at least rest up and let his wounds heal. Another important factor is that Kirk no longer has the "mistress" which has so long kept him from women. We have been told so many times that it is the *Enterprise* which keeps him from having a "flesh woman to touch, to hold," that it would be illogical for him not to have a lasting relationship now that the ship is gone. Unless, of course, there is a new ship waiting to take its place. Ironically, this seems the most likely scenario, that Admiral Kirk will assemble his crew on a new ship, perhaps a new *Enterprise*. Paramount realizes that most people are not going to pay five dollars to see Kirk, Spock, and McCoy sit around and say, "Remember the time . . ." One would hope, though, that there is a realistic gap between *Star Trek III: The Search for Spock* and *Star Trek IV*, to give them all a chance to recover from their adventure.

How will this transition occur? An alternative open to Starfleet would be to punish and reward the crew at the same time. They could do this by reducing each conspirator one rank. Uhura, Chekov, and Sulu would become lieutenant commanders, Scotty a commander, and Kirk would be a commodore and thus eligible for starship command. If Starfleet wants to reassemble the crew on a new ship, this would be an effective method. Starfleet might want to do this if the hostilities between the Federation and the Klingons and/or Romulans which were hinted at in *The Search for Spock* actually began. Kirk would want to follow in the footsteps of Garth of Izar, the great military strategist who is his hero, and Starfleet would certainly welcome his help. We have been told that the Klingons are "suing for peace in Organian space," and there may be retaliation for the crimes of Commander Kruge. On the other hand, the Organian Peace Treaty would prevent any open warfare between the powers, and it is more likely that covert activities will occur. Kirk may be sent to combat the Klingons' claim to the Genesis Planet, as he has already proved his skill in such matters in "The Trouble with Tribbles." Or he may be given the *Bird of Prey* for an espionage mission into Klingon or Romulan space, similar to that in "The Enterprise Incident." There are precedents in the series for "secret missions" for Kirk and his crew, and using such a plot would cause no breach in continuity.

Outright war with the Klingons would create a serious continuity gap, however. Such a development must be avoided if Star Trek is to remain distinguishable from the space-war movies which proliferate today. If the Klingons are to figure at all in *Star Trek IV*, it should be only as an invisible threat. They have already been used in the movie far more than they ever were in the television series, and the failure of the witless Kruge to provide Kirk with a worthy opponent argues for finding another villain.

If an alien race is to be featured in *Star Trek IV*, the Romulans would be an excellent choice. The Romulans have always been a more interesting people than the Klingons, and they are the only major race which has not appeared in the movies. Including the Romulans would also open up some intriguing possibilities for the half-Romulan Lieutenant Saavik. Perhaps she might be curious about the other race of her birth, and become involved with a Romulan. This could lead to a division of her loyalties between her Vulcan mentor Spock and the Romulan ways. The relationship between Spock and Saavik should be explored further. Perhaps Saavik will nurse Spock back to health, returning the favor Spock did for her after her brutal childhood. Robin Curtis, who portrayed Saavik in *Star Trek III: The Search for Spock*, made this interesting comment on the relationship: "Her devotion to him is *beyond* the ordinary . . . there is a certain effect Spock has on Saavik which has more to do with male-female feelings." Saavik had no choice but to help Spock through his *pon farr(s)*, but apparently she did not mind doing so. This brings us to one of the most obvious prospects for *Star Trek IV*, namely that Saavik will bear a Vulcan/Romulan/human baby. If this happens, what will her relationship be with Spock, who is once again old enough to be her father? Do such age differences matter to twenty-third-century Vulcans? Only the creators of *Star Trek IV* know for sure, but it is very doubtful that Paramount would allow such a relationship, which would seem (but not *be*) incestuous.

Summing up, we can detect a probable direction for *Star Trek IV*. The movie will begin with the exoneration of the conspirators. Spock and McCoy will have recovered, though each may retain some of the other's idiosyncrasies (to their mutual annoyance, of course). If Lieutenant Saavik appears in the film, she will probably not be killed off, and will thus become the first new character to survive three Star Trek films. The original crew will remain together, and it will be necessary for them to obtain a ship. How they accomplish this depends mainly on Admiral Kirk's status with Starfleet Command. If Starfleet is serious about retiring the *Enterprise* crew, Kirk will be forced to get his own ship. This might make him an outlaw, and the crew will then have to fight off the Federation along with any enemies they encounter. In this scenario, *Star Trek IV* might end with another great victory for Kirk, perhaps against the Klingons or Romulans. Starfleet might then finally agree to give Kirk a new ship and another mission, which he would either accept or reject (depending on William Shatner's plans). If Starfleet does not want to officially retire Kirk and his crew, but also does not want them on a starship, they may become secret agents for the Federation. The third possibility is that Starfleet will welcome Kirk and Company back into the fold, and give them a new *Enterprise* (or perhaps the *Excelsior*). Whether their new mission will be one of exploration or defense remains to be seen. Whatever happens, it is very likely that Kirk will have some kind of conflict with Starfleet in *Star Trek IV*, and we will thus learn more about the upper echelons of that organization.

Star Trek IV should be a self-contained adventure which completes the trilogy begun by *Wrath of Khan*. It should tie up all the plot elements that originated in that film, including Genesis and Spock's condition. And it should introduce some new, permanent characters to join Lieutenant Saavik as the future crew of Star Trek. This would give each of the actors an opportunity to make a clean break with Star Trek, if they wish, and give the creators of future Star Trek adventures the freedom to return to the original format. Only time will tell whether this course will be taken. Paramount may want to stick with the original cast as long as they are moneymakers, and might resist any new characters. The last two Star Trek films have consciously focused on the characters, and it may be that Star Trek will return to its original format only when it returns to television with a new cast. And Star Trek will eventually return to television, just as Sherlock Holmes and Frankenstein are continually revived . . . they have become permanent parts of our cultural mythology. In the meantime, though, we can look forward to another adventure with the original cast in *Star Trek IV*.

STAR TREK FANS—
THE BLIND SPOT

by Janeen S. DeBoard

You want controversy? You want an argument? You want Star Trek fans shouting at each other? You want to know the single issue about which Star Trek fandom is most divided? Simple: Just casually ask any fan what he or she thinks about doing Star Trek with a completely new cast. We guarantee you'll get an answer. A vehement, no-holds-barred, possibly loud, and very, very definite answer.

We here at Trek, *however, prefer to be more genteel. When the following article arrived, one of your editors averred, "This is one hundred percent right!" The other editor scanned the article and demurred, "This is one hundred percent wrong!" What does Jan DeBoard have to say about the controversy? Read on. . . . But please, no shouting, okay? There's enough going on here at the* Trek *offices!*

I was thirteen years old when Star Trek first premiered, and so that puts me into what I believe is a minority in Star Trek fandom: someone who watched and loved the show when it first ran on prime-time television, and who has kept up with it ever since through the animated series, the books, the conventions, and, finally, the motion pictures.

I was a fan in 1966 and I'm still one now; the characters have become old friends of mine, as they have for so many of us.

So many of us. This is a great part of what makes Star Trek unique, the fact that it is not, now, the creation or property of any one individual. The living essence that we call Star Trek is the end result of the thoughts and contributions of many, many people.

In the beginning, of course, there was Gene Roddenberry. But he knew, without having to think about it, that he alone was not Star Trek. It took the combined efforts of a lot of different writers, directors, actors, technicians, etc., etc., etc. And above all, it took courage, for when the time came that Gene Roddenberry could no longer produce Star Trek for us—the reasons why are unimportant—other hands took over. They did not always do as well, perhaps, but what matters is that Star Trek *lived*—it was not killed off under the guise of "no one can do this show except its creator." And we did learn, later, that other producers and directors are capable of turning out our mythology of the future to near-perfection, as did Harve Bennett and Nicholas Meyer with *Star Trek II: The Wrath of Khan.*

Where would we be now if we had refused to accept anyone but Gene Roddenberry as the producer of Star Trek?

The same is true of all of the Star Trek books and stories which appeared after the end of the television series. Suppose that only one person—it wouldn't matter who—had been allowed, under copyright, to produce further Star Trek fiction for publication. Think of the enormous gap that would be left in the Star Trek universe, the loss of the vast overview which we now have of these characters—all of it gained by having many people, not just one, examine and interpret them. We have everything from the strangeness of Marshak and Culbreath to the first-class polish of Vonda McIntyre to read, think about, and talk about—endlessly. And who knows how many fanzines and fan stories have been written, each adding its own ideas to the legend that is Star Trek?

The point is that in almost any area you can think of, the creative influence of diversity has touched Star Trek. The new music presented in the films, incorporating both old themes and new, has added greatly to the drama and feeling of the motion pictures. The beautifully refitted *Enterprise* is nothing more than a reinterpretation of this "character." The new uniforms reflect very well the respect and dignity which Star Trek has acquired over the years.

Change and growth, innovation and experiment—these are the things which have kept Star Trek alive for all this time. Nowhere in Star Trek—not in its writing, producing, directing, costuming, scoring, or special effects—has variation for the sake of keeping Star Trek a viable entity ever been resisted.

Except for one aspect:

The casting.

Fans who welcome a book by a new author or a film by a new director will screech in horror at the very thought of a new actor playing the role of any Star Trek character—even if it means condemning that character forever to exile or even death. No one new must be allowed to take on the role of Kirk, Spock, or McCoy; when it comes to the motion pictures, they are permanently closed to any other actor's interpretations.

It would be wonderful indeed if our favorite actors and actresses could go on portraying our friends for us indefinitely, but logic tells us that this simply cannot be. Actors grow old, they play other parts, they have other concerns (which are often none of our business). If William Shatner, for example, should no longer wish to do Star Trek, that is fine, that is his decision.

But should James T. Kirk have to die because of it?

If we never find the courage to allow someone new a chance, then we will be forcing these characters of our future mythology to grow old and die long before their own time, the twenty-third century, can arrive. Their yet-untold stories, countless in number, will never be seen; the generations which follow ours will never see any new films with these classic and irreplaceable characters. They will have new ones to watch and follow, to be sure, but they will not have Star Trek as it has been for the past nineteen years.

Step back into the past for a moment.

Suppose that in Shakespeare's time a very popular and talented actor had taken the part of Hamlet every time the play was produced. So great was his skill, so charismatic his personality, that when the day came that he was unable or unwilling to perform the role again the production of Hamlet was forced to close because audiences would accept no one else in the title role. What a great loss that would have been . . . for as we know, *Hamlet* was kept alive, and was even performed in space for the crew of the *Enterprise*.

A prime example of a character kept alive by a series of different actors is Sherlock Holmes. Although there were other actors who played Holmes before he did, Basil Rathbone played this role in the best films. He became firmly established in the part; audiences expected to see him and no one else. But as time went on and the stories remained popular, audiences wanted to see them despite the fact that Rathbone could no longer be Holmes for them. Was Sherlock Holmes killed off? Were the films and plays simply no longer done? Were new characters introduced to "carry" new stories through the same setting? Did the producers think that it was more important to get one particular actor than it was to once again bring a classic character to life?

Of course not.

By the galactic center, it was Leonard Nimoy himself who eventually came to play the role of Sherlock Holmes!

We are fortunate that a past generation was not so selfish as to deprive us of the character simply because its favorite actor was not available for the part.

Hamlet. Sherlock Holmes. Dracula. James Bond. King Arthur. Tarzan. Superman. How many times have you seen these classic characters played by different actors? Naturally, everyone has a favorite, but did seeing a different face from time to time really spoil the magic for you, or make the character any less real?

Would you rather not have seen them at all?

Over and over again, the lesson is the same: The character must continue, even though the actor who brings him to life may change.

This brings us, naturally, to the question of Robin Curtis as Lieutenant Saavik.

What we saw in this case was not an example of miscasting, nor is it proof that no new actors should ever play Star Trek characters.

What we saw was an actress who was ill prepared for her role.

By her own admission, Robin Curtis is not a Star Trek fan. She has seen none of the films or episodes, read none of the books. Apparently, she made a point of coming into the film "cold," so that she would have no preconceived ideas about what Saavik should be like, and therefore be a "clean slate" for her director.

She couldn't have been more wrong.

In most cases, whenever an actor is called upon to play a difficult, unusual, or unfamiliar role—a blind person, say, or a prehistoric barbarian, or any famous historical figure—that actor will spend considerable time in research and practice in order to play the role to the best of his or her ability. Marc Singer studied the ways of the blind before beginning *If You Could See What I Hear*; Arnold Schwarzenegger made a point of reading "Conan" stories and practicing horsemanship and swordplay before taking on the role of the barbarian. And anyone who is set to play a famous person from history is going to be sure to gain the proper background before attempting it.

Robin Curtis was given the task of playing the popular and well established character of Lieutenant Saavik—who is, no less, an alien. And yet, evidently because she did not want to have her portrayal of the role compared to Kirstie Alley's, she did no research, no homework of any kind, in preparation for it.

If she was truly so concerned about such a comparison that she could not watch *Star Trek II: The Wrath of Khan*, she could at least have read the excellent novelization of that film. This would have given her the background necessary for a proper portrayal of Lieutenant Saavik. She would have known that Saavik is not a pure Vulcan, always cool, logical, and seemingly emotionless; she could have brought out the fiery disposition and volatile temperament that are every bit as much a part of the character.

Curtis seems to be a capable actress and, admittedly, did bring a certain sensitivity to the role. We can hope, however, that in the future such ignorance and pettiness will not get in the way of Star Trek or any other stories.

As this is written, the *Enterprise* has been destroyed and her crew is in disgrace, little better than a band of outlaws. Their careers are ruined, and if they do return to Earth, it will only be to face charges of mutiny, sabotage, assault, grand larceny, and the galaxy knows what else. The end has already begun.

In view of this, who would not want to see Kirk, Spock, McCoy, Sulu, Scotty, Chekov, Uhura, and all the rest as they were in their youth, fresh from the Academy, each making his or her maiden voyage into space? Or Spock's life on Vulcan before he joined Starfleet? Or Kirk's first command? Or the countless other adventures of this time, which are at present unknown to us?

What did happen, anyway, during those last two years of the five-year mission? And at the end of it? And after the mission to V'Ger?

The only way we can ever hope to see these or other new motion pictures about the crew of the *Enterprise*—even if Kirk does somehow get back his ship, his crew, and his commission—will be if we allow new, younger actors and actresses to play the parts for us.

William Shatner, Leonard Nimoy, DeForest Kelley, and all

the other cast members of Star Trek have given us a marvelous gift: They have brought these characters to life with such skill, have given them such well-defined personalities, philosophies, and idiosyncrasies that new and capable actors and actresses could easily take on the roles and make them live for us again. This is the mark which a good actor leaves; this is the stamp of characters who do not deserve oblivion!

Thanks to these contributions, the characters now transcend any actor or actress, just as they have always transcended any writer, producer, or director. By using the dramatic device of flashback, we need not deprive ourselves of the delights of having the *Enterprise* whole and beautiful again, her crew once more the best in Starfleet. Or by picking up where *Star Trek III: The Search for Spock* leaves off, we can continue to explore Lieutenant Saavik as well and learn the fates of Kirk and his crew and follow any further adventures they may have.

How many years—real years, our years—might all of this take? It took some eighteen years to produce eighty-two "episodes." We must be prepared to allow the changes in casting to take place as they are needed if we want to keep Star Trek alive for more than just a few more months or years.

Star Trek could easily be just as popular in twenty, fifty, or a hundred years as it is today. It will be a tragedy of our own making if we deprive the next generations of the enjoyment and endless discovery of Kirk, Spock, and McCoy; of the eternal symbolism which is *Enterprise* and her crew.

How will the fans of the future feel about *us* if they look back to find that we insisted on destroying the heart of Star Trek instead of carefully preserving the magic we claim to love so well, simply because its cast was all too human and grew old?

As long as the stories continue to be well written—and we know that many people can write excellent Star Trek—and the new cast members care enough to properly research their roles, our timeless characters need not ever die. They can live on into new generations, as befits them . . . into the twenty-third century, and beyond.

BROTHER, MY SOUL: SPOCK, McCOY, AND THE MAN IN THE MIRROR

by Joyce Tullock

We've found that we really don't have to say much in these introductions to Joyce Tullock's articles. In fact, we kind of suspect that most fans just skip over them in their rush to read the article itself. Joyce is back again with an intense look at the eternal but ever-changing relationship between Spock and McCoy. Sound like the same old thing? If you think so, then you're not familiar with Joyce Tullock's work.

Star Trek is a saga of contraries. From its most obvious episodes to its most subtle, it consistently deals with the problems of our universe in a dual perspective. It's as if it were the very personality of man himself. It won't let us rest, in fact, for the very nature of the series (including the movies) has been a desire to face the positive/negative aspects of life and find a central ground. Even its main three characters are a kind of diplomatic equation; Spock and McCoy, the opposing natures of man, Kirk that "central ground." But in Star Trek's desire to take us along on the five-year mission—to discover not only the universe of space, but the universe of inner man—it has taken us on a very complete adventure in the greatest contrary of all: the logical and emotional mind of man.

In all the discussions of contraries, opposite viewpoints, and differing perspectives, we see a running theme. We see aliens who seek to be understood, we see evil that might not be so evil if viewed from another perspective, we see monsters who turn out to be more beautiful than beastly. Finally, we see difference and try to understand it. That's the magic and the heart of Star Trek, or any good science fiction.

And for many, the best of Star Trek involves this discussion of difference—sometimes referred to as "the unknown." But good science fiction always strives to make a human point by employing a somewhat nonhuman perspective. An attempt, perhaps, to discover the "unknown" within each man by taking the view outside of himself. In Star Trek, the very heart of this science fiction theme lies in the Spock/McCoy relationship. An unusual relationship which Leonard Nimoy once short-sightedly referred to as being the same as the Doc/Festus friendship of television's long-running *Gunsmoke* series. Nimoy came close, but he now himself admits that there is much more to the Spock/McCoy relationship than meets the eye. It is the perfect starting point, too, for a discussion of the way Star Trek deals with the complexities of the human mind.

Spock the alien is the aloof, quiet-minded sophisticate. Raised in a tradition of order and aestheticism, Spock grew up to be very much his father's son, a scientist dedicated to the concept of logic as a way of life. But it also fits into Star Trek's theme of contraries that Spock should choose to rebel, and against his father's wishes, join Starfleet. His reasons for this decision are, on the surface, unknown. In all other ways Spock seems to admire his father, and in "Journey to Babel," he struggles in his own way to gain his father's approval by choosing the course of greater logic over the feelings of a son for his father. He resists McCoy's pleas that he provide blood for his father during heart surgery, maintaining that to do so would take him away from his task as acting commander of the *Enterprise*. (Kirk has been wounded by a spy, and is temporarily unable to captain the ship, which is in danger of attack.)

Of course, this episode gives us some good Spock/McCoy stuff. We see the doctor, the "mere" human, openly feeling inferior and inadequate for the task he must undertake (more of that Spock/McCoy "man in the mirror" stuff). Sarek is dying, and McCoy, who has never performed heart surgery on a Vulcan, must now do so. There is an irony in this episode involving the emotion/logic theme in the Spock/McCoy relationship. At first, McCoy refuses to operate because he feels his lack of skill might endanger the patient. Then, when he gets his emotional, very "human" feelings of inferiority in hand, he knows he must operate and is willing to go ahead, but Spock refuses to take part, claiming (on behalf of logic)

that he has more important duties. Oh well, it's probably
really quite in character that the two are out of synch!

In this particular episode the Spock/McCoy conflict is rein-
forced by the presence on the ship of Amanda, Spock's
all-too-human mother. She backs up McCoy's point of view
where Spock's resentment of emotion is concerned. She reminds her son, not only in words, but by her very presence,
that he too possesses the qualities of being human. And by
giving the audience a flesh-and-blood Spock's mom to look
at, Star Trek accomplishes a mighty task. It gives Spock's
conflict and his half-humanness a very real backdrop on
which to build the character as a whole. Spock was, of
course, a well-established character in Star Trek by this time.
Nevertheless, Amanda and Sarek have continued to play a
very important, even magnificent part in the Star Trek mythology ever since, even to the point of becoming well developed in the amateur fan literature which began some time
after the series' demise. Jean Lorrah's works on Sarek and
Amanda are especially fine examples of what could be done
with characters who had appeared so briefly in the series.
And when we finally see Sarek again in *The Search for
Spock*, Mark Lenard's portrayal of him is so huge and powerful that his short part in the film seems somehow larger,
overshadowing even the performance of William Shatner.

Sarek and Amanda's marriage is a natural example of Star
Trek's tendency to seek a consolidation of differences and
understandings between peoples. Here we have two beings
who, by tradition, ethnic background, and even genetics, are
diametrically opposed—and yet they find a haven and a life in
one another's company. It is beautiful—a marriage which
defies all the rules of Sarek's logic, of Amanda's human
desire for overt sentiment. They have obviously found a place
which is neither of logic nor of emotion. It is likely that
neither has compromised beliefs to find that place. They have
simply grown together so closely, so trustingly, that they
have learned that there is another way to be.

In this way, Star Trek has provided a first step in a long
journey, toward an idea which must indeed take form in the
real world: the idea that great differences can be resolved to
the benefit and betterment of all involved.

But what of Spock? What did the marriage of Sarek and
Amanda do for him? Was it all good? It demanded, for one
thing, that he, evidently the first Vulcan/human, be born into
a world which was not entirely his. He quite literally was an

experiment in the consolidation of opposites and the unbiased blending of differences. Born of an important Vulcan sophisticate and his Terran wife, Spock no doubt started out in life as an oddity, rejected (so Amanda implies in "Journey to Babel") by his classmates and peers, probably not totally trusted or accepted by his father's friends and associates. As if Vulcan life was not lonely enough, Spock was an alien in his own world.

So Spock had to prove himself. It is too bad, in a way, that McCoy could not have known him as a child. (And remember, the original series plans called for Spock to be about a hundred years old. Strange to think, isn't it, that McCoy and Kirk could have been over fifty years his junior? But perhaps we should here dismiss the original concepts of Spock's age. Star Trek's writers and producers seemed to have abandoned it way, way back. And surely if Spock were really about a hundred by the time he joined the crew of the *Enterprise*, he would have already had enough life experience to have "found himself" as he finally does in *Star Trek: The Motion Picture*.) McCoy, had he known the young Spock, would no doubt have interfered enough in his upbringing to give him a clear example of the glories of being human. But to be fair, it is unlikely that a young Leonard McCoy would have been a good example. Even as a mature adult, the devil sparkles from his eyes. No, it's just as well that Amanda, with her human grace and wisdom, was the one to carefully guide Spock on behalf of human kind. She tried her best to give Spock a positive picture of his own half-human, half-emotional nature. She reminded him, no doubt, of his heritage as best she could.

But Spock had to live in a Vulcan world, not a human one, so, like all of us, he developed as best he could in order to be accepted, in order to be a part of the society around him.

Perhaps the knowledge of that can lead us to understand more about the Spock/McCoy relationship and how it works to bind two such "contrary" characters into an unlikely friendship. It's a funny thing about Spock and McCoy. Though their relationship is not very often the focal point of an episode, its undercurrent is so strong, so subtly pervasive, that it stands out in the memory of even the "fringe" Star Trek watchers. There is a reason for this, and we will get to that in a moment. (And wouldn't it have been nice, just once, to have seen an episode in which these two are thrown together alone for a good length of time in a hazardous or troublesome situation, where they could have discovered the "selves" in one another more openly. I suspect it would have happened if the series had been allowed to continue, or if it hadn't been necessary to give Mr. Shatner so much film time. We "almost" had it in "The Tholian Web," but someone somewhere along the line evidently felt that the audience only wanted to see the two of them bicker and make up.)

Leonard Nimoy and DeForest Kelley work well together. It is clear that they have great understanding and respect, not only for the characters each portrays, but for the character of the other. Perhaps that is part of that heretofore "unsung" Kelley/Nimoy magic: They each appreciate and perhaps even envy the character of the other. As actors, each clearly enjoys what the other does with his character—and they like to see that character do well. This makes for good underplaying of a delicate friendship. (Kelley's class and ability to underplay are his crowning glory in *The Search for Spock*. Though many scenes in that movie were his, they were also Spock's. Kelley never forgot that, and he played it that way. It is his finest work.)

Because Nimoy and Kelley have taken the time and effort to understand what the contrast of their respective Spock/McCoy characters is all about, they have gradually established that offbeat friendship as one of the major, if less swashbuckling, themes of Star Trek. In fact, we can pretty safely say that Kelley and Nimoy, more than any of the writers, producers, or directors of Star Trek, are primarily responsible for the development of that friendship. Some of the finest moments in film have come across this way—more through the patience and understanding of the creative mind of the performers than through anything blatantly intentional. And in a recent interview, Kelley reveals how closely he and Nimoy worked on the Spock/McCoy friendship, and that they would have liked to have done more were it not for Shatner's demands.

But the fact remains, regardless of all the nit-picky attitudes that may get in the way, that Nimoy and Kelley have worked consciously and unconsciously to create one of the most worthwhile, complex, and enjoyable subthemes in Star Trek. They have portrayed for us the existence of the differences within us all: the man in the mirror. With insight and warmth, they have taken part in the creative process, becoming true authors of the mood of friendship in Star Trek. They have taken the raw clay of Spock/McCoy and molded it into something very fine.

More important, they have provided, in Star Trek, the kind of theme which can either be enjoyed on the surface (the Spock/McCoy, Doc/Festus clashing of temper and wits) or appreciated on deeper thematic levels. The Spock/McCoy personality is itself a theme in Star Trek. An old theme, placed on science-fictional terms to make it all the more effective. As the "literature of ideas," science fiction and fantasy are extremely fertile grounds for the study of human personality. And it may be a lucky coincidence that Kelley and Nimoy seem to have a keen interest in the kind of acting which delves into the inner workings of the character. They both had a gut instinct for their characters . . . and what they mean to one another. There is no doubt that their portrayals of their respective characters are greatly responsible for the gradual script development and enhancement of the Spock/McCoy theme. After all, when Star Trek began, it was generally thought to be William Shatner's show . . . a fact which, whether Shatner accepts it or not, changed markedly, very soon.

Even as early as the first season, writers were taking advantage of the Spock/McCoy "feud" by allowing it to develop into something deeper. While in most first-season episodes the two seem to spend more time bickering than anything else, we do see a gradual development. We see them learning about themselves (and so, each other) in episodes like "Miri," "City on the Edge of Forever," and "Operation Annihilate." Not to say there is anything all that profound in the Spock/McCoy friendship in the first season. There isn't. But in the episodes mentioned, we do see the development of the McCoy character. We see his inner workings a bit more (the troubled McCoy of "City," the self-sacrificial McCoy of "Miri" who tries the antidote on himself).

In "Operation Annihilate," McCoy and Spock come closer than ever before in the sense of the mirror personality. Spock's courage in the face of pain is one of the main themes of the episode, as is McCoy's desperate struggle to save the Vulcan. And when the doctor experiences failure and (with a little encouragement from Kirk) guilt for having blinded Spock, we see his very, very human capacity for a kind of self-indulgent pain. When the doctor thinks he's responsible for blinding the Vulcan by acting too quickly to remedy his ailment, he becomes morose. It would seem outwardly ironic that Spock is the one who tries to reassure him. Ever so logically, he reminds McCoy that it is better to be blind than dead.

Could it be that Spock here is acting the part of the rational human mind? And that McCoy is portraying the emotional part? Why not? If you look at Star Trek as something more than just another action/adventure TV show, then it's hard to ignore what's going on here. We have the two most basic parts of the human personality juxtaposed. The ability to reason, the need to feel. And, by giving us clear, sometimes painful portrayals of the Spock/McCoy personalities, could Star Trek also be presenting us with a study of our own selves?

As a reader and writer of Star Trek articles and fan fiction, I've had occasion to talk to fans about this. It has been a favorite, secret topic of mine, one that seemed worthy of study. And over the years I've heard two recurring tales from Spock and/or McCoy fans. From avid McCoy fans I hear stories like this: "I was an isolated individual, shy, not used to admitting my feelings openly. But as I got into Star Trek, and watched McCoy work on Spock, I began to listen to him and apply what he was saying to myself. It's as though, in speaking to Spock, he was also talking to me. After a while, I began to look at myself more objectively. Maybe some of the things McCoy was saying to Spock applied to me as well. I began to examine my own outlook on life and open up a little bit. This may sound silly, but somehow McCoy made me like myself a little more. He also made me appreciate people more."

From the Spock fans, it goes something like this: "I guess I'm a Spock fan because I've never been a person who has a good deal of control over my emotions. I'm like McCoy gets sometimes, hot-headed, too quick with a sharp word. But watching Spock, seeing how he handles McCoy, I began to try to use logic to deal with my problems. And even if I can't be as logical as Mr. Spock, I admire his ability to keep in control in pressure situations. I guess I envy him a little."

It all seems to boil down to this: "I admire McCoy's ability to be open, to show his feelings." "I admire Spock's ability to use logic to solve his problems."

Now, when you put those two qualities together, you certainly do have the two most important aspects of the human personality. Put in the very simplest of terms, you have emotion and logic. And it happens that in Star Trek, as in real life, you can't really survive happily unless you have a fair capacity for both.

And sometimes I'll hear from an individual who relates that the "dueling personalities" of Spock and McCoy remind him of himself. It's as though Star Trek had provided people with a split-frame view of the human personality and allowed them to examine it without inhibition.

If this all makes Star Trek sound very therapeutic, I think, at times, that it is. There's nothing very startling in that. All good entertainment is a kind of therapy. In fact, that is its reason for existence.

Talking about "dueling personalities" . . . That's really how the Spock/McCoy friendship got started, most noticeably in the first season in an episode called "The Galileo Seven." In this episode the two quarrel viciously (or at least McCoy does). McCoy comes down hard on Spock throughout, in a manner that nowadays seems out of character. But that's only because the characters were still developing at this early stage. In so many words, Spock is accused of being heartless, insensitive, ambitious . . . and maybe not so logical as he'd like to be. All because our poor, noble Vulcan is doing his damnedest to save the crew and the stranded shuttle, Galileo Seven! But the pattern is established throughout that Spock is the one who acts on logic, and unlike McCoy, will not let his feelings get in the way of his judgment.

McCoy is very much "the heavy" in "Galileo Seven" where his interaction with Spock is concerned. And you'd be surprised how that upsets people! Especially those fans who think of Spock as only a superhero type. As for McCoy—thematically, he can get away with being nasty once in a while. He's so damned human, it's in his nature. If he gets cranky or blows his stack we tend to forgive it in him as we would forgive ourselves. It's natural for humans to "lose it," and we accept it, but when Spock of Vulcan does something "illogical"—look out! Some fans find it absolutely unacceptable, even insisting that it must have been an error on the writer's part.

Spock does something "illogical" in "Galileo Seven." He takes a chance when all else has failed. The shuttle is in a helpless position, unable to contact the mothership, the *Enterprise*, and so as a last-ditch effort, Spock ignites the last of the shuttle's fuel, causing a blast of power which is meant to tell the *Enterprise*, "We're here! Help!" The odds of the *Enterprise's* receiving Spock's dramatic message were . . .

well, we don't even want Mr. Spock to figure those for us. Let's just be glad it all worked out.

Nevertheless, Spock's behavior brings a question to mind. Was his action one of emotion or logic? We all know what McCoy would say: Deep within that logical Vulcan exterior lies a human's instinct to take a chance. There's no doubt that McCoy (never one to keep cool in a crisis) was more than a little pleased by Spock's very human behavior at the end of the episode. And while Spock insists that his last-ditch effort was really an act of logic, we find a kind of irony in knowing that it was in fact a very "McCoy like" thing to do. Humm . . . is the cranky doc actually getting to him a little bit? And so early in the series?

Maybe, maybe not. But in episodes like "The Galileo Seven" and "Operation Annihilate" we can see that Spock is certainly getting to McCoy. The Terran physician seems to have been in the fleet for a few years, but somehow Spock has more of an effect on him than the average alien. There may be a reason for this. To McCoy, the physician, the psychologist, Spock is no more classified an "alien" than Uhura or Sulu are classified as part of the "third world." Spock is an intelligent being, a patient, and gradually, a friend. Spock's Vulcanness doesn't bother McCoy—his humanness does!

Like Spock's mother, Amanda, McCoy wants the Vulcan to appreciate his own human heritage. It's very likely that McCoy even believes that of all the crew of the *Enterprise*, only one is a true bigot: Mr. Spock. For in rejecting his own human half, he is rejecting his Terran heritage. He is virtually saying to Kirk, McCoy, and the others, "You are my inferiors."

McCoy just doesn't seem to be the type to sit still for being called an "untouchable."

And yet, when you really think about it, he allows Mr. Spock to get away with a great deal. It's as though the doctor senses that the Vulcan needs someone to "berate." At least that would serve to make him a bit more human. So McCoy serves as a kind of therapeutic punching bag; someone with and to whom Spock can express all his rational and irrational fears about the state of being human. Like so many of us, Spock is terrified of being human, and more than anyone else aboard the *Enterprise*, McCoy seems to understand that. He understands it so much that he insists on calling Spock out on it—as would any good psychologist. Spock's struggle with his human nature has become such an important theme that it has now been the backdrop for two of the Star Trek films: *Star Trek: The Motion Picture* and *The Search for Spock*, although it might be more appropriate to say that *The Search for Spock* is specifically about Spock's struggle (and powerful friendship) with Dr. McCoy.

But in the first season episodes we see more of McCoy's view of Spock than Spock's view of McCoy. McCoy just doesn't seem to be a topic of discussion for those first season writers. They were too busy giving Kirk the lines and scenes Shatner wanted, and Spock the lines and scenes the fans wanted. No time for the eccentric ex-cowboy from the South. McCoy's main purpose (with a few exceptions, like "City on the Edge of Forever") seems to be that of providing tension—which he does well from the season's first aired episode, "The Man Trap," to its last, "Operation Annihilate." In some of those episodes, in fact, you're not all that sure which side the doc is on. He blusters, threatens, pouts, and explodes with a stubbornness and impetuousness which is almost a caricature of the McCoy of later episodes.

No doubt about it, McCoy had some growing up to do—and it is to DeForest Kelley's credit that McCoy did grow tremendously. He certainly got little help from script writers and producers. But McCoy had one thing going for him all along which none of the other characters did, not even Kirk.

McCoy had Spock. He had the Vulcan's continuous inner struggle with his human half. If Star Trek writers were going to explore the Spock personality, they needed some poor sap there to be the mirror of the mind, "emotional brat," the "friendly antagonist." Kirk couldn't do it. Nobody would believe it. Kirk was his friend! They needed a mirror-man to help Spock (and so the viewers) explore the humanness within himself. And for that, they needed a character who could be at once sympathetic and abrasive. They didn't need a hero, they needed an actor.

It's been said before, but it bears repeating here: Leonard McCoy is the most keenly developed, most well-rounded and complicated character of Star Trek. He has the advantage over Kirk and Spock in that he is not a hero as the Saturday matinee goers define heroism. His knees shake and his stomach quivers . . . and sometimes he wishes he were back home. And that makes him rea¹ enough, human enough, to represent that "other" side of th man-in-the-mirror friendship of Spock/McCoy.

As Spock, in many ways, is the man we would like to be, McCoy is the man we are.

Now, of course, some fans don't like that. They don't even like to "think" that they should relate to a character who is ill-tempered, sharp-tongued, distrustful, who can be openly afraid, who admits to feelings of inferiority, who . . . well, the list goes on. The being that Bones McCoy is doesn't appeal to those who turn to a hero for self-image. Nor has the good doctor won friends and influenced people by his open honesty with the good Captain Kirk. They see him (as have certain Star Trek writers, directors and producers) as being "too hard on Kirk." Many excellent scenes have been axed at the outset by persons who so identify with the captain that they cannot stand the thought of McCoy facing him with that powerful, often too-forceful honesty. McCoy sees too clearly, it seems, for the Saturday matinee audiences. And as we view the pulp-oriented Star Trek of the eighties, we can't help but wonder if the doctor belongs there at all.

The second season of Star Trek opened with "Amok Time." McCoy certainly did belong there. It was the doctor who first observed that something was troubling the Vulcan when Spock began to suffer the symptoms of *pon farr*. Unlike Kirk, who thinks of his friend Spock as being almost invincible, McCoy knows that he is, in essence, no different from anyone else. McCoy knows that the Vulcan has a breaking point, has weaknesses. It is only natural. And what concerns him throughout Star Trek is Spock's seeming denial of his own fallibility. McCoy is again the mirror-man, who sees the danger of that "other" part of the self: the logical, achieving part. The part which says, "I must succeed, I cannot be found out a failure." The part in each of us which, with all its logic, illogically maintains that fallibility is a sign of weakness. As if there were some great sin in being less than perfect.

As in *The Search for Spock*, the tension between Spock and McCoy is purposely underplayed in "Amok Time." The two are at odds, but quietly, and for one simple reason: each knows the other very well. Perhaps it's because they are men-in-the-mirror that they can see through one another's facade so easily. Kirk, for example, is too convinced of Spock's overall superiority to notice that there is a problem, while McCoy has been concerned about it for some time. Indeed, he's tried to get the Vulcan in for a checkup—only to be threatened ("You will cease prying into my personal affairs, doctor, or I shall certainly break your neck!").

But don't feel sorry for Bones on that count. Nothing could please him more than seeing the Vulcan blow his cool! Just once, even!

That fact seems to bother many Star Trek fans. And again we'll hear complaints about this or that episode where "McCoy was too hard on Spock." Poppycock! "Amok Time" is a perfect example of how McCoy's supposed "roughness" on the noble Vulcan is actually just the opposite. It is the truest sign of friendship.

Look at it from McCoy's point of view. He is a doctor, a friend (as Spock goes out of his way to acknowledge in "Amok Time"), and in a figurative way at least, he is the emotional side of that man-in-the-mirror who is Spock/McCoy. He has a deep, perhaps instinctive need to speak to the logical Vulcan from his own emotional perspective. At this stage in Spock's life, the only way he can experience emotion is through the man-in-the-mirror. McCoy, quite frankly, is his tutor.

He is shaking Spock to wakefulness at times, as one would shake a friend out of a dangerous stupor. It all makes even more sense if we look at it figuratively, digging a tiny bit below the surface of any given episode. Just as we'd dig beneath the surface of our own waking mind to find the secrets that lie within. So let's put aside our human prejudices for a time and think of Spock and McCoy not as two characters, but as a single mind, not totally human, not totally alien—one half ruled by the unswerving, comforting laws of logic and order, the other half its opposite, ruled by feelings that run deep and sometimes chaotically with impulse and emotion.

The cool, green-blooded Vulcan. The fiery, red-blooded McCoy. One may well represent our future, the other, most certainly our present. Together, on a figurative level, they could, indeed, represent those aspects of the mind which deal with logic and emotion. Like any single mind, they have their ups and downs, but mostly they work together well.

It's the popular thing these days to speak of the aloof Mr. Spock—his nobility, his isolation, his grand heroism in the face of a strange, often threatening universe. But the circumstances of Star Trek give one cause to wonder if that is so completely true. After all, our Vulcan is the embodiment of logic in a world where logic, order, and science have come to reign. From the "mental" perspective, he should be more at home on the *Enterprise* and in the twenty-third century than his mirror image, Dr. McCoy. Most of the time he is. His logical, scientific mind virtually lives and breathes the work to be done on the *Enterprise*. He thrives in the science of research. Yet, there are times (such as in "Amok Time") when we know all is not in perfect balance. We detect a loneliness, perhaps even a fear which, put in everyday terms, is childlike and vulnerable.

Could it be that the Spock we see at such times is the Spock of the figurative Star Trek? The "logical" half of the mirror-man? Look at him in "Amok Time": frightened, nearly out of control because of his lack of understanding of the ways of passion. And look who discovers his problem first: McCoy, the other half of the mirror-man. Here, perhaps, representing that part of the mind which recognizes, accepts and appreciates the passions of love and sex. In that case the "emotional mind" of "Amok Time" is quite literally taking charge, doing its best to handle that for which the "logical mind" is inexperienced and unprepared. The "emotional mind" does indeed take over in this episode of Star Trek, because it is in "its" territory. McCoy is able to save both Kirk and Spock at the end of the episode by injecting Kirk with a neuroparalyzer (to stimulate death, thus ending the "fight to the death"). He acts here as a passionate man, a friend, who is so "comfortable" with his feelings of love and fear that he can act for the good despite their influence. His mind is not "clouded" with emotion, but directed by it.

We see it happen again in many other episodes. Emotion takes over where logic fails, logic takes over where emotion fails. In "The Deadly Years," when Kirk, Spock, Scotty, and McCoy are exposed to radiation which causes rapid aging, Spock's logic carries the burden as long as it is physically able, but as the confusion of old age hits him, he is deeply troubled and distrustful of his own mind. In short, he's not used to being forgetful, or intellectually fatigued. But McCoy, always the emotional and erratic one, seems the least susceptible to senility. Well . . . maybe we should put it this way: If he's becoming senile, it doesn't bother him much. In his own, emotion-guided way, he takes his aging in stride. Of all who are affected, he alone retains the capacity to laugh at himself.

And if ever there was a clue to the most valuable aspect of human emotion, McCoy has just hit on it. McCoy, unlike Spock, has the ability to laugh at himself. And a man who knows enough not to take himself too seriously has a mighty edge indeed . . . regardless of what time he is living in!

But even that is not enough, in this century or in the twenty-third. McCoy knows that, and despite his stubborn outward desire to "put logic in its place," he recognizes that Spock's devotion to logic and order is to be respected, even envied by the supposedly more "sensitive" humans. McCoy, the emotional side of the mirror-man, has learned some hard lessons. He has grown to understand.

But McCoy hasn't learned the easy way. The emotional half, after all, is the part which has learned the fine-tuned and very intricate rules of the "game" of caring. So when it comes up against a strange, undiscovered "new" way of being—the way of logic—it faces a kind of psychic shock. Why is McCoy at first so leery of the Vulcan, Spock? Because while Spock is half human, he does not play by McCoy's "rules" at all. He doesn't even think much of them. And in his own, icy, standoffish way, Spock ridicules (without benefit of true experience) the very essence of McCoy's emotional being. It becomes a clash of souls.

It seems that as far as Mr. Spock is concerned, McCoy can do nothing right. Roles are strangely reversed. McCoy, the man of old Earth, is out of his territory, blasting into the unknown on a Starfleet ship built by the science of mathematics and logic, dedicated to the kind of discoveries most appreciated by the physical sciences. One wonders, at times, as Spock must have wondered in the early days: Why is the doctor even there?

But we discover, along with Spock, why McCoy is there. We see him wrestle with the mighty force of pure logic, we see it change him, mature him, guide him to believe at last that there is, indeed, something "more than the universe." Gradually, as the series develops, McCoy's distrust of Spock's logic becomes a grumbling admiration. Not only does the doctor see through Spock's outer facade of isolationism, he begins to understand that they are not so different after all. And McCoy will doubtless not forget that often it was as much Spock's logic as Kirk's courage which saved the day. In fact, in every episode from "The Man Trap" to *Star Trek: The Motion Picture*, Spock employs logic to help find the answers. But through his adventures Spock learns to work his logic carefully where McCoy is concerned. McCoy, it seems, must be dealt with on rather unusual terms. His friendship is a puzzle . . . even to the Vulcan.

In "Bread and Circuses," McCoy confronts Spock in one of his most angry, dramatic moments. He challenges Spock to "feel"—dares him to admit that he feels the human bonds of friendship for Kirk and himself. And when he chides Spock, saying that he "wouldn't know what to do with a genuine human feeling," the Vulcan takes it with a calmness and steady-mindedness that serves the mirror-man two ways. It shows McCoy, once and for all, that he is wrong. That if Spock at one time did not feel for his friends, he does now, despite the pain (and perhaps even shame) it causes him. Secondly, Spock's tremendous self-control provides a buffer for the powerfully emotional Dr. McCoy. Seen from outside, as a single mind working to keep balance, we can see that logic saves the entire spirit from a kind of hopeless self-destruction. Its purpose now, with the Spock/McCoy man-in-the-mirror, is to save the whole, when the part might cause serious damage.

Think back to some of the angriest moments of your life, whether it be anger with a loved one or heated frustration with traffic. Haven't you just once wished you could do or say something regrettable in a moment of anger? Something violent, irrevocable. Kind of makes you appreciate that logical side a little more, doesn't it?

Spock-the-prophet of *Star Trek II: The Wrath of Khan* gives McCoy a warning when the doctor gives way to one of his outbursts of emotion. They are discussing the horrible potential of the Genesis Device, and McCoy blasts angrily at Spock, saying, "Logic? He's talking about logic! We're talking about universal Armageddon!" Spock listens as a friend, clearly now enjoying McCoy's outburst, almost as one might relish the freshness of an unexpected thunderstorm. Then, with almost offhanded calmness, he issues a friendly warning:

"Really, Dr. McCoy. You must learn to control your emotions. They will be your undoing."

No kidding, Spock. No kidding.

Because Kirk's emotions are more tempered with logic (he is not part of the mirror-man), he was able to deal with Spock's death. He faced the pain and found reason to go on with his life. As Spock would have wanted. McCoy, on the other hand, was nearly dealt a death blow. Figuratively, without the "other side" of the mirror-mind, he was lost. As representative of the man of our own century, in Spock's death McCoy lost something which was too important. He lost Future; the part of the mirror-mind that represents the ability to control destiny.

At first, he was buried in grief, and in the turbolift scene which was cut from the third film, he showed that grief to Kirk. Maybe, if we're lucky, we'll get to see it someday. We only get a hint of it in *The Search for Spock* in an early scene where Kirk mentions his concern with the crew's "obsession" with Spock's death.

But that's just McCoy's luck, isn't it? It turns out he isn't so much "obsessed" as "possessed." Why is it that so often those horrible things that befall the emotional side of our natures turn out to be for the best? And why is it we can only see that after the emotional pain is over?

I suppose old Spock, if he'd been in a more corporeal condition at the time, would have calmly brought McCoy's own words back to him. "Remember, doctor, a little suffering is good for the soul."

McCoy's soul, coexisting with Spock's, is suffering as never before. And Kelley, under Nimoy's insightful direction, plays it with taste. (Though there must have been a few good laughs about the doc's situation between takes!) And through McCoy's journey of the mind, we discover the profound connection which has really always existed between Spock and McCoy. In *Star Trek II: The Wrath of Khan* we saw, in a few good scenes, Spock's gentle affection for the crusty, outspoken Earther. We see that Spock genuinely enjoys McCoy for the man he is and that he seems to represent something of unspoken value to the Vulcan. After the V'Ger experience, Spock has learned to respect the intense existence that is the emotional McCoy. He knows now that McCoy has presented him with the best of humanity and that, despite the doctor's human failings, man has not been found wanting. He appreciates McCoy—as we all learn to value that part of us that dares to feel . . . that part of us which makes us civilized. Perhaps, on some deeper level, the Vulcan has come to understand that McCoy has contributed so much to his own "emotional upbringing" as to be considered a psychic part of him. Perhaps in this one way, McCoy has become closer to Spock even than to Kirk. Certainly no two beings understand one another better than Spock and McCoy.

In *The Search for Spock*, McCoy becomes all. He is the mirror-man complete, struggling for survival in a world which doesn't even believe in his existence. (As Kirk's superior told him, "I never understood Vulcan mysticism, Jim.") It is a death struggle supreme, a battle to achieve peace, at the least, and the survival of the soul, at most. It may seem strange to some fans that McCoy was "chosen" to carry the soul or *katra* of Spock, but not when seen from the literary or interpretive sense. No good writer would have it any other way. There's just too much fertile ground, too much to explore, too many questions which can be touched upon, then left for the individual mind to discover more deeply. That's what science fiction, the "literature of ideas" is all about.

This all provides groundwork for another article, I suppose, on the Friendship of the three—how it works, and why Kirk can truly say that to have left Spock on Genesis would have meant to destroy his own soul. He knows about the mirror-man, all right. And he knows that the mirror-man, while not dependent on him, is still essential to his existence. He is tied to Spock and McCoy just as all the cosmic laws of the universe are tied to one another. His perspective is different; based on a greater balance now than either Spock or McCoy. He is the one in control, the one who dares to save this "new being" created by the meld of Spock and McCoy. He knows his friends well enough to accept that together, they just might be capable of pulling off a miracle. Always the Prometheus and the man of adventure, he senses the greatest discovery of all, and risks everything to achieve it: the discovery of Immortal Soul. Kirk, the true adventurer, represents in *The Search for Spock* that part of the human mind which has so far saved us from self-destruction. He believes in the friendship of the three of them, even when there is only reason to doubt McCoy's sanity, only proof of Spock's death. He is the "pure knight" of *Star Trek III: The Search for Spock*, the one capable of finding the chalice. Lucky for us that Kirk has always been the one to dare to reach outward, beyond Doubt . . . that ancient enemy of man's divinity.

The real beauty of McCoy's "sacrifice" in *The Search for Spock* is its human, down-to-earth perspective in a space-age setting. For on close inspection, McCoy's sacrifice is no sacrifice at all. As part of the mirror-mind of Spock/McCoy, his effort to save Spock is almost instinct. An act of survival. He is bound to Spock now through the meld in such a way that to separate their minds—other than through the Vulcan ritual of refusion, *fal tor pan*, would mean insanity and ultimate death. Like any man, he dwells, within the mind, in his own universe of life experiences. He cannot dwell eternally with that other universe that is Spock. There is too much subjective experience, translated—for the lack of a better word—as "difference," between any two minds, even the most tolerant, for long-term coexistence. That's why the Vulcans are so reluctant to perform the mind meld: to do so is to intervene in another's complete universe and to impose your universe on him! A painful, dangerous experience.

For McCoy, separation from Spock is the only answer. And it must be done carefully, for Spock is now virtually a part of him. His inner balance has been disturbed, then changed, so that to suddenly rip away the Vulcan's *katra* would be as destructive as allowing it to remain. This also serves to reinforce the concept of the mirror-man. On a figurative level, logic and emotion are separate functions, critically interdependent. To rip one carelessly from the other, just as to allow one to dominate the other, means insanity, psychological death.

So McCoy's stewardship of Spock's *katra*—his ultimate "sacrifice" on the altar of logic to Spock's rebirth—was simply the practical, natural thing to do. He didn't do it for Spock, although Spock must have known (at the time of the meld) that he was willing to, or he wouldn't have placed his *katra* with McCoy. McCoy did it for himself. To survive. And so mankind has taken another step. It has discovered that the "need" to give is a selfish thing. A matter of survival. It is a kind of evolution. A discovery, at least, of the necessity to care for one another . . . because it is logical.

In Star Trek, trust and friendship are practical concerns. Spock trusted McCoy with his soul, and his reward was the greatest gift of all: McCoy's open confession of friendship. And for all his blustering about "Vulcan logic," when McCoy found Spock had entrusted his essence in the most human hands for safekeeping, he held tight to that powerful and frightening "logical mind" . . . and carried it gently home.

It was the logical thing to do.

AND THE CHILDREN SHALL SUE

by Kiel Stuart

*A recent letter asked, "Just who is Kiel Stuart, anyway?"
Well, among other things, Kiel is director of the North Shore
Women Writers Alliance, and the assistant editor of* Undinal
Songs, *a collection of fantasy stories and poetry. Some of the
abovementioned "other things" include a raucous sense of
humor and an abiding affection for Star Trek. Those two
things are the reason why Kiel's parodies of Star Trek episodes continue to be among the most popular features in our*
Best of Trek *collections.*

*Hey, do you remember Gorgan the Friendly Angel? Thought
he was funny before, did you? How does the saying go? You
ain't seen nothin' yet. . . .*

Captain Jerk was already a little bit cranky and slightly on
edge when the *Enteritis* got a distress call from the Science
Stuff research team on the planet Tri-X. Had he possessed
any degree of clairvoyance at all, he might have spent that
day curled under blankets, sucking his thumb, instead of
charging to the rescue.

Tri-X was a regulation-issue blasted heath, not at all convenient to shopping, churches, and schools. When Jerk beamed
down with the landing party, he could see straight off that
something was amiss.

The clearing was littered with the bodies of research
scientists.

"Oh-oh," said Jerk.

Still alive, but looking as if he had just swallowed an entire
box of prunes, one scientist rose, gabbled a warning, and

pitched forward into the dust with a rattling wheeze. Lilies bloomed on his chest.

Dr. McCrotch knelt. "He's daid, Jim," he drawled, poking the corpse.

"I can see that," snapped Jerk, adding up the number of forms to be filled out, in triplicate. Great. "But why is he dead?"

"Y'all think *these* might've had somethin' to do with it?" McCrotch indicated several empty vials labeled "poison," which the dead scientists were still clutching in their hands.

Jerk shrugged. "I don't know. Could be, though," the captain added, as he ruminated over nearby rock outcroppings spray-painted with the warnings: Danger! Enemy Approaches! Look Out Behind You! We're In Real Trouble Now!

Suddenly from a nearby cave streamed a coterie of shrieking, giggling children. They surrounded the landing party, jumping up and down, clapping their chubby hands.

"Hi, I'm Bobby," said a gangling youth on the verge of acne. "And these are Tommy and Billy and Susie and Winky." He led the kids off to pay volleyball.

Jerk shook his head. Here they were surrounded by bodies and all they could think of was volleyball. Kids. Sure were resilient little things.

After the scientists had been properly buried, the kids set up a polo field around the gravestones.

"Funny," drawled McCrotch, "y'all would think them tykes would be a mite upset, playin' so close t' their parents' burial grounds an' all."

"Oh, you know," said Jerk. "Kids." McCrotch's comment caused him to pause, however. Could aught be amiss? Naah, he answered himself.

"Come, children," he called, "Time to beam up."

"Awww, we don't wanna," they chorused. "We wanna stay and play polo some more."

Shmuck set his jaw. "Should someone not tell the little bas—I mean, the little angels that they are dancing on their parents' graves?"

"Ah dunno," said McCrotch, leafing through a copy of *Psychology Tomorrow*. "Ah think mabbe it'd give 'em an Oedipal complex or somethin'."

"Leave it for now," said Jerk. "I'm sure nothing's seriously wrong." He wended his way to the transporter site, carefully stepping over the skull and crossbones labeled, Don't Say We Didn't Warn You!

Back aboard ship,, the gang of kids was foisted upon Nurse Chapel. She ground her teeth and tried not to reach for the paddle as they piled into one of the conversation pits, yanking her hair, smearing peanut butter on her uniform, setting off live blasting caps.

"All right, kiddies. This is the ice-cream machine." She flung a handful of cassette tapes at them. "Stick these in and get some."

They fell upon the machine, shrieking delight, jamming cassettes in, gobbling the resultant piles of sticky treats.

"Waah!" bawled Winky. "I got a trout parfait! I wanna chocolate double marshmallow cheese dip instead! Waah!"

"You can't always get what you want," spat Chapel. "How about a nice big piece of Aunt Neutrino's Neutron Star Cake? A solar system in every bite. Guaranteed to fill the black hole in your tummy."

"Naaw!" howled Winky, "I wanna double—"

"All right!" rasped Chapel, shoving the chocolate double marshmallow cheese dip cassette at Winky with twitching fingers.

In sick bay, the concerned officers were deep in conference. McCrotch hauled out a stack of reference books and explained the situation to Jerk.

"Them kids act lahk nothin' horrible's happened to their parents, and they ain't been poisoned, neither. Ah really don't think we should go pokin' round thangs we know nothin' about, so y'all oughta jess leave them be. Maybe. Ah guess."

Jerk sighed, departing for the conversation pit, to find Chapel and the kids.

"Heh, heh, put down that stiletto, Sistine," he said, hastily interposing his body between the mewling Winky and the tooth-gnashing Chapel. "Now, now. They're just a bunch of kids, and kids will be kids. You oughta know that, you're a broad." Grasping the nurse firmly, he steered her toward the ice-cream machine. "Get me a trout parfait, willya?" The heck with McCrotch's psychocological theories, he thought. Time to employ a little of that diplomacy and charm I'm so famous for.

Simpering down at Susie, Jerk said, "I bet you miss Mom and Dad now that they're worm food, huh, li'l orphan?"

Susie wrinkled her pert, freckled nose. "Mom and Dad were icky. That planet was icky."

"But Mom and Dad loved you," Jerk persisted. "And now they're pushing up daisies."

"Love is icky," said Susie, then swooped off, followed by the gang.

"Bzzz, bzzz," she intoned, "Guess what we are!"

"Juvenile delinquents," said Chapel, going for the stiletto again.

"Now, now," said Jerk admonishingly to Sistine. He scooped up the little tyke. "What are you, sweetie?"

"Killer bees!" she squawked, sticking him with one of her hairpins.

"Here!" Jerk abruptly palmed the moppet off on Chapel. "Kids. Women's work and all that," he muttered. Raising his voice over the sound of Susie's wailing, he said, "That's enough, nurse! Take them to their quarters."

He stared after the retreating mob, considering. Something odd might possibly be going on. You never could tell. But probably not, he decided as he headed back to the bridge.

The children were just as happy in their quarters. They formed a circle and began to chant:

> "All hail what we do.
> Call the lawyer, we will sue.
> Battery! Incorporate!
> Friendly lawyer, litigate!"

Suddenly, in a puff of smoke, an apparition appeared.

"Melvin the Friendly Lawyer!" they cried.

"Right," he said, adjusting his maroon polka-dot tie and the lapels of his navy pinstripe suit. "I present to you the plan. We must use this ship to reach Marcuswelby 12. There are millions of suckers there waiting for us to descend, and we shall be in clover, so do not take any guff, do I make myself clear? We will sue for palimony, we will sue for libel, we will bleed the universe dry, but in order to do so, we must take over the *Enteritis*, got me? So go forth and do that right now."

The Friendly Lawyer gathered up his papers and vanished in another puff of smoke.

Back on the bridge, Mr. Shmuck beckoned to the captain. "I have here in the records made by the Tri-X scientists. The tapes indicate their increasing anxiety, impending disasters, scary monsters, super creeps, and a lack of dietary fiber." He threaded the machine and started to run the tape.

"Interesting," said Jerk, leaning over for a better look.

Behind them, little towheaded Bobby appeared through the lift doors. Glaring at Jerk, he made a series of obscene gestures.

The tapes dissolved.

"Funny," said Jerk.

"Captain," puled Bobby, "Take us to Marcuswelby 12."

"Sorry," answered Jerk, patting the little towhead. "We gotta take you to a Starbase. Rules are rules. But don't cry. Here's a lollipop."

"But I wanna go to Marcuswelby. I wanna, I wanna, *I wanna*!"

"I think we should kill them," said Shmuck coolly.

"Hey! They're just kids," said Jerk. "We'll discuss this further in my quarters." He turned back to the wailing child. "Now, little Bobby, you stay right here on the bridge and pretend you are the captain. Won't that be fun, hunnn?"

The bridge crew beamed.

Little Bobby made another couple of high signs and changed the course to Marcuswelby. The crack bridge officers continued playing video Monopoly. "Cute," said Lieutenant Lulu.

"Cute," agreed Uwhora.

On other parts of the ship, the rest of the kids wrought similar havoc.

"Ain't dey cute?" grunted Assistant Chief Security Goon Bruno.

"Yeah, cute," mooed Top Chief Security Goon Gorgo, pausing to pat the head of Winky, who was melting the life-support circuitry.

In the captain's quarters, Jerk and Shmuck were deeply absorbed in another copy of the tape. Jerk's brow furrowed as he watched the scientists raving about enemies within, devils in the dark, and child-custody suits. "Pretty wild," he murmured. "But still, those guys were probably just nuts. I mean, they were eating an awful lot of sugary treats and I heard somewhere that sugar makes you schizophrenic or something, right?"

Shmuck heaved a long, whistling sigh, casting his eyes ceilingward.

"Well, have you got a better theory?" said Jerk indignantly.

"Yes. Whatever got them must have been swift and devastating, not to mention evil, and it is well known that evil seeks power by misleading the innocent." Shmuck casually stopped the tape in a freeze-frame of the kids. He nonchalantly pasted a big red arrow on the screen, pointing straight at the tykes.

"Gosh!" said Jerk. "Are you implying that the kids are involved?"

Shmuck zeroed in on another scene: the skull and crossbones. "According to legend," he said, "Tri-X was the home of a band of marauding lawyers, who, throughout the systems of Epsilon Indianapolis, shredded opposition and clients alike, to the last half-credit. Although the downtrodden folk were said to have arisen at last, disbarring the lawyers, legend also states that the lawyers lie in wait for fresh victims dumb enough to pay them a retainer fee."

"In that case," said Jerk, "maybe we'd better send down a couple of guys to see what really happened on Tri-X." He ran down a personnel list. "Okey-dokey . . . lessee . . . how about a security goon and a . . . right, geologist, lotta rocks down there. Shmuck, have 'em meet us in the transporter room."

Once there, Jerk issued last-minute instructions.

"Don't leave any gum wrappers lying around and try not to kill anyone unless you have to. Now wave bye-bye."

The two officers, dutifully waving, glittered away in a cloud of pixie dust.

"Oh dear," said Shmuck, "According to my readings, we no longer seem to be orbiting Tri-X. Therefore, those men were beamed into the cold black nothingness of space to certain death."

"Humm," mused Jerk. "Good thing we didn't go, eh? But someone on the bridge is in deep trouble!" They hurried off.

The kids were swarming all over the bridge, jamming chocolate bars and tadpoles into the instrument panels, dancing in a circle, chanting up the Friendly Lawyer.

Puff! He appeared, brushing off his lapels. "Habeas corpus," he droned. "The parties of the first part are on to us, so it is time for more drastic measures. Quid pro quo, we must cause their own private bogeymen to appear, and they will therefore be paralyzed with terror and rendered harmless. As I have taught you, the fear harbored deep within an individual can be turned against him to our advantage, and we shall soon be on Marcuswelby 12, knee-deep in wills, mortgages, title searches, and sequestrations." Having spewed forth enough exposition, Melvin vanished, scattering torts to the wind.

There was an uncomfortable silence. "Well, so what?"

said Jerk at last. "Mr. Lulu, just ignore anything you think you see and set course for Starbase 4."

But the helmsman sat frozen in his seat, petrified by a private and ghastly vision: Samurai Disco Maidens charged him, shish-kebabs drawn, ready to skewer.

Jerk whirled to Uwhora. "Contact Starfleece. Inform them of the crisis."

"Sure thing, honey," she purred, then stopped, terrified by what she saw in her compact mirror.

"Oh, no!" she gasped. "I've turned into Queen Victoria!"

Jerk shook her, partly to snap her out of it, partly to enjoy the topographic seismic waves.

"Captain, I be frightened," she whimpered. "Don't want to be no fat old honky queen married to no guy on no can of tobacco!"

Dropping Uwhora, Jerk backhanded Lulu. No use. "The Samurai Maidens will destroy us all if you do anything sensible!" cried the helmsman.

Even Shmuck trembled at his station. "Afterimages," he whispered, waving a hand in front of his face. "Vulgarian heebie-jeebies." In his hallucinations, the bridge crew appeared to be speaking of stocks and bonds. "This cannot be," he said. By a supreme force of will, he brought into play ancient and powerful Vulgarian mental disciplines, inserting his thumb and forefinger into a bottle of tranquilizers and swallowing the contents.

It worked. The purple haze cleared. He could hear the captain haranguing a security goon.

Little Bobby glared at the captain, focusing the rude gestures on him.

Jerk suddenly went green around the gills. He made little whistling, beeping noises.

Shmuck was at his side immediately. "We had better remove ourselves from the bridge before something awful happens."

Too late.

"Alas, poor Yorick," choked Jerk, "I . . . I . . . cannot . . ."

His eyes crossed. He reeled about, stammering, honking, bouncing off the walls. "I'm . . . I'm . . . losing . . . my . . . ability to act!"

"You never had any," murmured Shmuck, shoving him into the lift.

Jerk implanted his teeth in the handrail. "I . . . can . . . no

. . . longer . . . act . . . and I think, I think . . . that my pants are falling down as well." He peeled a large chunk of paneling from the wall and began to munch it, reciting scenes from Shakespeare and Becket and the lyrics of rock songs, all to no avail.

It was painful to see. A desperate act was called for.

Grabbing the captain's shirt, Shmuck shook him vigorously, slamming his head against the wall for punctuation. "Snap out of it," he advised.

Jerk's tongue lolled. His head wobbled. Suddenly, he jammed his nose close to the Vulgarian's. Chest heaving, lips trembling, eyes fluttering, he whispered, "Kiss me, my fool!"

Shmuck dropped him like a hot potato. "Sorry, captain, no can do. This is no cheap fanzine, and we are not in a Jerk/Shmuck story."

"Oh, okay. I'm lots better now, anyway. Now that I can act again, guess we better get down to auxiliary control and put things on manual override." He glanced into the mirror, smoothing his hair. "Gee, I bounce back quick, don't I?" he said admiringly.

They marched briskly out the door.

But Snotty had other ideas. "Get the ham-fisted, interfering idees awee!" cried the Chief Engineer. "Keep that awee frae me darlin' engines, or I will begin tae read selection fraw *'Th' Complete Worrks o' Rroberrt Burrrns!'*" He glowered at them, waving a huge volume of poetry threateningly.

"Robert Burns!" gasped Shmuck. "No, no!" He backed away, then turned and broke into a dead run.

"Well," said Jerk, "we tried."

Ensign Wackov leapt out from a shadowy corner. They pulled up short.

"Ceptain, I have been instrocketed to torture you end Meester Shmuck to death with a bad Rossian eccent!" His wig jiggled with ferocity.

"Yes, we can hear that," said Jerk, clubbing the youth over the head with a giant piroshky. "Hairbag," he muttered, then commanded, "Let's get back to the Bridge, Shmuck."

"And you've got them running around free," muttered Shmuck.

"Now come on," protested Jerk, "They're just kids."

The kids were all on the bridge, blowing their noses in the crew's hair. They set up a great yelp when they saw the captain and first officer.

"We wanna gota Marcuswelby 12, we wanna go, we wanna we wanna *we wanna*!"

"Well, you're not going, and we're not afraid of you, so how do you like that?" said Jerk. "Isn't that right, Shmuck?" Sotto voce, he ordered, "Put down that gun!"

"We are not afraid of you." Shmuck addressed the children as he somewhat reluctantly lowered his personal side-arm—a twelve-gauge, double-barreled, sawn-off shotgun of the type preferred by most anti-violence, peace-loving Vulgarians. "But your ally is afraid of us. He is a coward and shuns the legal clinics of Shylock and Lyers, where your consultation fees are always reasonable."

"What he said," added Jerk. "Go ahead, call the Friendly Lawyer. Prove it."

"We won't we won't *we won't!*"

"Captain," said Shmuck, "I can play back the reel-to-reel I made of the children calling upon Melvin. That should work admirably."

"Good idea."

A puff of smoke.

Melvin glared at Jerk. "Who summons me from small-claims court?"

"We do," said Jerk. "And we're not gonna take it. What do you think of that, buster?"

"You will shrivel before my greatness!" blustered Melvin. "Remember, I was the lawyer for late-night-talk-show host David Leatherman!"

Jerk cringed, but gravely stuck out his tongue in a defiant Bronx cheer.

"I will freeze your assets! I will read a deposition!" Melvin's jowls quivered.

"I have a swell idea," said Jerk. "Mr. Shmuck, as long as you're at the tape machine, why don't you show these tykes some home movies of their moms and dads? That ought to snap them out of it and break Melvin's power."

"I would prefer to show them the business end of a Fizzer," grumbled Shmuck.

"Now, now, Mr. Shmuck," Jerk chided, "They're just little kids."

"Do not show the films!" cried Melvin. "I forbid it! I will get an injunction to stop you!"

"Too late," said Jerk, "Grab some popcorn."

The house lights dimmed. Theme music swelled. On the

screen, scientists fiddled with test tubes and juggled petri dishes. Melvin quivered some more.

Five pairs of innocent blue eyes widened. Five freckled snub noses began to drip.

"Heh, heh!" sweated Melvin.

"Waah!" cried the kids. "Melvin killed our Moms and Dads!"

"Don't forget the chickies and kitties and puppies," added Jerk helpfully.

"Yeah! Waah! The chickies and kitties and puppies!" The kids wiped their streaming eyes on chairs, instrument panels, anything. "He's a bad man and he lied to us, waah, baw, snuck!"

"No!" Melvin was swimming in his own sweat and a pile of wrinkled documents. "We will sue them for breach of contract! We will tie them up in litigation for years! We shall prevail!"

"Bawww!" said Bobby. "You killed the puppies and we don't believe in you anymore!"

"No!" cried Melvin. "The jig is up! I'm melting!"

"Look at him!" gloated Jerk. "His pinstripes are dissolving! The polka dots on his tie are vaporizing! He's disappearing!"

"Hey!" cried Lieutenant Lulu. "The Samurai Maidens are gone. I can steer now."

"I'm not Queen Victoria any more!" crowded Uwhora. "I can put on some more eye liner."

"It seems a perfectly logical explanation to me," said Shmuck. "When the children stopped believing in Melvin, he and all his effects vanished just like that."

"Yup," said Jerk. "Happens all the time."

"My Feeler Gauges indicate that all is back to normal, Captain."

"Thank you, Mr. Shmuck," Jerk let out a long sigh and contentedly scratched his belly. He looked at the troop of sniveling youngsters, and a soft expression came over his face. Little Susie grabbed his sleeve and used it for a handkerchief.

"Well," he said, tousling the child's golden locks fondly, "now that the crisis has been averted, I see no reason why we can't tan all their little hides for being such an obnoxious bunch of precocious monsters. Mr. Shmuck," he asked as he transferred his hand to the nape of Little Susie's neck and handed the squirming child over to the Vulgarian, "would you and Nurse Sistene Chapel care to do the honors?"

"For once, captain, I shall be glad to hover in such close proximity to Nurse Chapel," said Shmuck, herding the kids from the bridge with a cattle prod.

Jerk gazed benignly at the departing throng, then turned to Lieutenant Lulu. "Mr. Lulu, set course for Starbase 4. I think I deserve a little nap after this one."

Soon the captain's snores echoed throughout the bridge, while the sounds of children being made to respect their elders wailed up and down the corridors of the *Enteritis*.

STAR TREK IN THE CLASSROOM

by Jeffrey H. Mills

Did you ever wish that you could major in Star Trek in college? Or at the very least, take a class wherein Star Trek was discussed seriously, enthusiastically, and on an adult level? Well, some time back students at Oberlin College in Ohio got just such an opportunity, thanks to the efforts of Jeffrey Mills. He tells us something of his experiences guiding a class of eager students through discussions about Star Trek and its "cultural relevance." We think you're really going to enjoy this article, and we suspect that it just might stir enough interest so that similar classes may appear in colleges and universities throughout the nation.

Imagine meeting twice a week for three months with twenty other people who are as delighted by or intrigued with Star Trek as you are: you watch episodes and talk about the development of the characters, you debate the significance of Federation principles and institutions, you discuss the importance of Vulcan philosophies and seek to understand the relationships between the world of the twenty-third century projected on the screen and the world we live in today. Sound like ecstasy?

Well, it *was* ecstasy, of a sort, for me to be able to bring all of the above to a group of students at Oberlin College in Ohio. Like many schools in the Midwest and elsewhere, Oberlin has an academic organization that allows students and townfolk to offer classes of varying subjects to other students and townfolk (and occasionally professors)—sometimes for credit, always for fun and the delight of learning. Thus, it was in spring of '84 that I taught a course through Oberlin's

Experimental College (EXCO) called "The Cultural Relevance of Star Trek."

Why would I want to do such a thing? And what *is* the cultural relevance of Star Trek? (These two questions were asked me eternally throughout the course of the semester when people discovered that it was I who was teaching *that course*.)

When the EXCO catalogs first came out, the appearance of something called "The Cultural Relevance of Star Trek" was greeted by a fair amount of laughs. "This is to be a serious study of the popular television show, Star Trek," my course description began. (Giggles.) "By looking at the characters, cultures, institutions, and events of the Star Trek universe, we will examine the various social, historical, moral, political (etc.) implications—or the *meaning* behind Star Trek." (Belly laughs, some rolling on the floor.)

In short, my course offering was responded to by many with cries of "Come on—let's get serious" (my intention exactly) or "Oh, God, those Trekkies are at it again."

I have always been fascinated by the fact that for every person who can't get enough of Star Trek there is another person who cannot get too little of Star Trek. There are quite a few people out there who despise everything about the show and who feel deeply offended if they are forced to watch even the tiniest fragment of an episode. I have never really understood these people (and they aren't always the same folks who hate science fiction in general) nor the great love-hate relationship between Star Trek and the viewing public that they help to create. As Spock would say, it is like nothing I have encountered before.

It wasn't these people I hoped to attract to my course—they would never sign up. There is another class of viewers that I hoped to attract. These are people who watch Star Trek and poke fun at it—filling in key moments with their own dialogue, pointing at alien makeup and costumes (pajamas, of course), laughing at tender moments and suggesting alternative motives to explain the actions of the heroes and villains on the screen. If you've ever watched Star Trek with a crowd on a public television, especially on a college campus, you know the type.

Along with the true fans of Star Trek, it was these people I had hoped to attract to the course. In fact, I got the idea for the course and the incentive to teach it while sitting through one of those public viewings. All around me there were people competing with one another to insert the best line the next time Kirk opened his mouth to speak. These viewers, I feel, do not understand Star Trek. They see a series of plot events tied together by a pretty neat ship, funny costumes, an arrogant captain, an eccentric doctor, and "that mellow pointed-eared dude." They do not see, and thus cannot appreciate, the things that Star Trek is saying—sometimes blatantly, more often with subtlety—about being human and living in society. Without understanding there can be no appreciation or learning. I had hoped to change that through "The Cultural Relevance of Star Trek."

As you readers and true fans of the show know, Star Trek is sophisticated. Despite the restrictions of prime-time television, Gene Roddenberry and his creative core (the writers, directors, production people, and actors who worked together to shape all that is Star Trek) managed to say some very interesting and provocative things about relationships between individuals, cultures, and nations; about the link between people and their machines; about alienness and the importance of preserving uniqueness; about social and political problems like racism and sexism. The institutions and philosophies presented throughout the show speak of mankind's problems and potentials. And though it projects the world of the twenty-third century, Star Trek teaches us important lessons about life in the twentieth century—lessons as relevant to the mid 1980s as they were to the late 1960s. Star Trek is not only sophisticated—it is intelligent.

As such, Star Trek is as at home in the classroom as it is in the convention hall. The voyages of the starship *Enterprise* provide us not only with excellent stories, but with valuable lessons as well. There is much to be gained from the formal approach.

Just as Star Trek is well suited to the classroom, the classroom is an arena well suited for Star Trek. Not only do students gain from regularly reading critical literature (of the sort found in *The Best of Trek* and elsewhere) and sharing the insights of a zealous course instructor, but they gain—tremendously—by throwing around ideas with one another. If you've ever talked with a friend about the themes and issues raised by Star Trek you know how enlightening it can be to share another person's ideas. Now imagine that multiplied by a factor of twenty or more. . . .

The act of teaching Star Trek in the classroom is a perfect, living example of the Vulcan philosophy of IDIC. The twenty students in my class came together to create great diversity: each of us brought different histories, different biases, different *uniqueness* to the classroom. There, our ideas built upon one another like bricks in a wall. Even when we disagreed (perhaps *especially* when we disagreed), or arrived at no conclusions, we understood Star Trek—and the world around us—all the better. True to the Vulcan IDIC, the meeting of minds (so to speak) fostered by the academic arena allows great possibilities for knowledge and meaning, and the beauty of understanding.

"The Cultural Relevance" was designed to study Star Trek concepts both for their intrinsic value—that is, how they relate to one another within the world of the twenty-third century—and for the insights they give us concerning life in the twentieth century. After all, you need to know what a "power principle" and a "prime directive" are before you can use them to understand situations in our own time. Thus, EXCO 282 was designed to study both the world of Star Trek and the world at large.

As a class, we met twice a week—once to watch (slightly edited) episodes aired from a local station and once to discuss the themes and issues raised by that episode and others like it. If I had my druthers (attention, all you potential course instructors) the best way to teach Star Trek would be to videotape the important segments from several episodes and group together those scenes which illustrate a particular point. It is a much more effective teaching method to have important scenes played out in front of students' eager eyes (e.g., "Here are some reasons you might call the Federation an imperialistic organization.") than it is to verbally remind everyone of these segments. Unfortunately, I did not have the resources for videotaping episodes (nor am I sure if it's even legal), but I was thankful for the weekly airing of Star Trek. It would be next to impossible to teach a weekly course on Star Trek without some sort of active viewing.

In a way, the opportunity to teach "The Cultural Relevance" was a dream come true for me. Ever since my high school days when I watched Star Trek episodes sandwiched between "Sesame Street" and "Space 1999" every afternoon (what a lineup!) I have studied the show and gained many insights into its significance. Star Trek is as dear to my heart as anything. Thus it was a great pleasure to be able to share my insights with others.

Yet the real pleasure (and the real challenge) was in allowing others to understand Star Trek for themselves. Rather than launching each class with a lengthy lecture, I most often eased into our subject by referring to a few episodes and dropping a few provocative thoughts. Then, if the discussion weakened, I inserted a fresh idea or a different angle to stimulate the conversation toward a new direction (as any good helmsman will do). This strategy I used for two reasons: First, by not overwhelming students with my interpretations I encouraged the shier people to take risks and suggest their ideas to the class; secondly, I felt it was important to stress the fact that different interpretations could be equally valid.

Some people came into ''The Cultural Relevance'' expecting to be *told* what *the* meaning behind Star Trek is. That is, what (specific things) were Gene Roddenberry and his creative core saying?

This was a misconception. There are, in essence, as many meanings to Star Trek as there are people. It is the same way with life. Many people run around trying to sell us their versions of life's meaning. But no—we must make our own meaning in life. We are all unique.

Star Trek is like a piece of art. Its shapes and faces are recognizable—as they are, say, in an impressionistic painting— yet the relationship between them defies objective meaning. The significance of a Picasso or a Monet depends on the viewer. And who could say, objectively, what the meaning behind Kubrick's *2001: A Space Odyssey* or Melville's *Moby Dick* is? We each do—in our unique ways.

One does not need to know the intentions of the writers and creators in order to gather meaning from Star Trek (or any other piece of art). If it is meaningful for you to understand the combined personalities of Kirk, Spock and McCoy as a working model of human psychology, then it doesn't make a bit of difference what Roddenberry or anybody else had in mind. If you feel that the *Enterprise* represents elements of Motherhood, then it doesn't much matter that its designers might not have thought about it.

And isn't that the beauty of it? Star Trek means different things to different people. As well, it can mean different things to us at different times in our lives. (I find, for instance, that the older I get, the more value I place on the relationship between Kirk, Spock, and McCoy—and the principles of friendship and loyalty they espouse.) Star Trek suggests different ideas, draws different connections, raises different feelings, depending on who you are and what you're all about. Star Trek can be a very personal experience.

There *are* parts of the show, of course, which suggest only one interpretation—the racial hatred in "Let This Be Your Last Battlefield," for instance—yet it is in how we apply these events and images to other parts of Star Trek and to our own lives that subjective meaning has its place. (The events of a single episode are, of course, less open to creative interpretation than the themes which run through several episodes.) For instance: Are there forms of prejudice within the Federation which this episode is inadvertently underlining? How is racial hatred an issue in the world today? And how do *I* deal with it? These are the questions which people will answer according to their own beliefs.

In order to prevent some students from becoming discouraged during the course of the semester by interpretations too abstract or radical, I made it known during the very first class that something as broad and complex as Star Trek can be interpreted on many levels, and that the act of doing so can be a very personal and subjective process. (This also meant that all interpretations were fair game, which allowed for more vigorous debate.)

To underline the point, I read to them a quote from the inside page of Karin Blair's *Meaning in Star Trek* where Gene Roddenberry says he learned much about Star Trek and himself from her book. Here we have the *creator* of Star Trek saying he learned a lot about *his creation* from a book written several years after the show had been cancelled!

Had Roddenberry missed something along the way that Blair's book enlightened him about? No, he was simply being introduced to another interpretation, another *meaning*, of Star Trek. Nor did he necessarily have to agree with her views in order to have learned something about his creation. (In fact, many of my students did *not* agree with Blair's views.)

This is because the classroom is in many respects similar to a shopping market. When we go into the market we see thousands of different items displayed on their racks and shelves, yet we purchase and bring home only those particular pieces which fit our personal needs and desires. But by knowing what other people eat and wear—we are all the more enlightened. The classroom effectively exposes the student to a wide spectrum of postulations and theories about Star Trek (or any subject). It is the task of the dedicated student to not only take home those interpretations which fit her personal needs but also to seek to understand those interpretations which don't jive with her own.

Why is this important? Why should we bother to understand alien ideas (alien here meaning simply "not one's own") which bore us or which seem ridiculously wrong? There are two main reasons. The first is knowledge for the sake of knowledge. Many people believe (and Spock is certainly to be included among them) that knowledge is in some respects a measure of self-development. In other words: *To know* is *to be*. The more we know, the more complete we are, the greater our possibilities are. (This is very much related to the Vulcan IDIC.) The act of learning—even learning about things alien—is an act of *becoming*.

Western culture has long taken great stock in knowledge. Learning was the greatest passion of the ancient Greeks. Ever since the scientific revolutions of the Renaissance, we in the West have been very busy performing our experiments in an attempt to understand the natural world around us. (Examination of the inner world of the human soul has, unfortunately, lagged behind.) The spirit of confronting the unknown (and overcoming the unpleasant) which sends the backpacker out into the forbidding wild (and sends starships out into the Big Black Beyond) is as much a cultural phenomenon as it is, say, a psychological phenomenon.

Roddenberry recognized the value of knowledge, and our thirst for it. "To explore strange new worlds, to seek out new life and new civilizations. . . ." If you consider the *Enterprise*, for a moment, as a *person*, her mission describes our own lives from Day One. We are born into a "strange new world" and begin a process of exploration which doesn't cease until we do. Roddenberry recognized that confrontation with the unknown is not only a very useful dramatic tool, but an essential human need, as well.

Of course, Kirk and his crew didn't always like what they found when they went exploring, just as students don't always like what they hear in the classroom. But (violations of the Prime Directive aside) the information brought back was still useful to the Federation. Ah, to know, to understand . . .

But knowledge for the sake of knowledge is not enough. (Yes, that was V'Ger's ultimate realization.) We must also know how to act. And thus, the second reason we must embrace alien viewpoints in the classroom (and in the world around us) is a matter of pragmatism. When we understand the full range of issues surrounding a Star Trek theme we can communicate more intelligently in circles where Star Trek is discussed. (And because many of Star Trek's themes are relevant to our own world, we can communicate more intelligently in circles where Star Trek is *not* discussed.) More important, we can better understand those people with whom we disagree and thus become better equipped to relate to them.

The importance of understanding other peoples' viewpoints as a guide to action cannot be exaggerated here. It is anthropology's greatest teaching and one of Star Trek's most useful lessons.

Picture the cultural anthropologist in the field, studying individuals of a primitive culture. The natives dance. They howl. They perform violent rituals and exhibit social patterns far different from our own. On the surface it all seems very strange, even perverse.

Yet when the anthropologist learns to see the world through their eyes, suddenly the dancing and howling and violence all seem to make sense. The anthropologist joins in their rituals and learns to relate to them without causing insult. And when he is immersed in the native culture, he sees that from *their* point of view it is *our* social patterns and violent rituals which seem so very strange, even perverse.

Now picture James Kirk in the mine shafts of Janus VI. He is faced by the rock-dwelling Horta which has killed several of the planet's inhabitants as well as members of his own crew. His first impulse (and official order) is to destroy the alien on sight. But he doesn't.

At some point during the search, Kirk becomes curious. He knows the Horta is not killing without reason. And he hears the troubled words of his first officer bemoaning the loss of uniqueness which the Horta's death would cause. So what does he do? He avoids the impulsive action.

By ordering Spock to mind-meld with the Horta, Kirk is seeking to see the world from the alien's point of view. And suddenly—the killing makes sense. From the Horta's viewpoint, it was the miners who had been killing. Though "The Devil in the Dark" is, on the surface, about the efforts of a starship captain to protect a group of miners (and later the life and offspring of an alien), this episode is more broadly about the wisdom of taking other people's viewpoints into consideration when finding solutions to interpersonal or international problems.

When the captain's life or ship are not in danger, he can

compete with the best of anthropologists. Kirk's compassion (call it humanitarianism if you like), seen in his desire to save the Horta, or to save Charlie X from the Thasians, or in his decision not to kill the Gorn, comes partly from his ability to see the world as others see it. If not, what would be the difference between the Gorns' blowing up Cestus Three and the Klingons' blowing it away? The difference is that the Klingons would destroy the base just to undermine the Federation (or just for fun), whereas the Gorn truly believed they were protecting themselves. This suggests that Kirk believes in an ethical system based upon intentions rather than results. Poor Charlie, for instance, didn't know any better.

To see the world as others see it. This is the key. The anthropologist in the field and James Kirk in the mineshafts of Janus VI both represent a model for the way we should lead our lives. The person who watches "Devil in the Dark" (or any other episode which explores the topic of "otherness") can apply its lesson immediately to becoming a better social creature—a more understanding father, mother, or child; a more insightful employer or employee; a better friend.

This same lesson has enormous possibilities when applied to a larger scale. Democrats and Republicans are more prepared to make productive compromises when they understand not only *what* the other wants, but *why*. If the global powers would seek to understand their adversaries (and not only around election time) rather than (un)comfortably standing behind their own dogma, the world would be a safer, more prosperous place. Conservative/liberal, capitalist/communist, Arab/Jew, black/white—all would benefit from taking the time and effort to see the world as their traditional rivals see it. Prejudice feeds on ignorance and fear. Kirk's treatment of the Horta presents an alternative.

This is not to say that understanding another's viewpoint will eliminate opposition. But it will help. With understanding comes a reduction in conflict. With a reduction in conflict comes an increase in the total harmony of the universe. With an increase in the total harmony of the universe . . . well, who knows the limitations of that one? It certainly sounds logical, though.

This is what I mean by the "cultural relevance" of Star Trek. Not only does Star Trek make intelligent statements about important issues of our day—issues like war, power, and prejudice—but it also offers us insights into the little problems we face in our daily lives. "Little" problems such as love, alienation, aging, loyalty to friends, and values. Both politically and personally, Star Trek offers us options for our own lives.

When we view the world as our alien neighbors do, we come to understand that there is more than one way to see an issue or an event. We come to understand that there are many spectrums which describe human thought and action, that differences are legitimate and special. Episode after episode, we are presented with intelligent and inquisitive aliens, cultures with different ways of thinking and acting, as if to say, "Look at all the variety of life out there!" By exposing us to such a great variety of possibilities, Star Trek helps us to appreciate the uniqueness of others, and the alien aspects of ourselves.

It's *okay* to be different, says Star Trek. It's okay to practice different beliefs or different rituals, to have different aspirations, to *physically be* different in a society dominated by norms. In fact, it's not only okay, it's great.

In Star Trek, such differences are not the cause of destruction but are instead a source of *con*struction. Earth of the twenty-third century is a *United Earth*. People of different ethnic backgrounds, of different politics, have embraced one another in peaceful and prosperous coexistence. They have reached out to unite with their alien neighbors in space. The many cultural backgrounds represented aboard the *Enterprise* (and presumably in other Federation vehicles/offices) is symbolic of the usefulness of differences. As Roddenberry says, if mankind survives to the twenty-third century he will learn to take delight in differences.

We have, of course, a long way to go in the next three-hundred years. Differences in our society are more *tolerated* than they are a source of delight. Our American Constitution has the roots for such delight, for instance, in its preservation of freedom of speech and religion, yet we have a long history of persecuting our minorities and singling out those who are different.

There is often great pressure to conform in our society. It is something Alexis de Tocqueville called "the tyranny of the majority." It is the phenomenon which causes millions of people to wear the same brand of clothes, get the same haircut, believe the same beliefs.

Star Trek tells us not to be afraid of the unique. It's okay to be a Vulcan on a vessel packed with humans. (This message is especially attractive to young people, most of whom are in constant search for identity.) To commit yourself to a fad or mass belief (simply for the sake of belonging—whether you realize it or not) is essentially to become "of the body," an automaton without individuality, dominated by something other than your own initiative. (I would bet that a statistical analysis of Star Trek's greatest fans would find them to be, more often than not, the type of person who does not fit into the common social cliques or easily participate in fads. Star Trek speaks to these people.)

Be yourself, says Star Trek. Allow differences to be not a source of alienation but a springboard for growth.

By watching Star Trek, studying it, and applying its lessons, we can make the world a better place. In this light, Star Trek almost becomes a sort of Scripture, doesn't it? Like the Bible, Star Trek has excellent stories with heroes and villains; it contains important messages and occasional thou-shalt-nots. What the Bible does in sixty-six books, Star Trek does in seventy-nine episodes. Of course, the focus is often different, but the method is the same: What remains up to the individual is interpretation and application.

Granted, the lessons in Star Trek are not perfect. Joyce Tullock has written in these pages about the tendency for Kirk and the Federation to "humanize" the aliens they encounter. This analysis is quite legitimate and is one example of how many of Star Trek's lessons are sometimes realized imperfectly. In other words, the Federation doesn't always practice what it preaches.

The same fault that occurs between theory and practice in American constitutional values occurs also in the realization of Federation values concerning the alien. "Where I come from," Kirk tells Alexander in "Plato's Stepchildren," "size, shape, or color make no difference." Yet equality is *not* fully realized within the Federation. Not until the movies, for instance, do women seem to have the same opportunities as men. (Neglected minorities are as alien in practice as outworlders.)

One of our best discussions in class concerned the image of women in Star Trek. The female has long been presented through the media (i.e., in advertisements and on prime-time television) as a seductress or a servant to the male will. Star Trek's treatment of women doesn't go much further than this.

Where do you place the blame? Place it partly on the audience that rejected the pants-wearing Number One (from the first pilot); partly on the businessmen who control what we see on television; partly on a long-standing imbalance in our culture.

Another Federation tenet not fully realized is the Prime Directive. On a few occasions Kirk interferes with the affairs of alien planets which he feels are not experiencing "normal development" (though Kirk and some viewers, in all fairness, may consider these actions to be "creative interpretation" of the Prime Directive rather than interference). Quite often the issue for Kirk is one of freedom. For instance, even though the people of Vaal enjoyed a society without disease, social violence, or war, they also had no choice in the matter. Kirk felt his job was to give them back their freedom, even though he would introduce all the historical evils into their society in the process.

By policing the freedom of other peoples, Kirk's actions take on American overtones. American foreign policy in the last twenty years or so has basically been to go into an alien country and slap some American freedom on it. The critics of this policy speak of the right of self-determination and argue against our version of "freedom" as a standard for other societies. The Prime Directive was designed during the Vietnam era with these criticisms in mind. Thus it is interesting that the show's producers allowed Kirk to violate the rule *at all*. (It is also interesting to note that most violations of the Prime Directive occur in the second- and third-season episodes, when Roddenberry had less creative control over the show.)

The occasional gaps between what the Federation preaches and what it practices are both disturbing and refreshing. They are disturbing because we don't like to consider our heroes as hypocrites; we don't want to believe that the noble values they subscribe to are unattainable. These faults are refreshing at the same time because we know our heroes are operating in the "real world." If everything the Federation or its representatives did was perfect, Star Trek would be reduced to a utopia; it would lose credibility and thus its ability to give us hope. As it is, we understand that mankind is still evolving in the era of Star Trek, still pushing toward the (elusive) ideal. We take comfort in, and are challenged by, such progress.

Since the filming days of the late 1960s bits and pieces of progress *have* been made toward realizing the Star Trek dream. Technologically, certainly, we are miles ahead of where we were. With the advent of the space shuttle, we have broadened our grasp on space, thus providing the next link in the (oh so achingly slow) evolution toward starships. The omnipresent computer seen in Star Trek has made great advances in the last sixteen years, changing the way adults fight wars and conduct business, the way youngsters play and learn. The computer has so very rapidly come to be accepted in our society that if Star Trek episodes were made today I imagine we would see errant computers more often *reprogrammed* than illogicked to death.

Social and political progress, unfortunately, does not occur as rapidly as technological progress. Human society is still plagued by war, greed, violence, and a whole scorecard of "isms." Faces have changed in sixteen years. Themes haven't.

It is a credit to the timeless quality of Star Trek's lessons that episodes filmed in the late 1960s can be used to illuminate problems in the mid-1980s. One student of mine, for instance, wrote an excellent paper in which he used the episode "Errand of Mercy" to examine the recent turmoil in Central America. In his analysis he used "Errand of Mercy" as a study of occupation and colonialization.

In this episode the Federation and the Klingons are competing for influence over Organia, just as the United States and the Soviet Union are competing for influence over El Salvador, Nicaragua, and much of Central America. This student concluded that from the point of view of the occupied party there isn't much difference between being occupied, or influenced, by one side or the other. (The Organians certainly didn't feel a difference.) The basic reality—stripped of all subsequent consequences—is that self-determination is lost. In practice, Central Americans have much in common with Organians. Not that they are twinkling energy forms of pure thought, but they are technological inferiors who in the process of having their freedom "enhanced" by two competing (technologically superior) superpowers are actually having it taken away.

Was the Federation on Organia because of an altruistic concern for the native people (promising defense, medicine, education), or was self-interest involved? This question must also be asked of the United States.

Another student wrote a similar paper using the episode "The Cloudminders" to examine apartheid in South Africa. By examining the circumstances which drive the exploited Troglytes to commit acts of terrorism one might also employ "The Cloudminders" to explain modern examples of terrorism in Ireland or in Lebanon.

Part of the beauty of Star Trek is this capacity to continue to examine cultural situations which occur years after the episodes were filmed. This timeless quality is one reason why Star Trek still flourishes on the airwaves after so many years.

The "Star Trek phenomenon," it is called. It is the phenomenon which sees a mere three-year television series burst into record-breaking popularity upon syndication and draw an ever-increasing base of fans (not just viewers, but *fans*) year after year. It is the phenomenon which brings characters back to the screen ten years after they believed they had left it for good. It is the phenomenon out of which arise hundreds of fan clubs and fanzines, conventions and collectors. It is the phenomenon which causes Star Trek to be the subject of major theses and, yes, academic coursework.

The classroom is one of the many places where fans can learn to appreciate and understand this wonderful thing we call Star Trek. The classroom is an excellent arena for the serious study of Star Trek. It allows students from diverse backgrounds to come together to watch episodes and share ideas. It encourages the review and production of critical literature. It engenders many of the values upheld throughout the series and opens up options for use in our own lives.

I am not the first one to offer a course in Star Trek—and I won't be the last. Wherever and whenever they come together, students of Star Trek all have one thing in common: Not only do they study the Star Trek phenomenon, but they themselves are very much a part of it.

STAR TREK IN COMIC BOOKS— ANOTHER LOOK

by Walter Irwin

A while back, we had the pleasure of meeting Michael Barr, the current author of DC's Star Trek comic book, at a convention. We gave Mike several different Best of Trek *volumes to aid in his research, one of which contained Walter and Leslie Thompson's long-ago article about Star Trek comic book adaptations. We mentioned that several readers had requested an update of the article to include Marvel Comics' Star Trek series, and Mike prevailed upon us to wait a few months so that we could include his efforts as well.*

About a year passed, then Walter sat down with G.B. and took on the almost herculean task of reading every *Star Trek comic ever published. Then the original article was slightly rewritten, and greatly expanded to include the Marvel and DC versions. It's taken a couple of years altogether, but we feel the end result is worth it.*

The adaptation of a movie or television series into comic book form is, at best, a difficult process. The special language of film, with its unique blend of graphic illustration, individual nuance, and storytelling shorthand, brings continuing characters to life in a manner which is extremely difficult to duplicate or even approximate in the comics medium. This is especially true in the case of Star Trek.

The problem seems to be that the series is just too popular; just about everyone knows what form the characters and situations will take, and any variance from that individualistic television style seems somehow to fall flat.

The biggest problem for the comic book writers is, of course, the creation of believable actions, attitudes, and dialogue for the main characters. We know how Kirk, Spock, McCoy, and the rest talk, respond, think. And if any of these seems the least little bit wrong, then the story just doesn't work. Because Star Trek's "world" is so well known, the author (and the artist) has the additional problem of maintaining consistency in supporting characters, technical jargon, the series "history," and so on.

From the artistic standpoint, there is the chore of having to constantly make sure the character renderings match up with the real actors. It is also difficult for the comic book creators to duplicate the special effects and high-tech hardware so essential to the series' "look"; the world of Star Trek in the comics always seems, somehow, to be a dark, cramped place. Also, there are just not many artists who can draw aliens that look both original and authentic. (To be fair, not many writers can create fresh or believable aliens, either.)

From the problems and restrictions listed above (and they are only a few, by the way), it would seem that it would be well-nigh impossible for any creative team to do a successful Star Trek comic book. Until the appearance in 1982 of DC's Star Trek series, this was true.

The first Star Trek comic series appeared in 1967 (cover dated October), about ten months after the debut of the television series. (This was about average for the time; comic book companies usually waited to see if the series was going to be a success before pouring money into an adaptation.) The publisher was Gold Key, the only company then regularly doing movie and TV adaptations. To the people at Gold Key, the adaptation process was simple: Buy the property, commission the writing and drawing of a story, and depend on the name to sell the book. A fairly simple process (and one which has accounted for many fine adaptations over the years), but when the writing and drawing are not based on research done on the original product, you end up with a bad adaptation. And, it follows, a very bad comic book.

Research for Gold Key's version of Star Trek seems to have been little more than the reading of some brief character outlines and a look at a few publicity stills. When reading the earliest issues, it is impossible to tell whether or not the creative teams had even seen the show. (In the case of at least one of the later artists, this proved to be true.)

Nevio Zaccara drew the first two issues of the comic; later issues were drawn by B. McWilliams and Alberto Giolitti.

Giolitti lives and works in Rome, so it was highly unlikely that he ever saw the series while he was working on the book.

(My research has failed to turn up a reliable source for the name of the writer or writers) of the Gold Key series, and I'm understandably loath to attribute such poor work to anyone on hearsay.)

The main fault for the poor quality of research and preparation probably lies with Gold Key's system of producing comic adaptations. Before condemning that system, however, it must be stated that this system *did* produce many, many fine adaptations of movies and television series over the years. It is just that, in Star Trek, Gold Key had hold of something more complex and more cared-about than their usual product. Their main failure was not realizing this fact and acting upon it.

Errors abound in the Gold Key issues. The blame must be equally shared by the company, the writer, and the artist (although it is likely that the writer lives and works in this country and should have been able to at least *watch* the show once in a while). However, many of the errors (but by no means all) would only be noticeable or disturbing to a Star Trek fan; many comic book adaptations have been successful, even in a series, without being mirror images of the originals. What the Gold Key Star Trek comic books lacked was good and entertaining story lines and art. The Gold Key series simply failed to capture *any* of the spirit of the series or what it was trying to say. The adaptation became space opera of the simplest kind, unabashedly aimed at a juvenile audience.

The cover of the first issue was a dull mishmash of stills from the show, capped by an unimpressive logo. It set the style for every issue to come. The featured story, "Planet of No Return," was a variation on the "bug-eyed monster" theme involving giant carnivorous plants. The standard, overworked elements of cheapjack sci-fi are present in force, including the capture of Yeoman Janice Rand by the plant creatures (rape did not seem to be out of the question), and an incredibly stupid and dull Kirk characterization. It could've (and probably had) made a perfect fifties bad horror movie. Unfortunately, just as the cover set the style for the following issues, so did the story.

The second issue did not see print until some eight months later, although it appeared to have been prepared at the same time as #1. This would suggest that the first issue sold only moderately well, as a second was not rushed onto the stands.

Too, Gold Key was apparently taking no chances; Star Trek had not been a runaway hit, and it is likely the comics company waited until the show was scheduled for a second season before continuing with the series. The next three issues appeared at approximately six-month intervals, and it was not until about #5 that Star Trek was added to Gold Key's regular schedule. Even then, the stories appeared sporadically.

"The Devil's Island of Space," the second entry in Gold Key's series, revolves about one of the oldest science fiction plot devices extant: "They Are Not What They Seem." (This device was destined to become a staple of stories to follow.) Kirk and his "boys" (he calls them that throughout the story) beam down to a strange asteroid where the inhabitants claim to be shipwrecked. But it is soon revealed that they are (gasp!) condemned criminals, and the asteroid is soon to be blown up as the method of their execution. A highlight of this tale is Spock joshing with Kirk.

Each of the Gold Key Star Trek comics was a variation on a classic science fiction theme, and usually a not too imaginative variation, at that. "Invasion of the City Builders," in issue #3, retells the horror which occurs when machines overrun their creators. Although this was one of Star Trek's favorite themes, in the hands of Gold Key's people, it deteriorated into a simple "chase" story, with the *Enterprise* crew trying to find a way to stop the rampaging building machines before they pave over the "last remaining ten thousand acres" of planet *Questionmark* (!).

In the middle of this silliness is a nice bit of characterization of the alien leader, who feels that his authority is being undermined by the saviors from the starship. This kind of subtle touch was seldom seen in the comic series.

By the time the fourth issue rolled around, it appeared that some fan feedback (or at least some pressure from Paramount) was being felt, for it prominently featured Spock, both on the cover and in the story. From then on, the Vulcan was featured as a full partner to Kirk, and handled just about as much action and dialogue. (This same thing had happened on the television series some time earlier.)

Following issues were no better or worse. Gold Key apparently was satisfied with sales, and Paramount apparently never objected to the product. (It must be remembered that such things as comic book adaptations were taken even less seriously twenty years ago then they are now; it is likely that no one at Paramount, outside of the legal department, ever even saw the comic books.) Throughout the entire sixty-one-issue run of Gold Key's series, the stories and art remained on a level well below that acceptable to most comic or Star Trek fans.

The splash page of issue #6 features a shot of meteors penetrating the hull of the *Enterprise*. Luckily, no one died when all of the air escaped from the ship. This issue also presents a cutaway view of the *Enterprise*, which, to judge by this drawing, would be about the size of a 747 jumbo jet and able to hold about forty people.

In the seventh issue, entitled "The Voodoo Planet," the crew finds a planet which is a complete replica of Earth, except that everything is made of papier-mâché! It is the work of one Count Dressler, who uses the replicas to perform a kind of grandiose voodoo; he destroys the papier-mâché Eiffel Tower, and the real one on Earth is destroyed. He is defeated when Spock reveals that Vulcans also know the arcane arts— Spock den does Vulcan voodoo and does in de voodoo man.

This story is most typical of the cursory treatment which Star Trek was given in the Gold Key series. Aside from the patent foolishness of reconstructing all of the buildings, etc. of an entire planet in papier-mâché, the scenes of twenty-third-century Earth were very contemporary, certainly no later than the 1990s. Add to this the spectacle of Spock researching through ancient Vulcan textbooks for references to his ancestors' voodoo practices, and then synthesizing a serum to give himself and Kirk "voodoo powers," and you have a perfect example of a story ground out without any regard or affection for the original.

This first series of Star Trek comics must be counted a failure, fit only for children and rabid completists. Even so, early issues command a surprisingly high price on the collector's market. If you feel you *must* read some of these stories, if only for a good laugh, you'd be better advised to pick up some of the later issues. The quality is about the same (often the artwork is much better), and they are fairly abundant.

The best way in which to read the Star Trek series back issues is in the the treasury volumes. Gold Key (through its Golden Press division) issued four thick volumes entitled "The Enterprise Logs" in 1976–77. These volumes reprint thirty-six of the first thirty-eight stories in chronological order. These "logs" can readily be found today, and are relatively inexpensive.

Gold Key published its final issue in the series in 1979. Throughout the final two years or so that Gold Key held the rights, there were constant reports that Marvel, DC, or even the then still-operative Charlton had purchased the rights. Fans, disgusted with the low quality of Gold Key's product, crossed their fingers with every rumor.

Finally, in late 1979, it was announced that Marvel Comics had obtained the rights to Star Trek, and would begin producing a regular series concurrent with the release of *Star Trek: The Motion Picture*. Fans were overjoyed. Even before the creative team was announced, Marvel promised that the series would be faithful to both the forthcoming movie and the television series. As a rousing kickoff to the series, Marvel would also product an adaptation of the movie, to be featured in a *Marvel Super Special*, an oversized magazine on quality paper. This same adaptation would also be spread over the first three issues of the new series.

Star Trek was placed on the Marvel schedule as a monthly title. This reflected the confidence which Marvel had in the property, and one can hardly blame them for it. Not only was Star Trek a favorite with comics fans, Marvel not unreasonably expected to pick up a large number of the legion of "Trekkies," many of whom did not read comic books at all. Marvel was reportedly paying a high fee for the rights (some reports say it was considerably more than they were paying for the rights to *Star Wars*), but the expected increase in sales would more than make up for the expense. Also, Star Trek was a prestige property for the company to have, "proof" that even Paramount Pictures and Gene Roddenberry considered Marvel to be Number One.

The script for the adaptation of *Star Trek: The Motion Picture* was done by Marv Wolfman, who would also be serving as editor of the title. Artwork was by fan favorite Dave Cockrum, with inks by the then-prolific Klaus Janson.

Star Trek: The Motion Picture proved to be less than enthralling, and the static quality of the film made for a comics adaptation which moved at a snail's pace. Wolfman's script, which included much dialogue excised from the final release print of the film—some of the best lines were cut; one wonders what Paramount was thinking of—was as fluid as the adaptation process would allow. Cockrum's art, however, was wildly uneven. Characters were almost totally unrecognizable in one panel, beautifully rendered in the very next. Page design varied between everything from standard six- or eight-up rectangular layout to double-page spreads with multiple inserts. Most irritatingly, the art was muddy, the fault of the use of too much black and lousy reproduction, even in the slick-paper *Super Special* edition.

(Sloppy reproduction and dark, overinked artwork continued to plague the series throughout its run, and contributed immeasurably to the disdain in which fans held the book. One of the things for which Star Trek was famous was its bright, open look, especially on the *Enterprise*, and the comic book made everything look dark, dank, and cramped.)

One gets the feeling that Marvel's people weren't really all that thrilled with the idea of adapting the movie, for the end result had a distinctly rushed and perfunctory look to it. (To be fair, it must be remembered that Paramount, because of in-house delays, was late in delivering scripts and stills to Marvel.) Perhaps everyone was looking forward to doing original stories with the beloved characters, considering the adaptation just a necessary chore to get out of the way before the fun began.

The first all-new issue was #4, cover dated July 1980. As if the previously published and overly long adaptation of the movie hadn't given the book a slow enough start, the series opened with a two-part story. "The Haunting of Thallus" (continued in #5, August 1980. "The Haunting of the *Enterprise*"). It is difficult to understand why an editorial decision was made to use a two-part story directly after the three-part movie adaptation; perhaps Wolfman and company felt that comics fans would not respond well to a book which did not utilize continuing stories.

Wolfman and Cockrum/Janson were the creative team, with Mike Barr taking over the scripting on issue #5. Even though the team had not yet found their footing with the series, this set the tone for all the issues to follow: Monsters, ghosts, and a healthy dose of pseudo science fiction.

The *Enterprise*, assigned to transport a dangerous alien prisoner back to the jail from which he escaped, encounters a "haunted house" floating around in space. When investigating, the crewmen are beset by near-invulnerable monsters (including the Frankenstein monster, vampire bats, werewolves, and the Official Marvel Version of Dracula). A beautiful young woman is found in the gothic manse, and rescued. All of these, including the woman, are proved to be the result of a new Klingon weapon (oh, did I forget to mention they showed up, too?) which can form corporeal monsters from the thoughts of a humanoid. The Klingons have captured a Starfleet scientist, attached him to their device, then used his subconscious memories to form monsters with which to attack the *Enterprise*. The alien prisoner, thanks to a surgical implant, is a "receptor" for these images. The mysterious woman was the first construct of the device; the Klingons allowed the young man to form an image of his "heart's desire," his late wife, in order to more easily subvert his will. All this information is glibly explained to Spock when he is captured by the Klingons; he then makes use of this largess by mind melding with the scientist, causing him to transmit an image of Spock, and informing Kirk to "destroy" the woman. Kirk does, and the psychic feedback causes the scientist to turn his creations upon the Klingons.

It doesn't make a heck of a lot more sense in the reading than it does in the telling, folks. The story was obviously padded to two-issue length, and characterization was lost in the never-ending battle against the monsters. The Klingons in particular were badly handled, gloating, gnashing their teeth, and spilling their plans and schemes to Spock in tried-and-true Marvel supervillain fashion. Also hampering the story was the use of several all-too-well-known Star Trek clichés, such as the mine meld, a secret weapon, and the warp drive malfunctioning at a crucial point. It was a disappointing effort. The series was now five issues old and had yet to produce a really good Star Trek story. Fans were beginning to get edgy and somewhat pessimistic.

The sixth issue presented a tale (again by Barr, Cockrum, and Janson) entitled "The Enterprise Murder Case." This was a little more like what readers expected: Spock made use of his intellectual and deductive abilities (at one point he refers to Sherlock Holmes), the crew dons cheesy disguises to visit the surface, and the events of the story are the result of actions taken by Kirk years before. Particularly welcome was the lack of superheroism action. Although this issue was not classic Star Trek, it was at least a step in the right direction. Readers could begin to hope.

The first really *alien* aliens appeared in issue #7, produced by a new creative team, Tom DeFalco writing and Mike Nasser drawing. (The continuing presence of Klaus Janson as inker provided a consistent look to the book.) The story was again nothing special (Marvel was showing a distinct tendency toward taking elements from two or three Star Trek television episodes and mixing them together), but it was at least an attempt at science fiction: Certain members of an alien race, rather than dying, evolve upward along the evolutionary scale. The effects of this on the society are, understandably, far-reaching and not all beneficial.

The Marvel Star Trek series now seemed to be approaching the kind of stories the TV series did so well. Unfortunately, with the next issue, Marvel proved that they could also do the kind of stories which the TV series did *badly*.

New scripter Marty Pasko was rejoined by Dave Cockrum (now inked by Ricardo Villamonte) for the "The Expansionist Syndrome," a simpleminded robots versus humans story ("mechs" versus "orgs").

The biggest flaw in this story was a subplot involving a young woman who was being ferried by the *Enterprise* to a Starbase for a heart transplant (Marvel's series saw the ship assigned to some rather humdrum duties). Feeling she was needed to help overcome the aliens, she leaped from her bed, knocked out Dr. Chapel, and escaped at phaserpoint. (She wasn't the superwoman she seemed—immediately upon reporting to Kirk now to solve the crisis, she swooned prettily into his arms.) Luckily, the "mechs" proved to be pretty nice guys after all, and théy whipped up a shiny new mechanical heart for the plucky lady.

This silliness was immediately followed by—you guessed it—more ghosts. Pasko and Cockrum, now accompanied by Frank Springer on inks, this time pulled a switch . . . these ghosts were *real*. Kind of. They were the surviving consciousnesses of victims of early transporter experiments, seeking vengeance upon the woman who had caused their deaths, Janice Hester! They were attracted to the *Enterprise* by the presence of her granddaughter, one Karen Hester, who was enough of a double for her granny to fool the not overly bright "ghosts." A boring and predictable subplot involving Karen's former involvement with Kirk made the issue even less appealing.

By this time, the hopes aroused in fans for a successful series by issues #6 and 7 were almost completely destroyed. Not only had the comics slipped back into mediocrity, but Marvel seemed to be less and less committed to them. The creative teams kept changing, and editorial direction (now under Louise Jones) seemed to be nonexistent. The series had no point of view and no internal consistency beyond the stock Star Trek characters and situations.

Perhaps the death knell for the series (from the standpoint

of both the fans *and* Marvel) was sounded in January 1981, with the cover of issue #10: Above a drawing of our favorite Vulcan brandishing a spear over a fallen alien opponent, a blurb shouted, "Spock—the Barbarian!" Michael Fleisher and Leo Duranona were responsible for this travesty, although the story inside proved to be little more than your stock capture-and-bondage shtick.

But that cover, and all that it represented, was enough for most readers. The "Trekkies" had probably long since quit buying the comic anyway, but the sheer crassness and so-what attitude which Marvel now displayed caused all but the most fanatic readers to drop the comic from their buying lists.

Nothing changed throughout the rest of the series except the creative teams. Pasko wrote the majority of the remaining issues, with assists by Alan Brennert (#12), Barr (#17), and J.M. DeMatteis (#18). Artistic teams changed more often: Joe Brozowski and Tom Palmer (#12), McDonnell and Gene Day (#14, 16). Ed Hannigan and Palmer (#17), and, somewhat surprisingly, Gil Kane (#15). Unfortunately, even Kane's fine inks were muddied up by poor reproduction, although he did manage to produce an *Enterprise* interior which at least looked as bright and airy as that on film.

The remaining issues—the series was canceled by Marvel with #18, having previously gone bimonthly with #15—never rose above the level of mediocrity set by #10. Only occasionally did anything of interest occur: The revelation in #12 that Yeoman Rand had married a formless alien intelligence (Kirk's amazed "It—I mean, he—*talks*?" has to be an all-time low for that character); the introduction of McCoy's daughter, Joanna, in #13, along with the news that she was engaged to a Vulcan (!); the sight of a little alien girl witnessing the transporter arrival of Kirk and company in #17 and thinking them to be "angels." These moments were few and far between, however, and the series ground its tortuous way to a halt with #18, cover dated February 1982. (In typical Marvel bravura fashion, the cover proclaimed, "Special Last Issue Collector's Item!" It's doubtful if anyone cared.)

The mistakes which Marvel made with its Star Trek series are almost too numerous to list. First and foremost among them, however, is the fact that the constant turnover of artists and writers never allowed the series to gain any kind of consistency, much less a fan following. Too, Marvel's adaptations consistently failed to capture either the feel or the intent of the *television series* (which was, *Star Trek: The*

Motion Picture notwithstanding, what readers wanted to see), nor were the characters ever handled in a believable or consistent fashion.

Most important, Marvel never made a serious attempt to do science fiction in the Star Trek series. Although superheroics were held to an absolute minimum, the creators seemed to never be able to forget that they were doing a *comic book*. The physiques of the men (and women) were superhero standard, dialogue was just as flippant, stilted, and redundant as a typical issue of, say, *Spider-Man*, and at least one fight scene per issue seemed to be a requirement. Real science fiction was most often discarded in favor of melodrama, in which ideas took second place to battles against monsters, machines, or all-too-humanoid aliens.

The Marvel Star Trek series was a failure, and all the more disappointing because it was not an *impressive* failure. Science fiction has always been a hard sell in comics, but if Marvel had chosen to go all out with Star Trek, breaking new ground and striving to capture the spirit and tone of the televised series, then fans of every stripe would have applauded. If sales had still not been good enough for the book to survive, so be it.

Marvel, however, apparently decided to aim the book at the lowest common denominator. Occasional posturing and posing aside, the series never began to approach any issues of substance—bug-eyed monsters, ghosts, gnomes, robots, and the occasional Klingon were deemed suitable enough opponents; one could hear the editors warning that ideas don't sell comics.

Back issues of the Marvel Star Trek comics can be found in plentiful numbers, and at extremely reasonable—even cheap—prices. (Many dealers simply put everything other than the first and second issues in the 25¢ bargain boxes.) Because it was in magazine format, the Marvel Super Special which adapted *Star Trek: The Motion Picture* may be a little more difficult to find, and consequently cost a bit more. From the standpoint of a Star Trek fan, however, the Marvel series is not nearly as collectible as are the Gold Key issues. And Marvel fans generally ignore them because they are not superhero comics.

Marvel Comics obviously never knew what it was doing with Star Trek, and fans were beginning to suspect that no comics company ever would. So it was with an overwhelming sense of ennui that fans reacted to the news that DC would begin publishing Star Trek. (Revived interest in the series by comics companies was due to the success of the second Star Trek film, *The Wrath of Khan*.) Even less reassuring to fans was the announcement that the creative team for the new series would be Marv Wolfman and Mike Barr, as editor and writer respectively. Both men had been associated with Marvel's series, and putting them in charge of the new effort seemed suicidal. Even the announcement that Tom Sutton would be the artist did not excite anyone, for his style, while distinctive, was of the same darkly inked school as Cockrum's and Palmer's. It seemed as if nothing would be different except the name of the company publishing the book.

However, at Wolfman's urging, the contract that DC negotiated with Paramount allowed for the use of all the characters and situations from the series and films. Fans knew that this one factor alone, if used properly, could make all the difference. Wolfman's idea, however, was to go one step farther, to use the best of both worlds. As he told Barr, "Don't be bound by the television format. Take the characters, the concepts, the universe, but do *comic book* stories, with comic book placing, subplots, even continued stories."

Barr took him at his word, and the series opened this time with a *four-part* story packed with characters and situations culled from the series. (Actually, the story line falls naturally into two parts of two issues each, essentially forming two interconnected stories.) The villains of the story are Klingons (again, as in the Marvel series, drawn in their horn-headed incarnation introduced in *Star Trek: The Motion Picture*). Among them are our old friends Captain Koloth and Admiral (Captain) Kor, as well as a new character, Konom, a Klingon pacifist. Subsequent issues bring back the Organians, and the rocklike Excalbians.

The involved plot opens with the Klingons building a massive space station in "wormhole space." With the assistance of Konom, the *Enterprise* crew destroys it, only to find that their actions have caused the Klingon Empire to declare war on the Federation. Checking in with headquarters, Kirk finds to his dismay that the commander of Starfleet is just as anxious to fight as the Klingons. Suspecting outside influences, Kirk goes to Organia for help, only to find it blocked off by the Excalbians. The Excalbians have caused the war to again test the relative strengths of good and evil. Kirk, working in concert with Admiral Kor, manages to free the Organians, then convinces the Excalbians to test their theories firsthand by fighting the equally powerful Organians. The challenge is accepted, and the two races vanish into limbo, bringing an end to the war, and leaving the Klingons and the Federation with the need to negotiate their own peace treaty.

The story proved pleasing to Star Trek fans, mainly because of the skillful use of established characters and history. There are several gaping plot holes—why would Kirk intentionally set off a war which could easily devastate the galaxy? —but all in all it was a very successful first effort.

The subplots which Wolfman requested were present in force. Konom, of course, remained as a continuing character, and gained a love interest in the person of Ensign Nancy Bryce. Bryce, in turn, is constantly at odds with Lieutenant Bearclaw, who blames both her father and the Klingons for his father's death. Needless to say, he isn't very fond of Konom. These characters are fairly well rounded, and have been used rather effectively as part of the supporting cast through the first half-dozen issues.

Other, still developing subplots include Kirk's reluctance to accept Saavik as a replacement for Spock (now effectively moot), Sulu's resentment at not receiving his own command, and Kirk's gradually increasing impatience with and repugnance for violence. Because of the necessity to set up the adaptation of the third movie between issues #7 and 8, all of these subplots are only just now being developed. It is obvious, however, that Barr plans to expand upon all of them in future issues.

Wolfman and Barr obviously realized that it would be a mistake to have every issue of the series be continued, comic book "style" or not, so the next two issues featured self-contained stories. The presence of the continuing subplots and the new crewmembers provided a feeling of continuity to the fledgling series which the Marvel series never achieved.

Issue #5 featured pretty standard "violation of the Prime Directive" stuff. A marooned captain, thought to be a god by native aliens, uses his phaser and advanced knowledge to end a war, heal the sick, etc. When Kirk and Company arrive, he naturally refuses to leave; they can't take him because it would mean fighting the populace. Events work themselves out, of course, but in this story we see a perfect example of the kind of faulty thinking which mars most comic book writing, be it science fiction or not.

When the renegade captain refused to leave, why didn't Kirk just return to the *Enterprise*, order Scotty to zero in on his one-of-a-kind readings, and beam him aboard? Never mind that perhaps Mike Barr never thought of this; it is something which has occurred so many times in the series (and in Barr's own Star Trek comics) as to be a cliché. Even the most casual Star Trek fan would think of it. It is this kind of mistake—which often can be taken care of with a line or two of dialogue—which ruined Marvel's adaptation. Barr has avoided such gaffes most of the time, but he and editor Wolfman must realize that only by remaining diligent and taking the time to read and reread the story from the *reader's* viewpoint can such errors and omissions be caught.

Issue #5 featured the return of Ambassador Fox in a story which told of the efforts of a terrorist group called "The Orion Victory League" to disrupt the Federation/Klingon peace conference. It turns out that the shape-changing agent is in reality Fox's estranged daughter. Barr makes the most of the fact that a man whose words have ended wars cannot talk to his own child, and rightly ends the situation ambivalently, if optimistically. Notable in this issue was McCoy's use of Kirk's allergy to Retinax 5 as a bluff, cleverly utilizing information from *Wrath of Khan*.

Issues #7 and #8 (the ones interrupted by the *DC Movie Special* adaptation of *The Search for Spock*) relate the history of Lieutenant Saavik.

Finding herself entering into *pon farr*, Saavik tells Kirk and McCoy of her background—found by Spock, taken to his family, matched to a male Vulcan child, Xon. Barr took no chances here. Most of his "past" for Saavik has long been taken for granted as a "given" in fan circles. The only new thing he added was the bonding with Xon, but as this is described as "imperfect," it can easily be dumped if plotlines require.

The story itself is a little awkward in construction, as it necessarily leads into the *The Search for Spock* adaptation. Actually, nothing much in the way of action happens until the second part of the story, when it's discovered that Romulans have developed a way to control the godlike powers granted by the energy barrier at the edge of the galaxy. Xon, whom a feverish Saavik has rushed off in search of, is undercover among the Romulans. Kirk rescues the pair, and tricks the Romulan vessel into entering the energy zone, where it will "wander helplessly . . . forever lost." (Don't bet on it, Dr. Doom fans.)

Although we're introduced to Saavik's betrothed and given a little of her background, nothing has really changed at issue's end. Better not to play with the characters at all than to have them go through typical DC/Marvel "appearance of change." The creators would be better advised to concentrate their efforts on the excellent supporting cast, or, if they feel readers demand some development in the main cast, do the kind of thing Barr is doing with Kirk: a gradual, developing shift in attitude that will not result in the person becoming too different, but will still affect the way he thinks and acts. Conversely, these new attitudes can and should be discarded or tempered when necessary, as in real life. This would be true characterization, of an even richer and more appealing kind than the series gave us. It must be done slowly and logically, however, and from all indications, Barr is doing so.

Tom Sutton has drawn all but one issue (#7) of the entire series, and has done an excellent job. He has managed to walk the thin line between photographic reproduction and comic book art, giving us representations of the main characters which look very much like their real-life counterparts, yet have a full range of emotion without a stiff, posed look.

The regular inker is Ricardo Villigran, and he has done a splendid job by removing much of the clutter from Sutton's art. His extremely varied linework has given the books a distinctive look all their own, and he is a valued part of the creative team.

Sutton's art is an acquired taste, and it's a well-known fact that many readers never seem to acquire it. His layouts and pacing are always interesting, however, though occasionally things become a bit confusing or a word balloon is awkwardly placed, and his visualizations of hardware, ships, aliens, and landscapes are always imaginative and fairly logical. He's obviously done his homework, and the care and attention shows.

Because the Star Trek series must, if it is to succeed, attract those who don't normally read comic books, the covers are even more important here than on regular comic books. Aside from an unduly cluttered cover on the first issue, Sutton's covers have been crisp and appealing, and are getting progressively better. But the best cover work on the DC Star Trek series—indeed, the best cover work of *any* Star Trek comic, from any company—is on the *DC Movie Special* adaptation of *Star Trek III: The Search for Spock*. It is a beautiful pen-and-wash by Howard Chaykin, featuring Kirk,

Kruge, and Saavik standing against a background of ships, the Genesis Planet, and a large profile of Spock. Let's hope this cover helped the issue to sell even better than expected. More attention needs to be paid to cover art on *all* comics, not just Star Trek, and increased sales is the surest way to gain that attention.

DC's Star Trek series is still feeling its way—a slight revamping is promised with the return of Spock; "new frontiers," Barr terms it—but things probably will not change very much as long as the present creative team stays on the book. So far, Wolfman, Barr, Sutton, and Villigran have given us the most consistently entertaining and artistically successful Star Trek comics series ever. With continued reader support, the voyages of the Starship *Enterprise* should continue to debark from the DC offices for quite some time to come.

As stated at the beginning of this article, adapting a television show to comics form is an extremely difficult and demanding job. In the case of Star Trek, only one of three tries has proven successful. The first, Gold Key, failed because the creators cared little about the original series, and did not even bother to check out the most basic facts. The second, Marvel, failed (even though the creators were originally enthusiastic) because it relied too much on the use of hackneyed plots and monsters-and-villains, as well as slipshod reproduction of halfhearted art. The third, DC, is so far successful because the creators have successfully merged tried-and-true comic book style and writing with well-known Star Trek situations and characters.

Perhaps the world will never see a perfect Star Trek comic book—perhaps such a thing is impossible—but DC is putting out a good product which will be more than acceptable to even the most hard-core Star Trek fan. The series performs the most necessary and important function of a comic book—it is entertaining. And when you get right down to it, be you comics fan, Star Trek fan, or both, isn't that what it's all about?

ALL ABOUT CHAPEL

by T. A. Morris

Nurse Christine Chapel may not have as many fans as some of the more prominent Star Trek characters, but there are more Chapel fans than you might think. And they are intensely devoted and quite vociferous in their support. If you aren't particularly enamored of Chapel, you might wonder why she would arouse such loyalty among her fans. Australian fan Teresa Morris's article should show you why, and who knows? You just might find yourself becoming a Chapel fan as well.

I have long had a liking for the Chapel character. Rather than being the typical blonde of fiction, she had the good grace not to gush, sigh in syrupy tones, or sprain her ankle at convenient moments so as to provide an extra problem for the hero to overcome. Or perhaps that's her problem. In "What Are Little Girls Made Of?" she and Kirk walk by a pit and the edge of it crumbles and falls toward bottomlessness, but instead of clinging to Kirk and flutteringly admiring his muscles, she puts a hand on a nearby rock and steadies herself. It is a sensible, if not very Hollywood, thing to do. Perhaps that is why Kirk, who is used to women who do cling, doesn't seem to know quite how to relate to her.

Of course, there is more to Chapel than not being a stereotype and her ability to keep her hands off Kirk while searching for her fiancé. The fact of her being there at the edge of that pit has a story behind it that tells us something about her. Chapel is actually a doctor in bioresearch and she has joined the crew of the *Enterprise* in order to search for her fiancé. He is the great Dr. Roger Korby, the Pasteur of archaeological medicine; the man who said that freedom of choice produced the human spirit, but who, nevertheless, is going to force a utopia on the galaxy by turning people into androids. He is a scientist, one of the greatest, and he combined this, when Chapel knew and loved him, with a reverence for life—just like someone else she falls in love with. Five years have passed since Korby went missing, but she has waited for him. Two previous expeditions have failed to find him; Chapel has been told that he is dead. She doesn't believe it. She believes so strongly that he is alive that she changes careers and comes looking for him. The curious thing is that she is right.

So, thinking more of her love life than anything else, Chapel seems to have stepped almost casually into a career aboard a starship. Kirk, on the other hand, sometimes makes allusions to his academy days, to how he was "a stack of books on legs" and "positively grim"; in short, how hard he had to work for his career. Chapel easily gained a position on a starship, and not just any starship, but the one going out on the five-year mission, the one going just her way. True, she seems to have had to accept a demotion to nurse in order to do it, but she has been given the rank of lieutenant. There is no telling what she might have become had she been more ambitious. No wonder she doesn't seem to be one of Kirk's favorite people.

It is quite understandable that Chapel should accept the position of nurse if that was all that was available to her, but how did she come by those nursing skills? They have to be learned: they don't come automatically even to someone who has studied enough to be a doctor of biology. Perhaps it is that she started out as a nurse and, finding the studies interesting, drifted further and further into them until at last she was being taught by Roger Korby and was inspired to become a doctor herself. Otherwise, she might just as easily have become a vet as a nurse. We are not given the details. The matter is left to speculation.

But when Chapel stands at the edge of the pit under the surface of Exo III, we know why she joined the *Enterprise* and, if we put the fragments together, we also know about her courage, and her loyalty, especially to love, and her brainpower (which should not go unobserved). What we don't know much about is why, having found and lost Roger, she chooses to stay on the scene of her loss and failure, still as a nurse. Her decision is made offstage, her story left largely untold, and we can only suppose that, for all her quiet and sensible attitude, there is something in the adventure of the mission that she really enjoys.

I love the bit in "Amok Time" where she ducks the flying soup. She comes running out of Spock's quarters and steps to one side and so, with great economy of movement and energy, is missed by the bowl of soup that goes sailing past her to splatter all over the opposite wall. It is such a simple thing to do, and so obvious, really, and she seems to do it instinctively in spite of her fright.

Then there is, of course, Spock. Vulcans love their women strangely, or so we've been told, but in "The Naked Time" Chapel is willing to take a chance with Mr. Spock. She says she knows he would not hurt her, and of course she says she loves him, and forever after she is thought of as the woman vainly loving the Vulcan and having little else to do. Loving someone who does not believe in emotions and who will never love her in return may seem unproductive and not too bright, but then, it is just possible that Chapel is one of those generous people who loves where she sees love is needed and not because it is "sensible" or profitable for her to do so. The words she chooses on this occasion are interesting, too. When she is moved by the Psi 2000 virus to murmur words of love and seduction, it is Spock's secret that she speaks of, her perceptiveness that is revealed, for she says she loves both his Human and Vulcan halves. Although the inner conflict Spock suffers is something that Star Trek audiences can all see and understand, within the Star Trek universe it is something he reveals only to a very few friends on a few, very rare occasions. It is Chapel's tragedy that she is never regarded as one of those friends. Yet, curiously, she knows. While others are struggling to understand the Vulcan, she knows and understands the conflict within him, and it casts a shadow over her, making her love something far more than the rather pathetic infatuation she is generally accused of.

In "The Naked Time" there is little doubt about what she wants from Spock, and yet in two other episodes we see her rejecting him while seeking his happiness. In "Amok Time" she knows that Spock must take a mate or die, but we don't see her taking some champagne to his cabin and trying her chances. Instead we see her smile when she hears that the ship is diverting to take him to Vulcan, where he must go, and she takes the news to him straight away. Standing over him as he lies on his bed, she will not wake him but turns away after all. Then he rises and calls her back, for it seems to him that she was trying to tell him something, but he never does quite hear her. It is not such a strange dream for a Vulcan to have, for they are telepathic, and perhaps it was an interpretation of an emotional projection he couldn't quite block out, a message from Chapel, who is only human and so could not have meant to send it. He tells her that it would be illogical of them to deny their natures, but she cuts his advance off by telling him that he is being taken to Vulcan after all. She does not let him continue on with something there is no longer any need for.

In "Plato's Stepchildren" the aliens take her from the *Enterprise* and put her in Spock's arms and (and this must have been flattering for him) she tells him she'd rather crawl away and die. Chapel seems to want Spock on certain terms, through a freedom of choice that could only be produced by the spirit in his human half. She just doesn't seem to have that driving selfishness that could get her what she wants. Or perhaps she knows the adage "If you love something, set it free."

We see Chapel always at work on something in the background, studying something. Perhaps she has technical manuals, too, although they are probably not on engineering. In "Return to Tomorrow" we see her helping the aliens who have transferred their minds into *Enterprise* officers' bodies, and in "The Deadly Years" helping to find the antidote to the ageing virus. Often we see her helping with operations, even when the surgery involves Spock's life. She remains professional, and if in "Operation Annihilate" she would have preferred to remove all the threads from Spock's spine, she can hardly be blamed for that. After Dr. McCoy's reprimand, she remains to do what she can.

Dr. McCoy often snaps at her for telling him what he already knows, although it must be her duty to give him a running report on what the diagnostic charts are saying while he concentrates on the actual surgery. That she manages to put up with Dr. McCoy is greatly to her credit, and, indeed, she seems quite fond of him; trying to help him in "For the World Is Hollow" by telling him a lot can happen in a year, and also in "Turnabout Intruder," where it seems that she would disobey an order from the captain rather than one from Dr. McCoy. The captain wants to keep Janice Lester's body sedated, and Chapel and McCoy know this is wrong. The captain and McCoy argue about it, and although the captain wins, it seems that Chapel could not quite bring herself to comply unless Dr. McCoy ordered her to.

We see some of her warmth in that episode, and in others such as "And the Children Shall Lead" (although in that episode we don't know where she went while the children were trying to take over the ship—perhaps they locked her up in a cupboard). In "The Changeling" she helps Uhura relearn her lost knowledge, and in "Obsession" we see her concern for a young crewman troubled by a guilt the captain has imposed on him. She persuaded him to eat by using psychology.

What we don't know, and are never told, is what she does for relaxation. For all we know her hobby could be barroom brawling.

There is another story that seems to happen for her off-stage, too. In "Amok Time," having already forgiven, or simply forgotten, the flying-soup incident, there is the part where she finds out that Spock actually has a wife on Vulcan whom he is returning to, and this is shortly after the scene where he makes some advances to her. The next time we see her is when Spock has beamed back to the ship and it is all over. What she thought of him between those appearances, how much it mattered to her and whether her idea of him had to change, we never know. We only see her happy for his sake, as if all is forgotten and the only really important thing is Spock himself: a man whose life she doesn't really have a right to try to share in. We see her smile when the men want her to leave. She dutifully does, leaving them to their male confabulation which they seem to have a need for—although there is little that they are going to talk of which she, as a nurse and a doctor of biology, doesn't know about.

We can only make guesses about why the Platonians in "Plato's Stepchildren" chose her for Spock, whose mind they took her from, and what Spock means when he confesses his distress at being unable to stop the Platonian games. The significance of his choice of words at that moment. "I have failed you," is something to ponder.

Equally interesting is his choice of mind to hide in when he is escaping Henoch's schemes in "Return to Tomorrow." How this plan was concocted and Chapel agreed to it happens offstage (or else, the story would lose its suspense). Perhaps other people were too involved with events to go unnoticed by Henoch, and others not involved enough to be risked in this way. Chapel, in spite of the flattery Henoch gives her, does manage to be overlooked by him. He doesn't search her mind; perhaps he can't. She has been hypnotized by him, but her mind is strong enough to leave her still vaguely aware that something is wrong. She doesn't know what it is that is wrong, but she does almost break through. Since Spock may also be controlling her mind to keep her quiet, we don't hear what it is she would have said to Dr. McCoy about her feeling.

So, finally, it should not come as a great surprise that in "The Lorelci Signal" she should hear Spock when he calls to her telepathically. The signs that she just might be able to do so have been there for a long time; really, from the time all those years ago when she was told Roger Korby was dead and did not believe it.

If I had to say in one word why it is that I like Chapel, I would say "courage." The fact that she stays on the *Enterprise*, the scene of her grief, is one example of that courage; the fact that she stays onboard when the heroes are too tired to hang on there anymore (Spock meditating on Vulcan, Dr. McCoy living in Georgia, Kirk behind a desk) is an extension of the same thing. She has frailties—which I call her "goofy" moments—as in "Return to Tomorrow" when she tells Spock, who, scoolboy-like, does not wish to discuss the sharing of their minds, "It was beautiful." Her courage is best summed up in those moments when Spock is brought into sickbay, and there is no time for her emotions, so she gets on with the work of caring for him. It is the courage of humanity that doesn't have to be perfectly brave or perfectly strong, but has to consider the best thing to do and then go ahead and do it. And if she takes a break for a softer moment sometimes, she can't be blamed for that.

Christine Chapel is a character whose time has come; I would guess that her popularity is increasing. People are recognizing her positive qualities, and no longer just thinking of her as a woman who is silent and dutiful, her world bound up in Spock, nor do they any any longer dismiss her altogether as not worth thinking about. Perhaps her intelligence and loyalty gives people something to think about, and perhaps her courage is something they can identify with. It is to be hoped that she will return in future Star Trek productions. While her character is often relegated to the background, her humanity helps fill in and make real the Star Trek world.

So, cheers to the Star Trek universe and the people who fill it and prop it up, and to Nurse Chapel who shows that love does not have to be selfish, nor courage only for heroes.

SPECULATION: ON POWER, POLITICS, AND PERSONAL INTEGRITY

by Sharron Crowson

Star Trek fans just don't consider the "why" of something, they take that one, but very long, step further and consider the "what"—that is: What was the cause of this event or action, and what will the ramifications of this event or action ultimately be? This is the kind of thinking which went into the whole Star Trek concept and many of the best scripts. In this article, Sherry Crowson gives some of the elements of Wrath of Khan *and* The Search for Spock *just such an in-depth examination.*

Speculations are conjectural considerations of a subject, and as such are often personal and subjective. As I watched the last two Star Trek movies, *The Wrath of Khan* and *The Search for Spock.* I was first caught up in the action and the adventures, in the wonder, humor, terror, and even grief that were part of the experience. After several viewings of both movies, I discovered I had time to look beyond the story and I found myself considering certain events and attitudes, speculating on causes and effects.

Consider Genesis. What are its causes and what effects will it have? Carol Marcus proposed the original project, the Federation funded it, and Starfleet provided men and material for it. Why?

Genesis is power, pure and simple, only nothing about it is simple. Imagine dealing with the political effects of being able to create whole worlds, or whole systems of worlds custom-tailored for any physiology. The Genesis team even thought it possible to create sentient beings, though they did not plan to do so in the initial trial. At best, the results would mean less hunger, more room, and more natural resources.

At worst, Genesis could, as David Marcus said, "be perverted into a dreadful weapon," capable of destroying populated planets, with the matter restructured into any form the destoyers chose.

Planets, resources, and people, these are the fundamentals of power. The Genesis Wave created the potential for all of them—made to order. But whose order?

Evidently Federation officials felt they were capable of handling the responsibility and directing such power, that the benefits outweighed the risks. However, they kept the research under tight security and used Starfleet both as workhorse and watchdog for the project. Starfleet's presence made the younger members of the Genesis team "nervous." Why should they have such an attitude? Carol Marcus was willing to give Starfleet the benefit of the doubt even when it seemed about to overstep its authority and take control of Genesis. The other members of the team were furious that their work would be taken from them, but didn't seem at all surprised at such a turn of events.

If you set aside the natural animosity which occurs in any situation where a person has to give up some control of his work, for security or funding or any other perfectly acceptable reason, the hostile reaction of the Genesis workers is still all out of proportion to the cause. Is it possible that the younger team members have some just cause to mistrust Starfleet? If so, what could it be?

To answer that question, it is necessary to take a good, hard, objective look at what we are shown of the Federation and Starfleet.

When the Federation suspects there might be something wrong on Regula One, Starfleet sends Kirk and his "boatload of children" to look into the situations. They are sent not because they are best suited for the task, but because Starfleet *has* to know what is happening to Genesis. Even Kirk, who is not known for patience, seems to question the wisdom of sending a training ship on a possibly dangerous mission. When he asks Spock for reassurance about the cadets, he gets command of the ship instead. It must have seemed like a mixed blessing at the time. Genesis must have made Starfleet "nervous," and with good cause.

Khan steals Genesis despite tough security for the whole project. An oblique example of that security is the fact that

Spock, "beyond the Biblical reference," knew nothing of the Genesis project until it became necessary for him to know. Spock was not only a top-ranking Starfleet officer, but also one of the Federation's leading scientific minds. We are left trying to figure out how Kirk knew of it; we might speculate that he kept in touch with Carol Marcus or had had some "need to know" when the project was first introduced.

Now the Federation's worst fears were realized. A madman, out to revenge himself on Admiral Kirk, took over *Reliant* and nearly destroyed the *Enterprise*, killing a number of young cadets. When Khan realized he could use the Genesis Device as a weapon, the *Enterprise* and its crew was saved only by the sacrifice of Spock.

The Genesis Device fulfilled its potential, creating a world and a small sun from the dust and gas of the Mutara Nebula. The premature detonation discarded all the experimental protocols and was monitored only by the *Enterprise*'s damaged sensors. Even given the evidence, as in *The Search for Spock*, that Genesis might be flawed, the idea, the basic premise might be enough to guarantee that someone, somewhere, might find a way to make it work. There is a state of the art to scientific endeavors that is perilous to ignore.

So Starfleet and the Federation found themselves in the unenviable position of trying to jam the lid back on Pandora's box. And how did they go about it? They panicked. They closed off the Mutara sector, tightened security, ordered the *Enterprise* personnel not to discuss Genesis, and scheduled a whole raft of hearings and debriefings. Sulu was replaced as captain of the *Excelsior*; Starfleet announced that the *Enterprise* would be decommissioned. Starfleet and the Federation were desperately trying to regain control of the situation, while Kirk and his crew paid the price.

If the Genesis Device hadn't been stolen and used as a weapon, the Federation might have had time to deal with the consequences of its success. There might have been time to answer questions such as: Who accepts responsibility for using Genesis? Who pays for it? Who decides when and how it will be used?

Saavik thought it might be possible to recreate the Glaezivers' home world, so that they might not die as a race. Even so noble a motive would take some examination. Those who control Genesis control power of a sort that's almost beyond comprehension.

And suppose, for a moment, that Genesis should fall into

enemy hands—a distinct possibility. Valkris obtained a briefing tape that showed her the bare bones of the Genesis project (though not the technical data).

What would the Klingons do with Genesis? They would use it as a weapon. The Federation was forced to consider that possibility almost before they had time to realize that Genesis worked. The permutations of the process are endless and terrifying. Genesis could be used to destroy living worlds, create slave races to carry on the battle, manufacture gems, crystals, and precious metals enough to disrupt entire economies.

So the Federation had to deal with the results of Genesis; it had to monitor what Genesis created and try to keep it out of enemy hands. A ship and crew were assigned to take Saavik and David Marcus back to research the Genesis World.

Whom and what did the Federation send to deal with the most explosive crisis of the century? They sent a single ship, the Federation science ship *Grissom*, commanded by J. T. Esteban. They were certain Captain Esteban would not act on his own initiative—he didn't have any. He couldn't breathe without calling Headquarters to see if it was allowed. Esteban was sent *because* he could be relied on to carry out policies and orders without hesitation, because he didn't have the imagination or courage to do anything else. Starfleet was taking no chance that it would not remain in complete control of the situation. Starfleet did, however, fail to realize that it takes courage and imagination to deal with the unexpected.

Commander Kruge's cloaked Bird of Prey was certainly unexpected. Though the *Grissom* probably had little in the way of defensive capability and even less offensive capacity, it would have been interesting to see how Kirk might have handled that situation. Kirk did manage to destroy a good portion of Kruge's crew with next to nothing functioning aboard the *Enterprise*. His actions took courage, initiative, and imagination—qualities singularly lacking in Captain Esteben.

Captain Styles, commander of the newest ship of the line, *Excelsior*, was another officer Starfleet chose to deal with a crisis situation. According to the novelization, Sulu was supposed to command *Excelsior*, but political fallout from Genesis made Starfleet back off and give command of the ship to Styles.

Starfleet's choice seems rather odd. Styles does not impress an observer as a man of action. He comes across as cool, and terribly smug, about the ship and his responsibilities. His affected mannerisms, that electronic swagger stick, for example, make him seem petty and a little ridiculous. Styles could not imagine a situation calling for a yellow alert in space dock. His lack of imagination made him slow to respond and slow to take the alert seriously. When finally convinced of the crisis, the theft of the *Enterprise* by Kirk, he checked out his equipment and admired it, yet you never heard him ask after any member of his crew. The yellow alert occurred during the night shift, and surely some personnel must have been off-duty or away from their stations.

Captain Styles relied on equipment (his "beautiful machine") and the new drive, rather than people and tested methods. He might have been able to catch the *Enterprise* on warp drive, or come pretty darn close, but, to satisfy his ego or curiosity, he used the transwarp drive, even if it meant overshooting *Enterprise* and doubling back. Kirk and Scott both seemed to understand Style's mentality and took cruel advantage of it by defusing the transwarp capabilities in such a way that use of it disabled all of *Excelsior's* power.

If Captain Styles represents the types of officer that Starfleet sees as most desirable, then it is obvious that Starfleet's priorities have changed drastically. It seems that the Federation wants to exercise strict control over the ships and crews; and to facilitate that control, Starfleet picks officers who are well trained but lacking in flexibility, creativity, and daring. It is hard to imagine that such control is possible, or even desirable, given the size of the universe and its diversity.

We see another example of this more rigid, "by the book" thinking in Kirk's conversation with the commander of Starfleet, Harry Morrow. Kirk went to him to get permission to take the *Enterprise* back to Genesis, retrieve Spock's body, and take it and Dr. McCoy to Vulcan. The commander saw only the dangers: The *Enterprise* might not hold together to make the trip, and an additional ship and crew, especially *that* ship and crew, might disturb the delicate balancing act they were performing. The Federation was trying to balance the need to learn more about Genesis against the possibility that more ships in the area might increase the danger of a security leak, or be interpreted as a unilateral move by Starfleet to take control of Genesis.

Morrow could not—or would not—understand the private needs Kirk was asking him to consider. The discussion of Spock's soul and McCoy's desperate emotional problems did not seem important to Morrow compared to the political issues surrounding the theft of Genesis and its implications. Morrow concluded that Kirk was devastated by Spock's death and the attack on his ship and that he wasn't in any condition to command a vessel; that McCoy's problems were open to interpretation and Spock's soul could not be quantified. Kirk decided that McCoy's life and Spock's soul were worth whatever he had to do to save them.

While Kirk talked to Morrow, McCoy was arrested and detained for discussing Genesis in public and trying to hire a ship to take him there. For Starfleet, the simplest, most expedient explanation for McCoy's actions was that he was overcome by grief and exhaustion. He gave Federation Security more than sufficient proof that he was not himself by resisting arrest and trying to disable the security officer—with a Vulcan nerve pinch. Sending McCoy to the "Federation funny farm" was Starfleet's handy way to dispose of an officer who had become an embarrassment.

In the novelization, McCoy wondered if he would get due process of law before being packed off to the "funny farm." We all know McCoy is a cynic, but his speculation has a certain aspect. He *was* incarcerated without a hearing. It makes you wonder if there were changes in the Federation that had McCoy worried *before* Genesis, possibly the same sort of changes that worried the young members of the Genesis team.

In the final analysis, the Federation and Starfleet seem to have grown into ponderous bureaucracies, conservative to the point of stagnation. The officers selected to handle new and possibly threatening situations are men who display no initiative, who follow directives and policies without deviation.

If Captain Styles is an example of what Starfleet wanted in a commander, it is not at all surprising that Kirk was not allowed to retain command of the *Enterprise*, though Starfleet had recommendations to the effect, he was more suited to command of a vessel than anything else. Starfleet was unwilling to support the example that Kirk would set for other captains; he would be an example of personal courage, daring, and imagination dangerous to the increasingly rigid status quo.

The Federation seems to have turned away from pursuing new and adventurous paths. Perhaps Spock's statement "The needs of the many outweigh the needs of the few, or the one" was not a personal belief, but a reflection of duty as defined by Starfleet. It was duty, so defined, that required the actions leading to his death.

Yet when Kirk spoke to Spock for the first time after the refusion, he reiterated and reaffirmed an essential tenet of freedom: "The needs of the one outweighed the needs of the many." For when a society stops considering individual needs, when individual beliefs and imperatives, even individual lives (McCoy might have died, Spock's refusion might not have been possible) are sacrificed, not out of necessity but for expendiency, then freedom is well on its way to being buried under rules, regulation, and red tape.

Kirk and his crew are in trouble not for the theft of the *Enterprise* or for mutiny, though those will probably be some of the charges, but because they are an unwelcome, possibly dangerous, reminder to the Federation and Starfleet of how things used to be, of how things *should* be, and what they have become.

Jim Kirk and the *Enterprise* crew may have outgrown Starfleet. They have the courage to act on their convictions, from an ethical sense of what is essential to personal integrity and honor. Rules and regulations will never come first with them; life, and the "chance for life," will always take precedence, and that is the way it should be.

"I intend to recommend you all for promotion . . . in whatever fleet we end up serving," Kirk said to his officers after stealing *Enterprise*. Maybe they do need another Starfleet to serve in, one not so bound "by the book." Or maybe they need to go back and take on the Federation and Starfleet, take them apart and rebuild them. They need to give those august bodies back the sense of adventure and lofty ideals that seem to have been lost somewhere along the way. Now, *there* is an adventure worth their effort, and it would be wonderful to see them succeed!

"APPROACHING EVIL" AND "LOVE IN STAR TREK"—A REBUTTAL

by Philip Carpenter

Below you will find the editors' favorite kind of article: one reader's reactions to and thoughts about a previously published Trek *article. In this case, Phil Carpenter takes a look at two articles, which he believes "say the same thing, although in different ways." Philip makes use of logic, a knowledge of Star Trek, and the respect and understanding one writer has for another's work to make his points. We think you'll enjoy reading Philip's article—but before you do, why not first dig out your copy of* Best of Trek #5, *and reread the articles he's discussing? Then you'll enjoy it even more.*

After reading *The Best of Trek #5*, I had to sit down and respond to Joyce Tullock's "Approaching Evil" and Walter Irwin's "Love in Star Trek." I was struck by the fact that they say the same thing, although in different ways. Miss Tullock gives her opinion of the system of morality in Star Trek, and Mr. Irwin gives his idea of the result of that system—namely, brotherly love. Evil and love are tied together through a complex process, with more implications than are mentioned in either article.

Miss Tullock's article is about evil—yet she doesn't define it, can't explain it, and can only conclude that it's just a vague matter of opinion. As Hamlet put it, "Nothing is good or bad, but thinking makes it so." And Hamlet was the biggest waffler this side of the ineffectual Kirk from "The Enemy Within." Star Trek was often guilty of this kind of moral timidity: the Gorn in "Arena" was obviously a bloodthirsty killer—no, wait, he was an innocent victim. The Salt

Vampire was a deadly monster—excuse me, he was just misunderstood. V'Ger was an annihilating juggernaut—oops, he just needed love. Miss Tullock applauds this uncertainty as "realistic," but is it really natural—or just a cop-out?

Since she doesn't even give a definition of evil, let me try. Something is evil if it opposes or destroys one's life. Conversely, something is good if it supports one's life. And since all sentient creatures must have the same moral rights—by definition—there is no right to violate another's rights, and anyone who tries to do so automatically shows his wish to live as a subhuman and forfeits his own "human" rights. That's why Kirk is justified in fighting Klingons, for instance—they act as animals, and may be treated as animals. (Granted, though, they're deliciously comic animals!) One of the first choices ever made by any sentient being is whether or not he will devote his life to the enhancement of life or to its destruction. If he chooses to destroy other sentient beings, he proves himself to be a savage. If he chooses to destroy himself, he will have failed his prime responsibility. Once this basic decision is made, all further choices are made on the grounds of what his goals should be and how he should accomplish them.

And what of the being who cannot make such decisions? The answer is V'Ger: powerful, supremely logical, yet having no values whatsoever, no purpose, no meaning. Such a being is inevitably destructive; since he does not value anything, he sees no reason to preserve anything. Only after Decker and Ilia combine with him does V'Ger become good. As Kirk said, "I think we gave it the ability to find its own sense of purpose."

Mr. Irwin thinks that we should value love as the foremost purpose—that love, sweet love, is what makes the galaxy go round. Actually, love, or any emotion, cannot be used as a value. Emotions are only the *results* of one's value system. It's a fine line, but one that humans have been tripping themselves on throughout history. Countless wars, massacres, injustices, and horrors have been started in the name of love.

Why, just take a look at "The Enemy Within," where a transporter malfunction splits Kirk into two halves, an Animal Kirk and a Weak Kirk. Is Animal Kirk evil because he has no love? On the contrary—he's chock full of love. He loves drinking, he loves Janice Rand, he loves starship command, and he certainly loves survival. So how can he be so evil? Simple. He uses emotion—that irrational, illogical quality—

instead of values as his motivation. Animal Kirk has the cart before the horse: Emotions must be the result of one's actions— *never* their cause. Weak Kirk realizes this. All his decisions (what few he makes) are rationally based. Any emotions— regret for the men, fear of his double, irritability directed at Spock—are the products of his premises: We must save the men. We must capture the double. We must maintain order.

But Weak Kirk is not completely good. He hasn't the courage of his convictions. He becomes a coward, which makes him as dangerous as Animal Kirk. He must be re-united. And when he is, the two evil halves become one good whole. Whole Kirk is good because he can make decisions rationally and stick by them. Yes, he has his Animal half, but that part is where it belongs. He listens to his emotions, but he is not driven by them. That's why I say that Kirk is not half good and half evil, but wholly good. It's a case of the whole being greater than the sum of the parts.

Values, not love, are what drive men. You can see this all through Star Trek—what a person loves is a dead giveaway to what he values. Kirk values the challenge and responsibility of starship command—therefore, he loves the *Enterprise*. Spock values intelligence, drive, ambition, and the skillful control of emotion—thus, he loves Kirk. McCoy values life, especially human life, and people who protect life—so he loves Kirk and Spock. Khan values destruction and subjugation—so he loves ruling others. Trelane of Gothos values a lack of values—he loves senseless games.

And what values drive Joyce Tullock? Her article speaks for itself: "Evil! Oh, how we love it! . . . We crave it, seek it out, revel in it." I do hope she wasn't serious—it's such a damning statement. But her article continues with a series of vacillations, hesitations, apologies, uncertainties, and ambiguities, and finally concludes, "Evil doesn't exist, you know? It's only a term we use to set moral boundaries!"

If anything is worse than evil, it must be moral uncertainty. Refusing to take a stand on anything has allowed dictators and criminals to plunder freely throughout the centuries. Star Trek had its fair share of flip-flopping, all right. Kodos the Executioner could never have carried out his plan of planetwide slaughter without his subjects thinking, "Oh, he must know what he's doing. We all have to make sacrifices, I guess. Why should I complain?" Eminiar VII, in "A Taste of Armageddon," carried out centuries of war wherein the leaders killed their own people and got away with it because nobody dared to complain. The Organians, in "Errand of Mercy," put on an act of being complacent Dagwood Bumsteads and promptly attracted every Klingon in the quadrant. It just goes to prove the old saying that all evil needs to triumph is for good men to do nothing.

Fortunately, not all Star Trek characters do nothing. One of the qualities which drew me to the series is how the main characters stand up and make themselves heard. They're courageous people with integrity. Just look at how quick Kirk and McCoy are to tell Khan in "Space Seed" or Apollo in "Who Mourns For Adonais?" or mischievous Harry Mudd just what they think of them. Spock commented on slavery in "Bread and Circuses": "I said I understood it. I did not say that I approved." And one of my favorite scenes with Uhura is in "Gamesters of Triskelion," where she is ordered to whip a slave. She flatly refuses. "It is forbidden to refuse," they warn darkly. "I don't care if it's forbidden or not," she retorts, "I won't do it!" She's a spunky gal.

It's good to have the courage of one's convictions, but first you have to make sure you know what your convictions are. That's what brings the Star Trek characters to life—they have a clear sense of values. That's what I liked about *Star Trek: The Wrath of Khan*. It explored Spock's relationship with Kirk. Every scene, every plot twist advanced the theme of Kirk trying to overcome his mortality, and showed how Spock gave him the strength to do so. It was well crafted in every area.

Yet, some things just didn't fit. It may be nitpicking, but it's the little things that trip me up, especially since they just weren't necessary. For example:

Spock's statement "The needs of the many outweigh the need of . . . the one." That's said twice in the movie, and both times it stops dead what would otherwise be a warm, moving scene. It's out of character. The perfectly rational, logical Spock could never reel off such an illogical, nonsensical statement. After all, what *are* "the many" besides a group of "ones"? If Spock actually believes that many ones can overrule the needs of a few ones, then he believes that some people have the right to trample the rights of other people. Talk about a blow against minorities! At the beginning of this article, I stated that all sentient beings, by definition, must have identical rights, and that if some beings decide to assume rights that are automatically forbidden to others (robbery, slavery, murder), then, logically, they cannot be rights. Spock *must* know this if he is the type of character whose life is guided by rationality. I can only conclude that this was a bit of hasty writing. The first time he says it is when Kirk apologetically requests command of the *Enterprise*. What Spock should have said instead was: "Logically, I have no need to command the *Enterprise*. I am qualified to lead a training mission, but not a deep-space mission. I am a scientist, but *you* are a leader. You *must* command—or waste your talents." The second time he says it is in the death scene in the engine room. A better line would have been "Do not grieve, my friend. I could not choose to avoid my death. It is illogical to mourn the inevitable. But I could choose whether or not you should join me—and it would have been a dreadful waste for you to do so." After all, that's the whole point of *Wrath of Khan*, although no one seems to have noticed it. Spock did not sacrifice his life because *he could not have avoided death anyway*. Had he not repaired the engines, he would have been torn apart in the Genesis explosion. It was simply logical for one to die if hundreds could thus be saved. It really wasn't a fair test for Spock. We still don't know (from the events presented in *Wrath of Khan*) whether or not he would give his life for Kirk and crew. In this instance, he just didn't have any choice in the matter.

Would Spock give his life for Kirk if he had a choice between saving himself or Kirk, but not both? According to Mr. Irwin, he should. Mr. Irwin states that the highest love any sentient being should feel is to give aid to another being at the expense of self. The only problem with this attitude is that it's been practiced all through human history and, without exception, has resulted in disaster. Ancient slaves killed themselves by exhaustion building temples and pyramids for their Egyptian masters. Japanese peasants and samurai willingly slaughtered themselves for the sake of their emperors, who expressed their gratitude by demanding more killings. Countless millions of Russians were put before the firing squad under orders of Lenin and Stalin "for the good of society" (or what was left of it). And just a few years ago, hundreds of innocent people willingly swallowed poison purely at the behest of a neurotic petty tyrant named Jim Jones. These are examples of what irrational "brotherly love" has done throughout history. And Mr. Irwin wants more of the same? Organia help us!

Actually, Mr. Spock *would* give his life for Kirk—not

because he's motivated by love, but because he's motivated by the proper values. He values Kirk so highly that to live without Kirk would be more painful than death. *Star Trek: The Motion Picture* should have settled that once and for all. No wonder Spock couldn't finish *Kolinahr*: all those years without Kirk had really done a number on him. He should have paid more attention to his feelings; they were screaming that Kirk was as necessary to his life as water and air. He should have remembered the lesson of "The Tholian Web," when he had a clearcut choice between bugging out, saving his own life, and leaving Kirk to die, or, remaining, risking everything for a friend perhaps already dead. *This* was what was missing from *Wrath of Khan*: the choice that would prove to us that Spock *would* give his life for Kirk's if necessary. Spock would have found the loss of Kirk more agonizing than any reward he might gain in the process. Spock was not moved by love, but, more precisely, by a process of logic in which love was the conclusion.

Incidentally, notice at the end of *Wrath of Khan* that Kirk is perfectly happy and recovering from Spock's death. Since Kirk can obviously live without Spock, but Spock could not live without Kirk, then Spock's love for Kirk must be greater than Kirk's love for Spock.

Speaking of Kirk, he had a similar choice in "City on the Edge of Forever," when he had to choose between Edith Keeler, a strong, intelligent, farsighted woman, or the entire future, including the Federation, his friends, and his command. It was such a close race between the two that he agonized over the decision until the last moment. Then we (and he) found out which he held more dear. He held Edith dear for the same reasons he valued the Federation and his position within it: benevolence, self-confidence, imagination, objectivity, rationality, and raw human drive. It was a hard choice, but fortunately Kirk decided which things were more important to him.

Everything (or everybody) that a person values is arranged in a hierarchy. No two things are valued exactly the same; they progress from least important to most important. Many neurotics create frustration and helplessness for themselves by not recognizing which values are more important, or that not all values are equally important, or that lower values should be sacrificed for higher ones if there is a conflict. Charlie Evans failed his test of adulthood because he couldn't understand what he needed to live in a society without resorting to mystical alien powers. He refused to take responsibility for his actions. And the Star Trek universe is about people who take responsibility for their own lives—they take credit for their triumphs and blame for their mistakes. Miss Tullock points out that many of us would like to blame our destructive, evil acts on something outside ourselves. "The devil made me do it" is the standard excuse—or any vague, mysterious unknown force which possesses us and jerks us around like puppets. But humans are not puppets and must not act as puppets. There are plenty of people in the world eager to pull our strings.

Evil is not something we must all be saddled with for the rest of our lives. Miss Tullock suggests that everyone has a naturally dark side that must be fought forever, which can be stifled, but never extinguished—on the premise that good and evil are black-and-white terms and that humans can never be totally either one. Well, it's true by definition that good and evil are black and white, but since they are absolute principles they cannot exist in some quantity or some combination. Either you are or you aren't. At some point, a person has to decide, "Yes, I will live my life to the fullest, to the benefit of my life," or else, "Yes, I will live for the purpose of destroying life, either mine or others." One can choose not to choose, but that makes a choice for evil by default.

One can make mistakes in judgment, or not have all the facts, or not have the intelligence needed to draw the proper conclusions, or not be perfectly wise, but there is no question on the most basic choice of a sentient being: "Will I dedicate my life to good—or to evil?" There's no doubt which choice Kirk, Spock, McCoy, and others have taken. Yet they've made plenty of mistakes and have suffered because of them. (If they had chosen evil, they would never have suffered for those mistakes. They would try to repeat them.) The evil crew in "Mirror, Mirror" don't make mistakes. They *know* the most efficient ways to make others suffer. It's not a matter of being a poor judge, or what effect your errors will have—it's what you *deliberately* do that shows your moral character.

Star Trek has often become bogged down in evading moral judgments—yes, I know it was necessary to do so for some of the story lines. But it has shown a glimmer of courage, of people who take a stand and can say, "Wait a minute, I think that is wrong.'' I'm glad Star Trek has gone as far as it has, and in all the science fiction I've read, I've never seen a more optimistic, exciting future. I applaud Mr. Roddenberry for his vision and truly hope it comes true!

THOUGHTS ON THE SEARCH FOR SPOCK

by Arden Lowe

By all rights, this article should have been in our last collection, as it was written, as Arden says, "on a first-impression basis" and intended to be read when the first flush of excitement about The Search for Spock *was still upon us. But it arrived just a few days after our deadline, and so missed being included in* Best of Trek #8. *However, we pulled the article from our files when assembling this collection, and discovered that Arden's off-the-cuff first impressions are still valid. See if you agree.*

I am writing this on a first-impression basis. So far, I have seen *Star Trek III: The Search for Spock* only once, and the novelization hasn't appeared in our bookstore yet, but I am on such a Star Trek high at the moment that I felt compelled to write.

Basically, what I have to say is that Leonard Nimoy is as fine a director as he is an actor, and, in the words of the Episcopal communion service, "It is right to give him thanks and praise." *The Search for Spock* is a terrific film! How nice to have someone direct the film who, through his own experiences, is so sensitive to the material with which he is working: and sensitivity is vital to this part of "the adventure."

The Search for Spock is, by and large, a much gentler and more introspective film than *Wrath of Khan*. Yes, there is a brutal murder, and the *Enterprise* is destroyed (sob), but the hateful, vengeful dynamism of *Wrath of Khan* is absent, and in its place is the feeling of brotherly love that was so characteristic of the TV series. Instead of going into space to thwart a raving lunatic, Kirk and his faithful officers set out like Robin Hood and his merry (*very* merry) men on their own personal mission—to rescue a beloved friend and respected officer. But it is the overall nonaggressiveness of their mission that sets the peaceful overtone to this film, and leads us up to quietly joyful resurrection at the end.

The best thing about *The Search for Spock*, though, is that it is such a terrific vehicle for the original Star Trek cast members! The script involves all of the characters to a far greater extent than either of the two preceding films, and it demonstrates the depth of their loyalty and friendship toward one another. Whether it is the simple act of having a drink at the home of their former captain (a *lovely* touch to the movie, I thought), or "borrowing" the *Enterprise* to find their missing friend, the film restates what the television series had already demonstrated—these people not only work together, they care about each other, too. No doubt Star Trek IV will open with the biggest court-martial in the history of the Federation, but I don't think that the defendants will mind too much. They did what they had to do, and they did it out of love. They, like Kirk, sacrificed everything out of love and friendship—just as Spock did in *Wrath of Khan*. It was, after all, their strong convictions that made them Starfleet material to begin with.

The script also added details that made *The Search for Spock* a true addition to the Star Trek legend. First of all, there is the humorous element. There was a great deal of humor in the course of the series—comical incidents, McCoy's unfailing sarcasm, and Spock's wry statements. Such humor was cleverly woven into the storyline of this film as well. For example, McCoy's feeble attempt at the Vulcan neck pinch saved the barroom scene; otherwise, it would have been far too much like something out of *Star Wars* to deserve being in a Star Trek movie. I'll remember to never call Sulu "tiny," and I now know how to keep a Klingon in suspense—kill him later.

Not only was humor abundant, but tiny bits of Star Trek trivia were used as well. For instance, Kirk initiated the self-destruct code we all remember from "Let This Be Your Last Battlefield." (I'll miss that old bucket—even if she was twenty archaic years old!) And poor Spock had to endure *pon farr*; probably more than once, I suspect. The nice thing was, although these little details helped to endear the movie to Star Trek fans, they were incorporated into the script in such a way that non-Trekkers would understand what was going on.

They were a logical (sorry) part of the story, and they were explained when necessary. One of the things I dislike about much of the Star Trek literature is the authors' smug "look what *I* worked into the story" attitude toward throwing in Star Trek details. Not so with *The Search for Spock*. It was a natural use of material.

The ending was as terrific as the script, of course. My special thanks to Walter Koenig, George Takei, James Doohan, and Nichelle Nichols for making their characters come alive for us once more. We really get to see their characters at work in this movie. Chekov and Sulu are as efficient as ever, and I rather suspect that they enjoy getting in trouble from time to time. And Scotty has mellowed so nicely! He is no longer the dour Scotsman from engineering; rather, he is more relaxed and has developed a sense of humor, although time has not altogether blunted his sharp tongue. For the first time since Star Trek hit the silver screen, we see how wonderfully assertive Uhura can be (I know there is a transporter operator who won't forget it), and also what a warm-hearted person she really is. I'm sure that by the time he reached Vulcan, Kirk really needed a warm welcome from an old friend.

Dr. McCoy is just as acerbic as ever—when he's himself, that is. While he is always good, this has to be one of DeForest Kelley's best performances. I wonder what Spock's "marbles" thought about being called "a green-blooded son of a bitch," though. However, we don't need to hear McCoy tell Spock how much he really cares for him. That acid tongue hides one of the warmest hearts in the galaxy, and that, thank God, hasn't changed. As in "The Empath," McCoy chooses "the danger" to help his friend, another instance of sacrifice on his part.

Admiral Kirk is grief-stricken, but his midlife crisis was indeed cured by Spock's death. It was his newly regained ambition that enabled him to defy Starfleet and help his dearest friend. (How ironic, though, that the only way Kirk and Company can go to Spock's aid is to put the computer in charge of the ship. It was the very thing Kirk dreaded when the M-5 unit was introduced onto the *Enterprise*.) As in earlier days, Kirk is able to put aside his grief so that he can command his ship, even though we all know how badly he is hurting. Imagine gaining a son's love and admiration, only to have him killed so tragically, and so soon after losing Spock (in a scene beautifully acted by Shatner and the rest of the cast). At least the fact that Spock and McCoy are finally together can give him what comfort time allows; but as in "Operation: Annihilate" and "City on the Edge of Forever," there really is no time. Once again, William Shatner is to be commended for his fine performance as Kirk!

Of course, Kirk is not the only grieving father. Mark Lenard's wonderful Sarek is far from being the nonemotional Vulcan prototype. He was almost irrational (gasp) when he visited Kirk's apartment, and, until Kirk remembered McCoy's bizarre behavior, was on the verge of hopelessness concerning his son. Sarek's admission that his logic was "flawed where my son is concerned" was probably the first time he had never come close to admitting he loved Spock. Yet, the usual Vulcan dignity and bearing were omnipresent. From Mark Lenard's performance, we understand that grief is as difficult for Vulcans as it is for humans. Actually, it must be worse for Vulcans since an emotional outburst would be considered distasteful.

I am sure that opinions on the "new" Saavik will be as diverse as Star Trek fans are themselves, but my reaction is mixed. Certainly, I missed Kirstie Alley's Vulcanoid austerity, and I think her physical features were more in keeping with the Vulcan/Romulan tradition, but Robin Curtis added a new perspective to the role, and did a fine job at that! Her Saavik, while crisply efficient, even when reporting David's death, was more comparable to the compassionate side of Spock's personality—the Spock who would tend to an injured or ill crew member . . . or chief surgeon. This quality was absolutely necessary for her new role in regard to Spock.

Spock, who was her chief mentor and guardian, is now her charge. She nurtures a child who needs to touch minds for security, a young Vulcan deep in the throes of *pon farr*, and tries to tend to a rapidly aging Vulcan man who is delirious in his agony. This Saavik was calmly compassionate, and most effective in her role. This entire episode will raise a lot more speculation on the relationship between Spock and Saavik, since there is a question as to whether or not Spock's *pon farr* resulted in a physical consummation between the two.

Christopher Lloyd did a superb job as Kruge! What I appreciated most was that, for once, a Klingon was shown to have more feelings than just bloodlust. (In fact, the Klingon who destroyed the *Grissom* was punished for his overzealous behavior.) But Kruge had a pet which he was fond of; and a lover. I am sure he felt personal grief for his lover's death, but a strong sense of duty is necessary for leadership regardless of what world you come from. And for a Klingon, to die in the line of duty is not only valorous, but honorable. However, it was nice to see that a Klingon who could callously, yet predictably, order a prisoner killed also had the capacity to feel a sense of loss for the deaths of his crew. Perhaps he felt a twinge of personal guilt not unlike that of another ship's captain of our acquaintance?

(Actually, I was hoping that Kruge would be more like Reverend Jim Ignatowski on *Taxi*. Kirk has always been up against equal or superior beings. Just imagine him facing an airheaded enemy who could phaser him to death by accident!)

I didn't discuss the ending earlier, because I feel it deserves special treatment. The beautiful symbolic ritual was as tastefully done as Spock's resurrection on the Genesis Planet. (I have to admit that I was concerned about how Spock's resurrection would be made plausible, but I needn't have worried. It was a nice touch to have Spock's friends act as "pallbearers" as they carried Spock, dressed in his burial robe, to the altar. It was also symbolic to have Spock stripped of his burial robe and dressed in white as a sign of his rebirth.

But what I liked best about the ending was that it wasn't overly emotional. I'm sure many fans were disappointed by this, but I wasn't. Kirk has always respected Spock's Vulcan reserve, and, though he was physically demonstrative at times, he avoided overt expressions of affection. That's why he was so surprised when Spock held his hand after contacting V'Ger. And at this sensitive moment, when Spock has just recognized Kirk, their normal relationship should not change. It would only have confused and embarrassed Spock. Kirk obviously means much to Spock by the very nature of the fact that he is the one person that Spock recognizes, as he was the one Spock reached out for after contacting V'Ger. The beauty in this ending was the joy on the faces of everyone as Spock, now reunited with them, stands in their midst. Could anyone think of a more fitting conclusion?

I also appreciated the fact that Spock was not fully recovered at the end of the film. He recognizes his friends, and they will help him, but he still has a way to go. One of the things I hated most about "Spock's Brain" was that after major brain surgery, Spock sat up, every hair in place, and resumed his duties. *The Search for Spock* is far more sensitive to the process of healing. It shows us that healing is multidimensional, that it is emotional as well as physical, and thus takes more time.

The only thing left for me to say is "thank you" to Leonard Nimoy, the Star Trek production crew, and the Star Trek cast for such a beautiful movie. Thank you for involving all the characters we know and love so well. Thank you also for showing us once again how strong the feelings of love and sacrifice can be. *Star Trek III: The Search for Spock* deserves its place in the Star Trek world! Live long and prosper.

MYTHOLOGY AND THE BIBLE IN STAR TREK— PART II

by Sarah Schaper and Mary Hamburger

We're kind of sorry that we must present this second half of Mary and Sarah's article before we've had a chance to get some reaction from our readers. (The manuscript for this volume goes to the printer several weeks before Best of Trek *#8 will appear on the stands.) We believe that the articles will draw a lot of mail, but we frankly have no idea whether that mail will be primarily positive, primarily negative, or primarily neutral. One thing we can be sure of, however, is that Sarah and Mary have done a terrific job of research, and are to be complimented for their dedication. We hope you'll enjoy this second half of the article just as much as you did the first.*

Many themes from mythology and the Bible were used in the episodes of Star Trek.

Myths are traditional stories that helped to explain to ancient societies mysteries about themselves and the world around them. Some of these myths were religious in nature, dealing with the origin of the cosmos and man and explaining the phenomena of nature. Other myths were stories of heroes or gods responding to their human nature and dealing with all their emotions.

The Bible is a collection of writings composed over many centuries. It is divided into two sections known as the Old Testament and the New Testament. The Old Testament begins with Genesis and the six-day creation of the heavens and the earth. It tells of the events which followed the creation of man, the actions of God, and the lives of the House of Israel. The New Testament deals with the life, teachings, death, and resurrection of Jesus Christ. It is also a record of Christian philosophy and belief through its beginning centuries. Both Testaments tell of God's promises of life and the hope of future generations.

Both myths and the Bible influence not only our lives but also our entertainment. These influences can be seen in Star Trek. So let's look at some more of these references with a theme-by-theme reference to Star Trek.

Paradise

In Star Trek, the *Enterprise* has come across many so-called paradises—places of peace, happiness, and eternal life or fantastic beauty, such as the "Shore Leave" planet where McCoy said, "You have to see this place to believe it. It's like something out of *Alice in Wonderland*." The planet Gideon in "The Mark of Gideon" had long ago been "a virtual paradise" where "people flourished in their physical and spiritual perfection." Landru's home planet in "The Return of the Archons" seemed like paradise to those who had been "absorbed" and were "of the body." Apollo in "Who Mourns for Adonais?" offered "life in paradise." However, all of the paradises in Star Trek turn out to have some fatal flaw.

Paradise seems to be a word of Persian origins, where it came to mean the king's private hunting ground—a grand enclosure or park, shady and well watered, in which wild animals were kept for the hunt. It was enclosed by walls and furnished with towers for the hunters.

In Greek it meant "garden." In the Greek Old Testament, it was used to translate a similar Hebrew word meaning "forest" or "orchard," as in King Solomon's pomegranate orchard or the Forest of Lebanon. It was also used for the garden in which Susanna decided to bathe because the weather was hot, and for the Garden of Eden. It was used in this sense in "This Side of Paradise," where Spock was able to enjoy the beauty of a rainbow, and in "The Apple," where the natives did not grow old and the landing party was reminded of the Garden of Eden.

The New Testament uses it three times to mean God's garden in heaven:

Jesus said to one of the criminals crucified with him, "Truly, I say to you, today you will be with me in The Garden."

St. Paul wrote, "I know a man in Christ who fourteen years ago was caught up to the third heaven—whether in the body or out of the body I do not know, God knows. And I know that this man was caught up into The Garden—whether in the body or out of the body I do not know, God knows. And he heard unspeakable things spoken of, which it is not lawful for a man to tell." (This sounds like part of the Prime Directive for undeveloped planets. References to space are not lawful to tell.)

And Jesus said, "To him who overcomes, I will give something to eat from the tree of life, which is in The Garden of God."

In English, *paradise* has three meanings: (1) an upper region of the heavens and the abode of souls of the righteous until the resurrection, (2) the Garden of Eden, and (3) a place of great beauty, perfection, and happiness—as in "The Paradise Syndrome," in which Kirk married Miramanee and said, "I've found paradise. Surely no man has ever attained such happiness." In "I, Mudd," when Mudd described his haremlike rock as "absolute paradise," he too was referring to the paradise that is a place of great beauty, perfection, and happiness.

The Soul

In "I, Mudd," Mudd called the android Norman a poor, souless creature. In "A Private Little War," after Nona, Tyree's wife, had cured Kirk, she said that her soul had been in contact with Kirk's.

In the New Testament as written in an early language, Koine Greek, the word for *soul* is *psyche*. (You couldn't pronounce it.) It is translated "soul," "life," "mind," or "person." A soul is a life complete with its thoughts and feelings both before and after death. That the soul is real and exists has been indicated by the measurements made by Dr. Duncan McDougall, a physician on the staff of the Massachusetts General Hospital. He "weighed" the soul by very carefully weighing six persons as each one died. Each person's weight dropped suddenly, in one or two stages, at the time of death. He found that the soul "weighs" a fraction of an ounce.

In "What Are Little Girls Made Of?" Dr. Roger Korby, Christine Chapel's fiancé, put his soul into an android body in an effort to achieve practical immortality—a new kind of heaven, and a new kind of paradise—but his scheme didn't work.

In "The Return of the Archons," the computer Landru was a marvelous feat of engineering capable of directing every act of millions of people. The original Landru had programmed it with all his knowledge, but he couldn't give it his soul with its wisdom, compassion, and understanding; and this would account for its soulless solution to all problems—machine-made peace and tranquillity, broken only by the emotional release of Festival.

"God formed man of the dust of the ground, and breathed into his nostrils the breath of life; and man became a living soul."

Jesus said, "Do not fear those who kill the body but cannot kill the soul."

And John wrote, "I saw the souls of those who had been beheaded of their testimony for Jesus and because of the word of God, and who did not worship the beast nor his image and did not receive the mark on their foreheads and on their hands. And they lived and reigned with Christ the thousand years."

Hell

In the episode "The Doomsday Machine," Commodore Decker called the doomsday machine "the devil right out of hell." The word *hell* is generally used in the King James Version of the Old Testament to translate the Hebrew word *Sheol*, which means simply the place of the dead, without reference to either reward or punishment. In the King James Version of the New Testament, the word *hell* is used to translate two words: (1) *Hades*, generally meaning the same as Sheol, the place of the dead, and (2) *Gehenna*, the place of punishment for evil deeds, named after the Jerusalem garbage dump. Different translations handle these words differently and, generally, better. But for any peoples on planets gobbled up by the doomsday machine, it was death, the place of death, and doomsday for them. Doomsday is the day of final judgment.

In "The Menagerie," when Captain Pike did not drink the nutritious liquid his keepers prepared for him, they punished him by making him experience what he thought hell would be like, with flames and agony. This could have come from a story Jesus told about a certain rich man and a beggar named

Lazarus. The rich man refused to share anything with Lazarus, or help him in any way. Lazarus died and was carried by angels to be with Abraham. The rich man died and was buried; and in the place of the dead, where he was in torment, he looked up and saw Abraham at a distance and Lazarus with him. The rich man called out, "Father Abraham, pity me and send Lazarus to dip the tip of his finger in water and cool my tongue, because I am in anguish in this flame."

The Sons of God

In "Bread and Circuses," Kirk, Spock, and McCoy had just beamed down to a very Earthlike planet where the Prime Directive was supposed to be in full force, and McCoy said, "Once, just once, I'd like to land someplace and say, 'Behold, I am the Archangel Gabriel.' " But perhaps Gabriel had already appeared on this planet. In the Bible the Archangel Gabriel appeared at least twice to Daniel, once to the father of John the Baptist, and once to Mary, who was to become the mother of Jesus. Each time Gabriel appeared, he brought very important and prophetic news.

This planet had a society like a twentieth-century Roman Empire. The outcasts seemed to be sun worshipers. Back aboard the ship at the end of the episode, Spock said, "I wish we could have examined that belief of his [Flavius'] more closely. It seems illogical for a sun worshiper to develop a philosophy of total brotherhood. Sun worship is usually a primitive superstition-religion." But, as Uhura revealed from radio and television broadcasts she'd overheard from the planet, it wasn't the sun up in the sky they worshiped; it was the Son of God, Christ. And the word was spreading only now.

These Son worshipers sometimes referred to him as the Light, and would glance upward when talking about him as if they had seen him ascend into heaven and were expecting him to return that way. In the Bible, Jesus said, "I am the light of the world. He who follows me will not walk in the darkness, but will have the light of life." After Jesus rose from the dead, as his friends were looking on, "he was lifted up, and a cloud took him out of their sight. And while they were gazing into the sky as he was going, behold two men stood by them in white robes, and said, 'Men of Galilee, why are you standing looking up into the sky? This Jesus who was taken up from you into heaven, will come the same way you saw him go into heaven.' "

Perhaps you have been taught that Jesus was the *only* Son of God. The Greek New Testament does not say that, but only that he was the only-of-his-kind Son; that is, he was the only one of his kind. Job mentioned "the sons of God" who came to present themselves before the Lord. And Jesus repeatedly referred to himself as the Son of Man as if there were other sons of God, and as if he were only the one for man, that is, for humans. In that case other planets might have other sons of God.

Concerning "The Return of the Archons," *archon* means "beginning," "being first," "leader," or "ruler," and was an appropriate name for an early starship. Later it came to mean crew members of that starship. On Landru's planet there was a prophecy of the return of Archons to free the planet from Landru and his talking image. Jesus is called "the Archon of the kings of the Earth" in Revelation 1:5, and on our planet there is the prophecy of Jesus' return and his freeing of Earth from the control of the "beast" and his talking image.

Reminders of Jesus turn up in many episodes, in the form of teachings, a Christmas party, and quotes—"Out of the mouth of babes" in "A Piece of the Action," and "the lilies of the field . . . they toil not, neither do they spin" in "The Trouble with Tribbles."

Blessings (Beatitudes)

In "Arena," the Metrons had Kirk fight the Gorn captain. When Kirk refused to kill the wounded Gorn, he obeyed the command "You shall not kill," and showed the advanced trait of mercy. In the same way in "Spectre of the Gun," the Melkotians had Kirk fight the Earps, but he did not try to kill them even after they had tried to kill him. The Metrons and the Melkotians approved of his mercy and showed mercy to him. Jesus said, "Blessed are the merciful, for they shall receive mercy," and "With the same measure [*metron* means "measure"] with which you measure, it will be measured back to you," which means that you will be treated as you treat others.

Another beatitude, "Blessed are the peacemakers, for they shall be called sons of God," is seen in "Errand of Mercy," when the Organians were peacemakers, and Spock said of them, "Even the gods did not spring into being overnight." The Organians repeatedly denounced violence, as does God in the Old Testament. And the Organians have other characteristics of children of God or of God himself—knowledge, omnipresence, power, and light. "Those who are wise will shine like the brightness of the heavens, and those who lead many to righteousness, like the stars forever and ever."

Kor and Kirk had been threatening war against each other, as Paul (Saul) had been threatening destruction aginst the church. The Organians put a stop to the violence and said, "Please leave us. The mere presence of beings like yourselves is extremely painful to us."

Kirk asked, "What do you mean, 'beings like yourselves'?" The Organians explained that millions of years ago they had been humanoid, but they had developed beyond that. The humanoids saw the Organians become very bright lights, then disappear.

Similarly, Jesus put a stop to Saul's violence. As Saul was going to Damascus to get rid of the church there, suddenly he saw a light from heaven brighter than the sun shining around him, and a voice said, "Saul, Saul, why do you persecute me?"

And Paul said, "Who are you, Lord?"

And the Lord said, "I am Jesus, whom you are persecuting; but rise and enter the city, and you will be told what you are to do."

"Sinner Repent"

"There is joy in the presence of angels of God over one sinner who repents." There was quite a bit of sinning and repenting in Star Trek. It was often Kirk's lot to persuade the sinners to repent; fortunately he could be quite persuasive. He persuaded the Vians to show mercy in "The Empath," persuaded the children to give back the communicators in "Miri," and even persuaded the Klingons to cease hostilities in "Day of the Dove."

But he found it impossible to persuade Bele and Lokai of the planet Cheron not to hate each other, "And sin, when it is full-grown, produces death."

The people of Cheron destroyed each other, and Spock reported from his scanners, "Several very large cities. All uninhabited. Extensive traffic systems barren of traffic. Vegetation and lower animals encroaching on the cities. No sapient life forms at all, captain."

"You mean the people are *all* dead?"

"Yes, captain—all dead."

The Old Testament description of the destruction of Sharon:

> Woe to you, O destroyer,
>   you who have not been destroyed!
> Woe to you, O traitor,
>   you who have not been betrayed!
> When you stop destroying,
>   you will be destroyed;
> When you stop betraying,
>   you will be betrayed . . .
> Look, their brave men cry aloud in the streets;
>   the envoys of peace weep bitterly.
> The highways are deserted,
>   no travelers on the roads.
> The treaty is broken,
>   its witnesses are despised,
>   no one is respected.
> The land mourns and wastes away;
>   Lebanon is ashamed and withers;
> Sharon is like a desert.

In "The Ultimate Computer," Dr. Daystrom, the inventor of the M-5 computer, believed that killing, murdering, was wrong and contrary to the laws of man and God; so he programmed this information into his computer. When the computer was convinced that it had murdered hundreds of people, it left itself open to the penalty of death to atone for the sin of murder.

The story of "Charlie X" suggests the story of the prodigal son. Both took what had been given them for survival, went far away, misused it, got into trouble, and then repented. But the stories end somewhat differently. The prodigal son went gladly back to his father. Charlie X pleaded to go with the humans, but the Thasians had to take him back home with them by force.

Possession

In "The Lights of Zetar," the Zetarians entered Mira Romaine's mind and tried to take possession of her and function through her, and they caused her to apparently foresee future events. Captain Kirk spoke to them, and they answered using her voice. After they were forced to leave her, she became normal again.

This was somewhat like a spirit of future-telling or "a spirit of Python" which inhabited a Greek slave girl whom St. Paul and his friends met. In Greek mythology, people who were supposed to predict future events were said to have a spirit of Python. The Greek slave girl earned a good income for her owners as a soothsayer. She followed Paul, shouting, "These men are servants of the highest God, who are telling you a way of salvation."

Paul became annoyed and said to the spirit, "I command you in the name of Jesus Christ to come out of her." Then the girl became normal and was of no more use to her owners.

Similarly, in "Wolf in the Fold," the entity that was Jack the Ripper had entered and possessed Mr. Hengist before he left his home planet, Rigel IV. When the entity abandoned Mr. Hengist, it left him dead, then entered the ship's computer. It was driven back into Hengist's body and beamed into deep space.

Jesus met a man who was demon-possessed, who for a long time had worn no clothes and lived in the tombs. Jesus commanded the demon to come out of him. The man fell down before Jesus and cried out loudly, "What's with me and you, Jesus, Son of the highest God. I beg you don't torment me."

Jesus asked him, "What is your name?"

And he said, "Legion, for we are many." And they begged him not to command them to go into the abyss (space without bottom) but to let them enter a herd of pigs there on the hillside, and he let them. Then the demons left the man and entered the pigs, and the pigs rushed down a steep bank into a lake and were drowned. People from the city went out to see what had happened and found the man sitting at the feet of Jesus, dressed and in his right mind.

Other episodes use a similar possession theme. Gorgan, "the friendly angel," led the children and they led the crew in "The Children Shall Lead." An entity that lived on hate possessed the Klingons and the humans in "Day of the Dove." Janice Lester possessed Captain Kirk in "Turnabout Intruder." And Sargon, Thalassa, and Henoch transferred from orbs into the bodies of Kirk, Spock, and Dr. Ann Mulhall in "Return to Tomorrow."

God and His Commandments

"In the beginning God created the heavens and the earth" —that is, the universe and everything in it. In "Metamorphosis," when Nancy Hedford was near death, the Companion cured her and combined with her. Spock said, "Companion, you cannot create life."

The Companion answered, "That is for the maker of all things."

At the beginning of "The Empath," Spock played back a tape in order to find out what had happened to the missing geologists. On the tape, one of the men said, "I don't think I can stand another week of this God-forsaken place."

Then there was an earthquake, and the other man said, " 'In his hands are the deep places of the earth.' Psalm 95, verse 4. Looks like he was listening." This seemingly obscure Bible verse may have been a favorite for a geologist.

Other people in Star Trek have shown their belief in God:

Apollo in "Who Mourns for Adonais?" demanded to be worshiped as a god, but Kirk refused and said, "Mankind has no need for gods. We find the one quite adequate." Kirk obeyed 'the commandment, "I am the Lord your God, who brought you out of Egypt, out of the land of slavery. You shall have no other gods besides me. . . . You shall not bow down to them or worship them."

In "Where No Man Has Gone Before," in addition to the sin of considering himself a god, Gary Mitchell sinned when he contemplated "the death of an old friend," and tried to disobey God's commandment "You shall not kill."

He lacked compassion; and as Kirk told him, "Above all, a god needs compassion."

"The Lord is good to all, and his compassion is over all that he has made."

When Kirk was explaining the Prime Directive to the Capellan leader in "Friday's Child," he said that we have laws, "and the highest of our laws states that your world is yours and will always remain yours. This differs us from the Klingons. Their empire is made up of conquered worlds. They take what they want by arms and force."

"You shall not steal" is another one of the Ten Commandments. The Klingons steal.

During Kirk's trial in "Court-Martial," his lawyer, Cogley, mentioned the Bible and other documents and said, "These documents all speak of rights, rights of the accused to a trial by his peers, to be represented by counsel, the right of cross-examination, but most important, the right to be confronted by the witnesses against him, a right to which my client has been denied. . . . The most devastating witness against my client is not a human being. It's a machine.''

Another of the Ten Commandments is ''You shall not bear false witness against your neighbor''; but the computer log of the *Enterprise* had been giving false witness against Kirk.

If Cogley's Bible was a Catholic one, it told about the trial of Susanna, who was accused falsely. Daniel examined the two false witnesses separately so that they could not hear each other and proved Susanna's innocence.

Marriage

In the beginning of ''Balance of Terror,'' Kirk had the happy privilege of officiating at a wedding aboard the *Enterprise*. ''From the beginning of creation God 'made them male and female. For this a man will leave his father and mother and be joined to his wife, and the two will become one flesh.' So they are no longer two, but one. Therefore, what God has joined together, let man not separate.''

Christine Chapel wanted to get married. Elaan, in ''Elaan of Troyius,'' didn't—at least not to the man picked out for her—but in her words, she was ''a bribe to stop a war.''

In Ambassador Petri's words, ''That creature, Elaan, is to be the wife of our ruler to bring peace. . . . To obtain peace at the price of accepting such a queen is no victory.''

In King Solomon's time, daughters of rulers were often given to the enemy to make peace. This is why King Solomon had so many wives. He made a peace alliance with the king of Egypt and married the Egyptian princess. Then he made peace alliances with all the surrounding foreign towns and married their leaders' daughters. To obtain peace at the price of accepting seven hundred wives was no victory because they led him astray with their detestable gods.

In ''The Paradise Syndrome,'' Kirk married the chief's daughter because tribal law betrothed her to the medicine chief. He loved her and said, ''These last few weeks my love for Miramanee grows stronger with each passing day.''

The New Testament says, ''Husbands, love your wives,'' and ''Wives, submit to your husbands.'' Miramanee was submissive to her husband; she even thought he was a god.

In ''Amok Time,'' Spock returned to Vulcan to take a

wife. He called T'Pring his wife, but his relationship to her was less than a marriage, yet more than a betrothal, and it could be broken only by divorce. This is like the custom Mary and Joseph were living under when Jesus was born. Their betrothal could be broken only by divorce. "Mary had been betrothed to Joseph, but before they came together, she was found to be pregnant by the Holy Spirit; and Joseph her husband, being a righteous man and unwilling to make an example of her, wanted to divorce her privately. But as he considered these things, behold, an angel of the Lord appeared to him in a dream, saying, 'Joseph, son of David, do not be afraid to take Mary as your wife, for what is conceived in her is from the Holy Spirit.' "

T'Pring chose to divorce Spock by choosing the challenge and choosing Kirk as her champion. Divorce on Vulcan is a violent thing, and it nearly got the captain killed. " 'I hate divorce,' says the Lord the God of Israel, 'and covering one's garment with violence.' "

The Ultimate Crisis

When Sargon was explaining the ultimate catastrophe that destroyed his civilization in "Return to Tomorrow," he said, "We survived our primitive nuclear era, my son, but there comes to all races an ultimate crisis which you have yet to face. . . . One day our minds became so powerful we dared think of ourselves as gods."

A New Testament prophecy says, "The Day will not come until the final Rebellion occurs and the man of lawlessness appears, the son of destruction. He will oppose and exalt himself over everything called a god or worshiped. He will even sit down in the temple of God and proclaim himself to be a god." He will also have enough power to convince people of his claim.

"Star date Armageddon." Armageddon will be the Earth equivalent of the ultimate crisis Sargon was speaking of, a battle of the future that the participants will have little chance of living through. The word *Armageddon* is from *Har Magedon*, which means "Mountain of Megiddo," which would be Mount Carmel in Israel. "A Taste of Armageddon" was a story of two planets that had been carrying on an orderly war with computers for five hundred years. But a taste of Armageddon will be a taste of:

"The sixth angel poured his bowl on the great river Euphrates, and its water was dried up to prepare the way for the kings from the east. And I saw, out of the mouth of the dragon and out of the mouth of the beast and out of the mouth of the false prophet, three unclean spirits as frogs; for they are demonic spirits, performing signs, who go out to the kings of the whole world, to assemble them for war of the great day of God the Almighty. . . . And they assembled them at the place that is called in Hebrew, Armageddon.''

In ''The Paradise Syndrome,'' the planet where Miramanee lived was threatened by another kind of catastrophe. An asteroid was on a collision course with the planet; and she said, ''The wind is only beginning. Soon the sky will darken. The lake will go wild, and the earth will tremble!'' Kirk suggested they go to the caves.

Compare ''The Paradise Syndrome'' to the prophecy in Revelation:

''When he opened the sixth seal, there was a great earthquake; and the sun became black as sackcloth of hair, the full moon became as blood, and the stars of the sky fell to the earth as a fig tree drops its late figs when shaken by a great wind. The sky disappeared like a scroll being rolled up, and every mountain and island was moved out of its place. Then the kings of the earth and the great men and the commanders and the rich and the strong and every slave and every free man hid in the caves and among the rocks of the mountains.''

The people on Miramanee's planet were very much afraid, and they expected the wise ones to send a god to come and save them. Jesus said, ''On the earth there will be distress of nations in perplexity at the roaring of the sea and the waves, men fainting from fear and anticipation of what is coming on the world; for the powers of the heavens will be shaken. And then they will see the Son of Man coming in a cloud with power and great glory.''

Beaming Up

The transporter operates by converting matter to energy and reconverting the energy to matter in another place. St. Paul wrote, ''The Lord himself will come down from heaven with a command, with an archangel's call, and with a trumpet of God; and the dead in Christ will rise first. Then we the living, who are left, will be caught up together with them in the clouds to meet the Lord in the air; and so we will always be with the Lord.'' This future event, which will happen before

Armageddon, is called "the translation" or "the rapture" by some Christians; but it could also be thought of as "the beaming up."

The Epistle of Barnabas was written a few years after Revelation and was considered scripture at Alexandria in Egypt but not at other places. It indicates that the return of Christ will be two thousand years after his birth. Whether this is accurate or not, at least it won't be too many years before we find out.

Life in the Future

The life span for humans in our future millennium will become well over a hundred years as it was for the beings in a number of Star Trek's episodes, such as the Kohms in "The Omega Glory" and the Vulcans in "Journey to Babel." Spock's father was only 102.437, measured in our years.

> Never again will there be in it
>   an infant that lives but a few days,
>   or an old man who does not live out his
>   years;
>   he who dies at a hundred
>   will be thought a mere youth;
>   he who fails to reach a hundred
>   will be considered accursed.

The title of the episode "And the Children Shall Lead" is adapted from this verse in Isaiah:

> The wolf shall dwell with the lamb,
>   and the leopard shall lie down with the kid,
>   and the calf and the lion and the fatling together,
>   and a little child shall lead them.

Nova

In "All Our Yesterdays," the sun of Zarabeth's planet, Sarpeidon, was about to go nova, and the whole planet was about to be destroyed by the exploding sun.

"The day of the Lord will come like a thief, and then the heavens will pass away with a roar, and the burning elements will be dissolved, and the earth and the works on it will be burned up."

The mission of the *Enterprise* is to explore strange new worlds and to seek out new life and new civilizations. "Then I saw a new heaven and a new earth, for the first heaven and the first earth were gone. . . . And I heard a loud voice from the throne saying, '. . . Death shall be no more, and neither mourning nor crying nor pain shall be any more. . . . Behold, I make all things new.' "

References to Biblical People and Their Stories

Numerous names from the Bible are used in Star Trek. Ruth from "Shore Leave" and James are examples. The Ruth in the Bible was the young Moabite widow, a woman of worth, who said to her Jewish mother-in-law. "Where you go I will go, and where you stay I will stay. Your people will be my people and your God my God. Where you die I will die, and there I will be buried." James was the name of two outstanding men in the Bible. One James was an apostle of Jesus whom Jesus surnamed Son of Thunder. Being an apostle was a dangerous occupation, and James was the first apostle to be martyred. Herod Agrippa I had him put to death with a sword. Another James was a brother of Jesus and became the bishop of the church at Jerusalem. One day when all the Roman rulers just happened to be out of town at the same time, the Jewish leaders had James killed by stoning because he had been preaching about Jesus. Both the stoning of this James and the stoning of James Kirk in "The Paradise Syndrome" resulted from claims about a god who bled (Jesus and James Kirk), who was the object of intense jealousy, and who wasn't saving his people.

In the episode "Miri," Miri and Jahn lived on a planet so similar to Earth that it had had an almost parallel development. Miri and Jahn are variant spellings of New Testament names. Mary was the mother of Jesus; John was a favorite disciple of Jesus.

In "Patterns of Force," the warlike Ekosians, patterned after Nazi Germany, were out to destroy the peaceful, more advanced Zeons, who took the place of the Jews in the story. The Zeons have Old Testament names with variant spellings: Zeon is a variant of Zion, Isak of Isaac, Abrom of Abram, and Davod of David.

In "Journey to Babel," the neutral planetoid on which the council of ambassadors of Federation planets was to meet was code-named Babel because of the many languages spoken there. When the earth had one language, the men of Shinar decided to build themselves a city with a tower that reached to the sky. But the Lord confused them by giving them different languages and thus scattered them over the face of the whole earth. Therefore the name of the city was called Babel (meaning "confusion").

In "The Mark of Gideon," the planet Gideon was so full of people that there was no place to be alone. Odona said, "There is no place, no street, no house, no garden, no beach, no mountain that is not filled with people." The population had to be reduced.

In the Bible, Gideon was the leader of thousands and thousands of people (32,000 men) ready to fight the Midianites. So God said to Gideon, "You have too many men for me to deliver Midian into their hands. In order that Israel may not boast against me that her own strength has saved her, announce now to the people, 'Anyone who trembles with fear may turn back.' " Twenty-two thousand men went home, but ten thousand stayed. Then God said to Gideon, "You still have too many men. Take them down to the water for a drink. Separate those who scoop up water with their hand from those who get down on their hands and knees to drink." Three hundred men scooped up water to drink, and the rest were sent back home. With these three hundred men, God delivered Midian into their hands.

Lazarus, the time traveler in "The Alternative Factor," seemed to have recuperative powers that amazed Dr. McCoy, and he seemed independent of time and death. Lazarus in the Bible was raised from the dead by Jesus. Concerning time travel, in Revelation 1:10 the author, John, said, "I became, in spirit, in the Lord's day," and then he described what he heard and saw. Since "the Lord's day" means "the day of the Lord" and refers to a future time, time travel into the future is a possible interpretation here.

In "Metamorphosis," Zefram Cochrane asked, "What did they call it—the-'Judas goat'?" before he went out to call the Companion so it could be betrayed, rendered harmless, and possibly killed. Judas, one of Jesus' disciples who had been with him continually for three years, betrayed Jesus with a kiss; and *goat* refers to the scapegoat.

In "The Gamesters of Triskelion," when Spock started to beam down to that dangerous planet, McCoy volunteered, "Well, Mr. Spock, if you're going into the lion's den, you'll need a medical officer."

Spock said, "Daniel, as I recall, had only his faith, but I welcome your company, doctor."

Daniel was thrown into a den of lions for praying to God three times a day when it was against the law to pray to God. The king said to Daniel, "May your God, whom you serve continually, rescue you!"

The king spent a sleepless night in his palace and returned at daybreak and found Daniel, who said, "My God sent his angel, and he shut the mouths of the lions. They have not hurt me because I was found innocent in his sight."

King Solomon's Wisdom

In "Whom Gods Destroy," "Lord" Garth took the form of other people in order to deceive. When he took the form of Spock in order to deceive Kirk, Kirk realized which was Spock and which Garth by their actions and what they said. Later, Garth took the form of Kirk in order to fool Spock. As he fought with the real Kirk, Spock had to decide which was which. Spock was waiting for a victor and ended up getting hit on the head. He was finally able to distinguish between the two by their behavior. Kirk told Spock that letting himself get hit on the head was not exactly a method of which King Solomon would have approved.

In King Solomon's time, two prostitutes came before the king and claimed to be the mother of the same baby boy. To test them, King Solomon ordered the baby cut in two. The real mother quickly protested and gave up her claim to her baby so that it would not be harmed; so Solomon gave the unharmed baby to its real mother.

In "The Squire of Gothos," Uhura's beauty and color reminded Trelane of the Queen of Sheba. The Queen of Sheba visited King Solomon to ask him difficult questions because of the fame of his wisdom, and his relation to the name of the Lord. She "arrived in Jerusalem with a very numerous retinue, and with camels bearing spices, a large amount of gold, and precious stones. She came to Solomon and questioned him on every subject in which she was interested. King Solomon explained everything she asked about, and there remained nothing hidden from him that he could not explain to her." She was overcome with admiration. They exchanged gifts and she returned to her own land.

Spock

Spock can be compared to a true classical mythological hero. The word hero is from the Greek *heros*, and in Greek mythology and legend meant "a man of great skill, strength, and courage." Here are the characteristics of a classical hero:

1. The mother is a royal virgin.
2. The father is a king.
3. The father is often a near relative of the mother.
4. Circumstances of conception are often unusual.
5. The child is reputed to be the son of a god.
6. There is an attempt to kill him, usually by his father or paternal grandfather.
7. He is spirited away before he can be killed.
8. He is reared by foster parents in a far-away country.
9. We're told nothing about his childhood.
10. Upon manhood he returns to his future kingdom.
11. He is victorious over a major power.
12. He marries a princess—often the daughter of a predecessor.
13. He becomes king.
14. He reigns uneventfully for a time.
15. He prescribes laws.
16. He loses favor either with the gods or with his subjects.
17. He is driven from the throne or the city.
18. He meets with a mysterious death.
19. Death is often on a hilltop.
20. Children, if any, do not succeed him to the throne.
21. His body is never buried in the ground. It is put in a tomb or sepulcher.
22. There is often more than one sepulcher.

Some of these characteristics apply to Spock, but if you modernize them and move them up into Star Trek's time, then:

1. Spock's mother is a teacher on the planet Vulcan but is human, which makes her unusual like a royal virgin.
2. Spock's father, Sarek, is from an important family and is an ambassador, a position of leadership.
4. Circumstances of Spock's conception are admittedly unusual.
6. Spock had a falling-out with his father. They didn't speak to each other as father and son for eighteen years.
7. Spock left his home planet, Vulcan, and joined Starfleet.
9. We're told little about Spock's childhood except that he had a pet sehlat with six-inch fangs.
10. At Spock's *pon farr* he returned to Vulcan to claim his bride, T'Pring.

11. Spock's victory is over his "self." He survives his internal struggle between his Vulcan and his human halves because his intelligence wins out over both.
12. Spock was betrothed to a girl from an important family.
13. Spock proves to be a true Vulcan in spite of his human mother.
14. Spock's times at command of the *Enterprise* are rather uneventful.
15. He gives orders.
16. When in command, Spock is often criticized by those who must obey him.
17. Spock readily gives up command to Kirk.
18. He meets with an unusual death.
19. His death occurs in space.
20. Spock's children, if any, will not succeed him.
21. His body is not buried in the ground.
22. There will be more than one funeral.

Although both Kirk and Spock are heroes in the series, Spock is the modern classical hero. There are similarities between Spock and Jesus as heroes, and dissimilarities. Both Spock and Jesus had human mothers and nonhuman fathers. Both have superior intelligence. Both can do things that we cannot do. Both were critical of humans' hardness of heart. In "The Immunity Syndrome," Spock sensed the deaths of four hundred Vulcans aboard the starship *Intrepid*. McCoy asks him about this, and Spock said, "I've noticed that about your people, doctor. You find it easier to understand the death of one than the death of a million. You speak about the objective hardness of the Vulcan heart, yet how little room there seems to be in yours."

Again in "The Immunity Syndrome," when the captain thought Spock was dead, he said that Spock gave his life in the performance of his duty. Jesus risked his life for three years in the performance of his duty. Both of them finally sacrificed their lives to save others. Since Jesus was raised from the dead, it was not surprising to see Spock resurrected.

But Jesus is real and divine. Spock is fictional and an ordinary mortal of the "be fruitful-and-multiply" type in his own Vulcan way. Spock was less emotional; and he certainly spoke to his father less than did Jesus, who prayed often; and Spock made occasional errors. Spock said that he did not believe in angels. Jesus was helped by an angel after his temptation by Satan, and again when he was praying before his crucifixion. Their resurrections were different. Jesus was granted immortality. Spock is still a mortal—like the man whose friends were burying him, but when they saw a gang of bandits, hastily threw his body into the tomb of Elisha the prophet. When the body touched Elisha's bones, the man came to life and stood on his feet.

Some people identify with Spock because he is an alien. So, in a way, was Jesus, who said, "My kingdom is not of this world," and to his disciples, "You are not of the world."

Logic

Spock accepted a philosophy that is logical and beneficial. He said that Vulcans were once a people who were "wildly emotional, often committed to irrationally opposing points of view, leading of course to death and destruction. Only the discipline of logic saved my people from extinction."

The message of the Bible is also logical and beneficial. We get our word *logic* from *logos*, "reasoning, thought, mind, message, or word." *Logos* is used in the beginning of the Gospel of John to mean the Word of God, that is, Jesus. "In the beginning was the Logos, and the Logos was with God, and the Logos was divine."

Mind Probing

Spock occasionally used an ancient Vulcan technique to probe into the mind of another person or some creature. He would touch the face of the person or touch the creature. In "Dagger of the Mind," he described it as a "personal thing to the Vulcan people, part of our private lives." To Van Gelder, he said, "You begin to feel a strange euphoria. Your body floats. . . . Open your mind. We move together, our minds sharing the same thoughts."

Since God is everywhere, he touches us. He enters our minds and knows our thoughts and feelings that are too deep for words. "The mind [Logos] of God is living and active, sharper than any double-edged sword, penetrating even to a division of life and breath, of joints and marrow, and discerning the thoughts and attitudes of the heart. And no creature is hidden in his sight, but all are open and laid bare to his eyes." He knows us better than we know ourselves.

Love

"The City on the Edge of Forever" is a Good Samaritan story. Edith Keeler (Sister Edith Keeler in the film credits) helped people on old Earth in 1930 at the 21st Street Mission. She hired Kirk and Spock because they showed up there with no money. She was a most uncommon person gifted with insight. She believed that in the future, men would "find ways to feed the hungry millions of the world and cure their diseases." To McCoy she became ". . . a friend. When you showed up here, you looked like you could use one." She ran the mission because "It's necessary."

McCoy said, "Well, it was for me at least. You may have saved my life."

Edith obeyed the command "You shall love your neighbor as yourself."

A lawyer asked Jesus, "And who is my neighbor?"

In reply, Jesus said, "A man was going down from Jerusalem to Jericho, and he fell among robbers, who stripped him and beat him and departed, leaving him half dead. And by chance, a priest was going down that road; and when he saw him, he went by on the other side. And likewise also a Levite, when he came to the place and saw him, went by on the other side. But a traveling Samaritan came toward him; and when he saw him, he had compassion. And he went to him and bandaged his wounds, pouring on oil and wine; then he put him on his own beast, led him to an inn and took care of him. And the next day he took out two denatii [two days' wages] and gave them to the innkeeper and said, 'Take care of him; and whatever more you spend, I will repay you when I come back.' Which of these three seems to you to have become a neighbor to the man who fell among the robbers?"

And the lawyer said, "The one who had mercy on him."

And Jesus told him, "Go and do likewise."

Edith Keeler took Dr. McCoy in and took care of him as the Samaritan helped the man beaten up by robbers. Her request to Kirk, "Let me help," also shows this kind of love. It is expressed in the Greek New Testament by the word *agape* (pronounced a-ga-pay), the kind of love meant in the injunction "You shall love your neighbor as yourself." This kind of love and compassion is not something you "fall into" or a feeling or an emotion; the person loving may or may not be emotional. This kind of love corresponds to the Vulcan philosophy or way of life that is beneficial. It is like God's love for us that is for our lasting good. "For God so loved the world that he gave his only-of-his-kind Son, that whoever believes in him may not perish but have eternal life."

The other kind of love mentioned in the New Testament is *philiam*, friendship and affection.

In order to change history back to what it should have been, Edith Keeler had to die. Spock and Kirk knew that, but it was hard for Kirk to accept it. In order for our history to be what it was to be, Jesus had to die. He knew that, and while he was still with his disciples, he began to teach them that he must suffer much and be rejected by the Jewish leaders and that he must be killed and on the third day be raised to life again. He said this plainly, but the disciples could not or would not accept it.

Gem, the empath in the episode "The Empath," also demonstrated, "You shall love your neighbor as yourself," when she healed Kirk and McCoy by touching them, a manner of healing reminiscent of the manner of healing used by Jesus. Her nervous system was so sensitive and responsive that she could feel their emotional and physical reactions and heal their injuries. The Vians were testing Gem to see whether the inhabitants of her planet were worthy of survival. She had three good examples of compassion to learn from—Kirk, who was willing to sacrifice himself for his friends; Spock, who decided to go with the Vians after Kirk was asleep; and Dr. McCoy, who actually went with them. She also had the background of her own culture, a culture the Vians decided was worth saving, on the basis of her behavior.

A gem, such as a pearl, is prized for its beauty, value, and perfection. Scotty realized that Gem was like the "pearl of great price" and said, "Do you not know the story of the merchant? The merchant who, when he found one pearl of great price, went and sold all that he had and bought it?"

Jesus said, "The kingdom of heaven is like a merchant in search of beautiful pearls, who, on finding one pearl of great value, went and sold all that he had and bought it."

In Star Trek, there are many examples of the *agape* type of love: in "The Immunity Syndrome," when Spock said, "Do not risk the ship further on my account"; in "The Tholian Web," when the captain stayed behind so that other crew members could beam back; in "Errand of Mercy," when the Organians stopped a war even though the presence of humanoids was quite painful to them; and possibly in Spock's actions in "The Menagerie," though friendship, too, could have been involved here. But in "The Menagerie" we saw that Kirk confused the kinds of love when he accused Spock of flagrant emotionalism. Spock was not as guilty as the captain thought he was.

At the end of "Requiem for Methuselah," after Reena's death, when Kirk, Spock, and McCoy were aboard the *Enterprise*, Kirk said he wished he could forget her, and then he went to sleep. Dr. McCoy enumerated to Spock all the things that Spock would never know, simply because the word *love* wasn't written in his book. McCoy said he wished Kirk could forget her, and then he left the room. Spock gently probed Kirk's mind and found out what McCoy said he would never know; then he performed an act of love, that is, *agape*, by changing Kirk's memory so that he would forget Reena. But Spock would have said that he was being "beneficial."

In "The Corbomite Maneuver," Kirk beamed over to the little alien ship with Bailey and Dr. McCoy to show Bailey the face of the unknown, and to treat the enemies' wounds if necessary. Kirk said to McCoy, "What's the mission of this vessel, doctor? To seek out and contact alien life and have an opportunity to demonstrate what our high-sounding words mean."

"Love your enemies, do good to those who hate you, bless those who curse you, pray for those who insult you. To him who strikes you on the cheek, offer the other also; and from him who takes your cloak, do not withhold your tunic also. Give to everyone who asks you; and from him who takes your things, do not demand them back. And as you wish that men would do to you, do to them." This is the Golden Rule.

"We come in friendship" and "We come in peace" are recurrent themes all through Star Trek. The *Enterprise* decontaminates planets, delivers vaccine, and answers other distress calls. The Vians valued the capacity to love others shown by Kirk, Spock, and McCoy, who protected, trusted, hoped, and persevered.

But the things that love does not do have also been superbly illustrated in Star Trek. Miranda Jones had to get rid of her jealousy before she could form a mind link with the Medusan ambassador in "Is There in Truth No Beauty?" "Lord" Garth bragged that he was master of the universe and that his fleet was out there waiting for him in "Whom Gods Destroy." Proud Apollo puffed himself up until he was about twenty feet tall in "Who Mourns for Adonais?" In "Elaan of

Troyius," the men of Elas were arrogant, and the Dohlman, Elaan, was rude and had to have lessons in courtesy and Troyian customs. Sylvia in "Catspaw" was self-seeking. Trelane in "Squire of Gothos" was easily angered. The android Stella Mudd kept count of all of Harry Mudd's faults, and this was multiplied five hundred times in "I, Mudd." Kor, the Klingon in "Errand of Mercy," thought that war would have been glorious, and he would have delighted in doing wrong. In "The Return of the Archons," the prophecy of the return of Archons to destroy Landru was fulfilled and became obsolete. Telepaths in "The Menagerie" and other episodes have ceased to use languages. The knowledge of the pilot Captain Christopher was obsolete in the *Enterprise*'s time period in "Tomorrow Is Yesterday." And the children in "Miri" had been going their childish ways for three hundred years.

St. Paul wrote, "Love is patient, kind; love is not jealous, does not brag, is not puffed up, is not rude, is not self-seeking, is not easily angered, does not count the bad, does not delight in the wrong, but rejoices in the truth. It always protects, always trusts, always hopes, always perseveres.

"Love never fails; but as for prophecies, they will become obsolete; as for languages, they will cease; as for knowledge, it will become obsolete. For we know in part and we prophesy in part; but when the perfect comes, the partial will be obsolete. When I was a child, I talked like a child, I thought like a child, I reasoned like a child; when I became a man I gave up childish ways. For now we see through a mirror obscurely, but then we shall see face to face. Now I know in part, but then I shall understand fully, even as I am fully understood. And now faith, hope, love remain, these three; but the greatest of these is love."

TREK ROUNDTABLE
LETTERS FROM OUR READERS

As you may have guessed, we editors read many, many times more letters than we could possibly publish in the Roundtable. Being able to do so is one of the greatest pleasures we get from our hobby; we never cease to be astounded, and enthralled by the fact that you readers take the time and effort to write to us. Often the mail includes unexpected bonuses: drawings and cartoons, photographs, Christmas cards, wedding or birth announcements, handmade jewelry, Enterprise models, movie posters and press kits, fanzines, clippings, and small items of interest in the science fiction field such as stamps, coins, NASA literature, etc. One generous fan even sent us a jar of her delicious homemade jelly!

You needn't go so far as all that (though peanut butter lover G.B. insists on equal time!), but we do want you to send a letter to Trek Roundtable. The Roundtable is the leading fun forum for discussion of Star Trek and related matters, but it only continues to remain so if you readers continue to write. So let us hear from you, but for now why don't you enjoy the following letters.

Randy Holland
Charlottesville, Va.

You stated in *Best of Trek #6* that you wanted to hear from your readers. I would therefore like to respond to an article in that book.

The article to which I refer is, in my humble opinion, one of the worst articles on Star Trek ever to appear in your usually fine collections. I am speaking, of course, of Rowena

G. Warner's "Plausibility of the Star Trek Universe and Technology." The article is useless, and when it isn't busy being ridiculous, it is just wrong. Now, I don't intend this letter to be just a vague critique of Ms. Warner's article; I intend to demonstrate just how poor her work is by a careful examination of it. Also, let me assure you that, as is all too obvious in Ms. Warner's case, I am not a scientist. I don't even have a technical background. I am merely a scholar of Star Trek who has an interest in science. With that established, let's look at Warner's article.

Warner's explanation of warp drive is hopelessly truncated. All she does is say that objects cannot accelerate to light speed in normal space, that the *Enterprise* does not travel in normal space, and that therefore the ship is not constrained by Einstein's Special Theory of Relativity. That is simple. Any child can say that. What takes a degree of imagination and thought is to say *how* it does it. For an example of a more intelligent discussion, see *The Making of Star Trek the Motion Picture*, where Mr. Puttkamer talks about warp speeds. Thus Warner's failure to explore how, within the confines of relativity, warp drive could work renders her discussion, not an examination of the plausibility of warp drive, but a mere conclusion that it works.

The article's discussion of subspace radio is also shorter than I would like. As with warp drive, Warner simply says that if a way is found to make radio waves travel faster than light, then subspace can exist. But how it does or whether we can do this—Warner lets that remain a mystery. Again, we don't so much have a discussion of technological plausibility as we have a childish statement that "if we can invent something that does what we see in the show then it is possible." That's not a discussion, that's a conclusion, despite her conjectures about "wave guides."

Warner shows a stunning lack of research skills when she talks about the matter-antimatter engines. She states that "the existence of antimatter has not been completely substantiated." This is, in a word, wrong. Antiprotons were observed for the first time at the six-billion-volt bevatron in Berkeley, California in 1955! After this incredible mistake, she launches into a wild discussion of dilithium. She suggests that dilithium has a special "field" around it which causes hydrogen to convert itself into antimatter. This would be an interesting trick, but even more interesting is how the dilithium could ever exist in open air. Since our atmosphere contains hydrogen, anytime dilithium contacted our air, it would start its presto-chango routine. But as soon as a hydrogen atom was converted into antimatter, it would explode into pure energy the moment it contacted *any* matter—such as the crystal itself! The result: Warner's dilithium would create a series of explosions upon exposure to air which would destroy the crystal as well as anything nearby. Evidently Warner did not take the two or three minutes to realize the implications of her suggestion. But given the rest of her article, that is to be expected.

Take for example Warner's explanation of Yonada. She suggests that it is a whole planet with an asteroid shell around it. She then says that such a planet would not need a life-support system. Well, how does she expect the planet's ecosystem—which she has supporting life—to continue to function without the benefit of a nearby sun? Far more reasonable is the explanation that Yonada is a spaceship, complete with life support, merely resembling an asteroid. But alternative explanations are not to the point; the point is that Warner was too taken with her own theory to see how silly it actually is.

Warner begins her discussion of the Romulan (and now Federation) cloaking device by saying that no present theory would account for it. This, as is so often the case in this article, is wrong. "Balance of Terror" itself establishes the conceptual framework from which to construct a theory. By selectively bending light *around* a ship, it would appear to be invisible. Of course it would still radiate heat and its mass would affect space, but it wasn't until "The Enterprise Incident" that the cloaking device was perfected, effectively masking a ship from all sensor contact. So instead of listening to the episode and theorizing from that, Warner begins to discuss combinations of tachyons and photons. Although her explanation never accounts for the dual nature of the photon (being both a wave and a particle simultaneously), and she never even mentions the word *photon*," it still fails for purely logical reasons. Warner has her screen turn light into "litachyons" (don't ask me, I didn't write it) and this field "would prevent light from reaching and reflecting off" the ship. The problem is that this would also leave a large black spot in space; not an invisible ship, but the outline of one. So, as is becoming depressingly common, Warner's explanation does not make sense.

Warner discusses ion power, tachyons, silicon life, and

surgery, but adds nothing more than can be found in *The Making of Star Trek* or an encyclopedia. But more than that, she doesn't really discuss their plausibility, she merely says that "it might exist."

The only subject which Warner addresses with any semblance of logic or rationality is the time warp in "The Naked Time." But even then, while she gives an explanation of it, she fails to investigate or even discuss the implications of her explanation.

Finally, mercifully, Warner discusses her last topic. Parallel and alternate universes, she calls it. This is probably her most ridiculous, inane, and senseless discussion. For instance, she says that the mirror universe in "Mirror, Mirror" is antimatter. Why she says this is a mystery to me, since she admits that it has no basis in the episode. Probably she is thinking that since the characters we know as "good" were "evil" there, that they must be composed of "anti" particles. This is rather childish and an example of her unthinking approach to the whole article. But there's more! She wonders why our characters are not destroyed upon touching something "tangible" in the antimatter universe. (Air would be sufficient, Ms. Warner; it wouldn't have to be anything "tangible.") To explain this she says that matter and antimatter only cancel out if they contact a "mirror" object. This is absolutely wrong! *Any* amount of positive matter coming into contact with *any* amount of negative matter results in annihilation. For it is the individual particles whose charges cancel, not the object as a whole. In short, Warner's understanding of antimatter is ludicrously limited.

Actually, it appears that Warner's understanding of almost everything is limited. Going through her article, it seems evident that her "research" was confined to one, maybe two magazine articles per subject and *The Making of Star Trek*. And in building her explanation based on this "research," she obviously did not think about it very long. If she had she would have easily seen how illogical some of the points are. And when she isn't being illogical, she is merely duplicating already known information. Add to that her truncated discussions and egregious errors in science and we are left with a silly, poorly written, useless article.

Now, perhaps this response seems rather harsh. It probably is. But it infuriates me that tripe like Warner's article should find its way into a supposedly intelligent and thoughtful publication. That it should make its way into the "Best" that the publication has to offer is a damning indictment of the editors.

I sincerely hope that, as editors of *Trek*, you will in the future examine articles such as Ms. Warner's a little more carefully before allowing them to escape into print. After all, articles like this one serve no purpose other than to promote ridicule and derision of the series and those who hold it dear.

*****Randy, your response isn't too harsh, but we feel some of your language is. Namecalling and snide remarks have no place in legitimate criticism. Articles are chosen for our magazines (and consequent "Best of" editions) on one basis only: Will Star Trek fans enjoy reading this? We don't feel it's necessary for us to judge scientific accuracy or even the internal logic of such in an article. Our primary interest is in entertainment. Our secondary interest is in eliciting response and comment, to run articles which will stimulate debate among our readers and fandom in general. You certainly can't deny that Rowena's article did its job in that department, can you? —The Editors *****

Betty Catherwood
Longwood, Fla.

As a Star Trek lover (and science fiction fan since childhood), I have enjoyed reading most of your *Best of Trek* books. Though my interest in Star Trek has waxed and waned over the years, it has recently been reawakened since I have been able to watch most of the original episodes once again (my favorite being "The Menagerie").

The articles in *Best of Trek* are highly enjoyable (very enlightening and occasionally amusing). I love the letters written by the fans—they inspired me to write my own! I wish I could write an article such as "Star Trek: A Philosophical View" by Michael Constantino (*Best of Trek #7*). It was excellent and sums up many of my own feelings about the show. Barbara Devereaux's article, "In Search of Star Trek Fiction" (also in #7), was of interest and is helping me to be very selective in my reading, as I have read very few of the novels and short stories based on the series. (What I have read has been recent.) A good many of the novels in her review don't seem worth reading; however, a few do seem appealing.

A discussion in *Trek* of William Rotsler's *Star Trek Biographies* would be interesting (this book was mentioned in

Ms. Devereaux's review). The author has Kirk's date of birth as the year 2132 and Spock's in the Vulcan year 503, which translates (says the author) as our year 2084 (Vulcan 519-2100 Earth time). This would make him forty-eight years older than Kirk! I will grant that Spock may be older than Kirk even by a number of years, due to Vulcan physiology, but I hardly think he is nearly fifty years older. His human mother appeared in "Journey to Babel" to be a woman perhaps in her early fifties. Of course life spans in humans might be longer a couple of centuries from now and she could actually have been much older. But I hardly think she was pushing a hundred! Also, it has been my understanding that the Star Trek voyages took place in the *twenty-third* century, not the twenty-second; however, the series was often vague about it.

The article by Jennifer Weston, "Of Spock, Genes, and DNA Recombination" (*Best of Trek #5*), was, to quote Spock, "fascinating." But if Spock couldn't sire children, why his bonding with T'Pring? (He couldn't possibly be the father of Zar in Ann Crispin's book, *Yesterday's Son*, either!) However, Ms. Weston did hold out hope in the matter and perhaps by the twenty-third century that problem will have been solved. My vote as a potential mate for Spock would be for the intellectual Droxine of Stratos ("The Cloud Minders"). He was obviously very attracted to her (and not only to her mind!) and there were no outside influences at work here (very unusual for him). They would have made the perfect pair and I'd like to think they met again. Incidentally, Leila Kalomi ("This Side of Paradise") said she met Spock on Earth, not Starbase Eleven as Leslie Thompson stated in "A Brief Look at Spock's Career."

"Jim's Little Black Book" by Walter Irwin (*Best of Trek #2*) was interesting reading, though I agree more with Beth Carlson's view ("A Woman Looks at Jim's Little Black Book"—*Best of Trek #4*). Both articles were written before Carol Marcus entered the scene in *Wrath of Khan*. This affair obviously took place not long before Kirk took over the *Enterprise*. It was my understanding from the movie that he had known, at least for a time, about their son David. (I don't think this was just a casual fling with Kirk; he must have been in love with Carol, but he could not give up his career for her. And she couldn't follow him all over the galaxy, especially after David was born. Perhaps the captain had spent time with his son in years past, perhaps when he was a small child—David apparently knew of Kirk—but Carol did not want her son to know Kirk was his father.) It's a pity David was killed off in *Star Trek III: The Search for Spock*. I can't understand the reasoning here, as there were possibilities for more stories. The relationship between David and Saavik, as well as that of Kirk and his son, could have been explored more fully. Shame on Harve Bennett! Actually, I'd like to think there were twins born to Kirk and Carol Marcus and that the survivor will show up in a future movie (played by Merritt Butrick as before, of course.)

As a fan I could not help but like *The Search for Spock* very much. With Leonard Nimoy at the helm it couldn't be anything but a success! But I'm wondering just how well this movie is faring with non-Trekkers. Certainly it lives up to Star Trek ideals, but it is essentially a movie to get Spock back with us. (I felt it totally unnecessary to have killed him off in the first place!) I missed Spock's not being present in the film until the last—a very happy ending, thank goodness! But *The Search for Spock*, as sequel to *Wrath of Khan*, probably leaves those persons not familiar with the television series or with *Wrath of Khan* quite puzzled as to what is going on—so perhaps it's not quite the box-office draw it could have been.

I am now awaiting the next movie. Sure there will be one—we can't be left in suspense about what happens to Kirk and company when they return to Earth! I would like to see them pardoned, of course, and Kirk should take command of another ship. Any ship can be renamed *Enterprise*, but Star Trek without Kirk or Spock (or anyone other than William Shatner or Leonard Nimoy portraying them) would be hard to accept. This is also true to a lesser extent with the other crew members. (It certainly would never be the same without DeForest Kelley as Dr. McCoy!) The theatrical movies take over two years in production, so there can't be too many more filmed with the original actors, unfortunately, as they are getting older. But I wish it could go on forever! If it does continue for many more years I would rather see a completely new cast of characters than have other actors take over the roles. It would never be the same for me, but at least Star Trek and its vision would not die.

*****Aside from her comment about Leila Kalomi, Betty also wondered why discrepancies of "fact" appear in articles published in* Trek *and those in other publications, such as Bill*

Rotsler's fine Star Trek Biographies. *It's simple: Different authors offer differing interpretations of Star Trek lore. It's all part of the fun; a way of filling in the blanks, as it were, and increasing our enjoyment of our hobby. The more the merrier, we feel, and if discrepancies or disagreements crop up, why then, that's what forums like this Trek Roundtable are for! —The Editors* *****

Cynthia Caswell
Louisville, Ky.

I disagreed wholeheartedly with Kyle Holland in regards to his article called "Indiana Skywalker Meets the Son of Star Trek" (*Best of Trek # 7*).

I can only say we must have seen two different Star Trek movies. I didn't care much for *Star Trek: The Motion Picture*, yet I loved *Star Trek II: The Wrath of Khan*. To me, the second film held truer to the relationship of Spock, Kirk, and McCoy. It was like seeing old friends. The first movie made them seem like complete strangers trying to act like old friends.

Star Trek: The Motion Picture made Kirk out to be an incompetent fool who couldn't understand what was going on. I agree that being behind a desk can make a man rusty, but like the saying goes, "It's like riding a bike, you never forget how to do it." The film also made Spock seem like a machine. He didn't even respond to Kirk's "Welcome back, Mr. Spock." He seemed cold, distant. Not like the Spock we know and love. The only time he even resembled the Spock of the series was when he was in V'Ger in the space suit.

Also, in my opinion, the changes to the ship and uniforms are a much-needed improvement. The uniforms are much more becoming to the people in them than were the drab blue jumpsuits worn in *STTMP*. The ship, in the first film, seemed too much like a shell showing the girders holding it together.

I am an avid Trekker; I have watched every episode at least a dozen times. What about you, Mr. Holland? I mean, any man who has seen any of the episodes would be appalled by the treatment of Spock and Kirk. One who isn't has not understood the true meaning of Star Trek.

I grew up with Star Trek and I may be considered too young to judge (I'm eighteen years old), but I feel you are not giving *Star Trek II: The Wrath of Khan* a fair assessment.

John A. Mariani
Glasgow, Scotland

First, may I say how much I've enjoyed your *Best of Trek* paperback collections; as a British reader, these are all I've been able to obtain—at hugely inflated import prices. Fellow SF readers think I'm crazy, but I find the books of great interest.

I enjoy the wide spectrum of articles you publish; from the in-depth character analysis/histories, to the "pseudo-scientific examinations, to the many thematic and dramatic explorations of the program. Amazing that all of this should stem from one series!

The main reason I'm writing is to share my views on something you may regard as "old hat" by now, but nevertheless I'd like to join in the ongoing *Star Trek: The Motion Picture* debate. ITV, the independent British television network, recently premiered *STTMP*. Having seen a video, I already felt the film looked better on the small screen. However, I was pleasantly surprised as scene after scene, previously unseen but read as part of the novel, flickered by. I scoured my *Best of Treks* to find only brief mention of an ABC extended version, which, I guess, was what I was treated to. Perhaps these brief additions, mostly non-Kirk/Spock/McCoy and nonvisual effects, helped me appreciate the film more.

At this point, I must admit that I too was one of the many (judging by your Roundtable) fans who were disappointed by the film. Indeed, I often used the awful joke of referring to the film as "the slow motion picture." Equally, I loved *Star Trek II: The Wrath of Khan* and praised it as "being as good as a TV episode." *Star Trek III: The Search for Spock* was similarly welcome.

If I may digress (as is my wont) and discuss the latter two films. The thing that annoyed me most about *Wrath of Khan* was my nonfeelings about Spock's death. I definitely felt sad about the demise of the *Enterprise*. Irrationally, I (and I'm sure many others) hoped to serve on board that ship, and now it's gone. But what an important "death" that was in terms of the rising and advancing of Jim Kirk's spirit! BBC TV is currently repeating all the Star Trek episodes in sequence and I caught "The Naked Time"—in which Kirk vows to the ship that he'll "never lose you—never!" How dramatically we saw him fight to regain the ship in *STTMP*; and equally, how he finally breaks his pledge in *The Search for Spock*. People are now more important to him than a ship or, indeed, a career. I'm sure your regular contributors will express how we all feel about the developments of *The Search for Spock* far more eloquently than I.

Back to *Star Trek: The Motion Picture*! Us Federation fans/hardware fans finally saw the *Enterprise* and all its technology as it was meant to be seen.

There is one main theme in *STTMP*—the search for God or the creator. However, as is obvious in the novel, there is an important parallel between V'Ger/Ilia/Decker and Spock-Vulcan/Spock-human. V'Ger's flight mirrors Spock's. The film portrays the coldly rational, logical machine that has done all it can with its current resources and mode of operation (learn all that is learnable/achieve *Kolinahr*; and let's make no bones about it—ouch—despite Bones' jibe, Spock was just about to "graduate" at the start of *STTMP*), but it knows something is missing. V'Ger, through Ilia, merges with Decker to obtain humanity. Spock "merely" accepts that which was always a part of him. The film is, simply put, the most important single event in Spock's life (unless you consider his subsequent scientific resurrection!). The fans, who then thought the next time we met Spock he would be a grinning jackanapes, failed to realize that although Spock has finally accepted his human half, he has not rejected his Vulcanity. The two sides are no longer at war; rather, he melds them both into a workable, comfortable whole, and it is this Spock we see in *Wrath of Khan*. For fans to simply reject the events of *Star Trek: The Motion Picture* and "pretend it never happened" is to ignore all of the above.

There can be little doubt that *STTMP* is far too long; even Shatner has been quoted as saying so. A judicious 15-30-minute editing job would have increased the pace without damaging the story one jot. As it stands, however, *Star Trek: The Motion Picture* is definitely a film which improves with repeated viewings.

I have my own theory about the film which I'd like to share with you. As we all know, when a new live-action Star Trek was proposed it metamorphosized from film to TV series to TV movie and finally into a big-budget film. Probably because of the success of *Star Wars*, sci-fi (urgh!) movies were/are big business. So, *STTMP* got a megabuck budget. As good guys like the Great Bird of the Galaxy were behind *STTMP*, they didn't want just another space epic like *Star*

Wars—which is, after all, just good guys versus bad guys and lots of fighting and laser blasts. They wanted a film with an important theme. Personally, I think they came up with one. I think, though, they would have loved to have done *2001*! That is the movie that *STTMP* tries to emulate on many levels: the visual effects, future technology, and even thematically with the birth of a new, improved kind of human.

What awaited the *Enterprise* was not an elegant black monolith but a beat-up old Voyager!

Well, that's it! Just wanted to add my voice to a debate which I am sure will go on.

Naturally, I'd love to see this letter printed in a *Best of Trek*, but whatever you decide, thanks for wading through it! Thanks again for *Best of Trek*—I'll continue to haunt the SF specialist stores and snap up any future tomes—Keep up the good work!

Laurie Tomlin
Clearwater, Fla.

I have loved Star Trek from day one, back in 1966, but I didn't know until late 1983 that your *Best of Trek* books existed. What a find!

Add me to your list of everybody who's interested in a list of all the Star Trek fiction. After reading Barbara Corrigan's letter in the Roundtable section of #6, I got started trying to find some of the books she mentioned. I really liked *The Entropy Effect*, too, so I thought anything else she liked must be good reading! Which reminds me: Why don't we see any of the novels critiqued in *Best of Trek*? I could really get into that; maybe I'll write an article myself. Some of the fiction—for example, in the Timescape books by various authors—is definitely better than others. The ones I enjoy most, understandably, are the ones in which the characters are kept as true to the original series as possible. Some of them have a too-stern Kirk, a too-thick brogue for poor Scotty, and just plain wacko Spocks! The novel that read the most like original Star Trek to me was *Web of the Romulans*, by M.S. Murdock—down to the corny subplot about the ship's computer falling in love with Captain Kirk!

I love comparing the ideas put forth by your *Best of Trek* contributors with my own. I was especially interested in some of the views of Spock's death. Here it comes again: another gushing fan of Joyce Tullock! Her articles (most notably

"Friendship—in the Balance," *Best of Trek #4*), are always thought-provoking and always just plain fun. I agree with her that Spock has been too "humanized" in *Wrath of Khan*. In a way, it's good to see him finally, apparently, at peace with himself; but as Joyce says in "The Alien Question" (*BOT #6*), are they *sure* that's what they really want to do? I thought she expressed it perfectly when she said, "It is the *continuing* inner conflict which makes him live in the minds of the viewers. The intrinsic nature of his character requires that he always feel a bit different, a bit out of place." Sure, *we* know that human is human, Vulcan is Vulcan, but Spock is *Spock*!—but can we really expect that Spock, as logical as he is, will *ever* be able to realize that about himself?

I have always most enjoyed the episodes of Star Trek in which Spock was Spock. By that I mean that I was always just a bit irritated with the "in love" Spock of "All Our Yesterdays" and "This Side of Paradise," and the excitable, early version of Spock in "Where No Man Has Gone Before." Do you think there's any chance that Spock's brush (more than a "brush"—say *experience*) with death in *Wrath of Khan* could return him to *normal*?

Allison Drury
Hamilton, Ont., Canada

I found the *Best of Trek #7* just in time. I was beginning to recognize the earliest stages of "Star Trek withdrawal." The symptoms are especially acute coming a month after the opening of *The Search for Spock*. After seeing the movie twice, tracking down all the reviews, articles, and magazines and reading and rereading Vonda N. McIntyre's excellent novelization, it was hard to accept that the movie fever was getting out again. I found myself wandering aimlessly around bookstores and magazine racks looking for new Star Trek books that likely won't be in the stores for some time.

Your *Trek* books are always fun to read because they give me a chance to see what other Star Trek fans are thinking about various aspects of the Star Trek universe. I've been teased unmercifully in the last few weeks because of my Star Trek obsession (my enthusiasm got the better of me in the weeks leading up to *The Search for Spock*), and it's good to read about other Star Trek fans coping with their non-Trekker acquaintances, too.

As usual, I found myself wrinkling my brow over some of

the more controversial articles in your book (Kyle Holland's two articles come to mind) and astonished, as well, at how close some *Trek* writers came to my own thoughts (especially Barbara Devereaux's analysis of Star Trek fiction).

You asked for ideas for future *Trek* articles and I'd like to suggest a few:

1. Star Trek Folksongs. As a guitarist, I would be interested in learning about the folksinging that is said to be all the rage at Star Trek conventions. Would it be possible to have someone write about a cross-section of Star Trek folksongs and how we noninitiated folksingers can get ahold of these songs?

2. Fanzines. Everytime I order a copy of the Star Trek Welcommittee's Directory, I am overwhelmed by the number of Star Trek fanzines available. It would be interesting if someone could outline the best of the Star Trek fanzines and available fanzine classics from the past. I would also enjoy a follow-up to Barbara Devereaux's fiction article. New Star Trek novels are appearing on the shelves these days at breakneck speed (just finished Duane's *My Enemy, My Ally*; Duane has a marvelous grasp of the *Enterprise* crew).

3. Saavik. Is there anyone out there willing to take a shot at writing a profile on Saavik's tangled character? I find her the most interesting Star Trek character to appear in years, but everyone who portrays her or writes about her seems to have a different idea of what Saavik is all about.

4. Artwork. I hope you will return the art section to your future books. My own copy of the Star Trek needlepoint picture that you outlined in one of your earlier books still hangs proudly on my wall.

*****We'd love to run a folksong article, Allison . . . We're just waiting for someone to submit one to us. As to fanzines, we don't feel that we're qualified to judge which are the "best"—heck, we kinda like 'em all! We'll always be willing to publish any good articles on zines, however. In the meantime, we hope you enjoy Ingrid Cross' look at fanzine writing and production, "The Three-Foot Pit," included in this volume. Saavik's character has been discussed pretty thoroughly in these pages, but we just don't as yet know enough about her to justify a full-length article. We'd love to have the artwork return to these pages as well, Allison, but the decision to remove it was based on several factors, not the least of which was economic. —The Editors *****

Eric van Beaumont
Fairborn, Ohio

I have just completed reading *Best of Trek #7* and have found it up to your usual high standards. I have been a Star Trek fan from the beginning and am glad it has finally received the credit and attention it deserves. In your introduction you ask for comments or ideas and I have a few that I cannot keep to myself any longer. I also unfortunately do not have the time, resources, or talent to pursue them, so I give them to you.

The first one deals with Mr. Scott. Many has been the time that Captain Kirk and Mr. Spock have beamed down to some new planet to face adventure, danger, and beautiful females, always leaving Mr. Scott to mind the store. Often this is the wisest move Kirk will make that day. Never can I recall an instance when Mr. Scott has made a mistake while in command, and I can remember several occasions where Kirk and Spock owe their lives to the ever-diligent Mr. Scott. I would enjoy reading a tribute to Mr. Scott's command capabilities by one of your fine writers.

My second idea will require more time and effort on your part. I have noticed in my collection of *Best of Trek* books that a large percentage of your writers are female. In some instances, such as *Best of Trek #7*, it is well over half female. I find this fascinating, considering that science fiction as a whole is a male-dominated pastime. I would be interested in your ideas why Star Trek has such a strong female following. I would also be interested in the average characteristics of a trekkie: age, sex, race, education, etc.

I have one final question for you which has bothered me for some time. Why are non-Federation starships always used on your covers? I do like them, they are quite colorful, I just don't see the connection.

*****Your suggestion about Scotty was a good one, Eric, but we asked ourselves, why limit it to him? So we have an article in preparation which takes a look at the command capabilities of all the* Enterprise *officers (even Dr. McCoy!). That percentage of female fans which you mention is probably larger than you think; more than half of our readers are women, and women probably make up more than two-thirds of hard-core SF fans. Whether or not this information warrants an article remains to be seen, but we can tell you right now that science fiction fandom and Star Trek fandom over-*

lap far less than most people believe. True, the ships on our covers are ''generic'' in style, but that is the connection— they give our books a distinctive and attractive look which is designed to keep readers from confusing them with Star Trek fiction from other publishers.—The Editors*****

Michelle Ross
Muskogee, Okla.

I'm the kind of Trekker who, even though I collect Star Trek things like mad, never writes about being a fan to anybody, and its only logical that I stop being a closet Trekker!

I also wrote because it seems that so many of the people who write in have a wish to meet one of the actors involved in Star Trek. I also share this dream and at a convention in February of 1983, I got to meet Mr. James Doohan.

My father had taken me to the convention as a sort of early birthday present. I had spent nearly an hour walking around, awestruck at everything I saw. Finally after blowing all but $25 of my grand savings, I saw some sort of auction was starting. I told my father to come with me as I ducked through the curtains, curious to see what was going on. James Doohan himself was talking to somebody who, in turn, was talking to the one and only George Takei.

Soon the auction began and Doohan and Takei traded chores of auctioning off several different items. During this time I had unstuck my feet from the floor, grabbed my father's hand, and sat down.

Then Mr. Doohan began to auction a large movie poster from the first movie. I immediately knew that I *had* to own that poster. But my hopes were quickly overshadowed by the rising price of the poster; $25, $35, and on up it went. My father knew how badly I wanted it so he tried several times to bid on it. But, alas, we were in the back of the room and Mr. Doohan's hearing just wasn't picking him up. Finally, as the price reached $50, several men who sat around us and had heard my father's unsuccessful tries at reaching Mr. Doohan came to our aid. They stood on their chairs and at the top of their lungs yelled, ''Hey, Jimmy. You got a young lady over here who wants that poster. So sell it to her, for Pete's sake!''

So, I had my poster. An extra treat was added in that while

trying to sell the poster Mr. Doohan had jokingly said he would autograph the poster and kiss the person who bought it. He must have forgotten about the latter because he and George Takei signed it and he went to sit down. But one of his assistants had not forgotten and reminded him. He then introduced me, and Mr. Doohan gave me my promised kiss.

I was higher than a kite on the ride home. I had accomplished a dream, and, who knows William Shatner and Leonard Nimoy might be next!

Thank you so much for publishing the books to which I could send the story of one of my fondest memories!

Julia Arch
Pocasset, Mass.

I've just finished reading your *Best of Trek #7*. I enjoyed it as I did the other six. I have been an avid Star Trek follower since its very inception. I only missed two episodes in the three years of its prime-time run. (Considering that I was in high school at the time and that the programming times were less than ideal, I thought I did well to miss only two.)

I missed the animated series, since I was in college at the time and no longer a TV viewer. Through most of the seventies my passion for Star Trek went no further than viewing the reruns that were intermittently shown in syndication.

Then to my immense pleasure, they revived Star Trek with the movies, as well as with a fairly regular release of books. I have endeavored to collect all the stories published once I became aware of their existence, so that now I've read a good many of them, though I've not had access to all. I even tried writing some of my own—another indication of my profound addiction, I fear.

I find it fascinating how the various analyses, discussions, and other comments represented in your books reflect the IDIC inherent in the Star Trek world. The depth and variety of human experience found in Star Trek is reflected in the number of different themes fans can legitimately document in the 'series. One of the reasons Star Trek succeeds is that it serves as a mirror to our own humanity and human potential. (The term ''human'' being used in the broad sense, as Admiral Kirk used it at Spock's funeral.)

I don't always agree with the various opinions expressed in your articles. But I respect the thought and consideration evident in the preparation. It's a pleasure to have my mind engaged in enlightened discussion, challenged to defend my view or adapt it to new evidence.

Colin Lewis
Edinburgh, Scotland

Well, you asked for it! I am a devoted fifteen-year-old Scottish Trekker. I felt compelled to write to you before I saw *Star Trek III: The Search for Spock*, or at least before it opens here.

The following is a sort of personal history of Star Trek in my life which I also had to get down on paper. Don't go away halfway through it—please!

The first thing I remember was a Star Trek annual I had, which subsequently vanished, but I remember it had a picture of Kirk very like one of the drawings in *Best of Trek #2*, "Target Practice" by Steve Fabian. It is taken from "Where No Man Has Gone Before," I think (having just recently seen the episode on TV).

I then remember watching Filmation's animated episodes— especially "Practical Joker," and "Counter-Clock Incident." Then I saw my first actual episode (or part of it) on someone else's portable TV: "A Private Little War." Most of this was when I was still between seven and ten years old, so my recollections are sort of vague, but I especially remember the Mugato jumping Kirk.

I heard about *Star Trek: The Motion Picture* from a friend of one of my brothers (I have two, six and eight years older than I). I wanted to go, but it never turned out that way. Then I saw the Great Bird's novelization of the film in the local library. It was the Severn House hardback, and along with it were James Blish's Star Trek #9 and #10, also by Severn House. I borrowed all three for months on end, devouring every detail.

Then in a bookshop in town, I spotted Bantam Star Trek Fotonovels #1 and #12 ("City on the Edge of Forever" and "Amok Time"), but because "City" was pretty dogeared, I left it and bought "Amok Time." I have regretted not buying it ever since. (They're out of print now, aren't they?) Anyway, I had already bought most of the Blish collections at this bookshop when suddenly the Star Trek books started to peter out. So I wrote to the bookseller in London from which

I got *STTMP* in paperback. I loved the photos! (The hardback didn't have any.)

But the final awakening arrived with *Star Trek II: The Wrath of Khan*. It was great! I just reveled in actually seeing Kirk, Spock, Bones, Scotty, Sulu, Uhura, and Chekov in action. And then, of course—Spock's death. I was shocked; I couldn't believe it. I hadn't known anything about it beforehand. I think it was right that he died *to save the ship*. (I don't mean that he deserved to die, or that I wanted him to—nothing like that. I guess I'm a little confused with *The Search for Spock* so close. His death seems temporary, almost, so forgive me.)

It was just after *Wrath of Khan* that I discovered my local science-fiction bookshop! I just started buying and buying until my bookshelves were sagging with the weight, and then more. I thought your ST fiction review was especially welcome. I tend to agree with most of it. Yes, Vonda McIntyre's two works are gems (so is her third, I expect—I was glad to hear she was doing *The Search for Spock*). Her prose is so perfect, every nuance is just right (very important when writing about someone else's universe and characters which are so well known).

My favorite article in *Best of Trek #7* is Deanna Rafferty's "Another Look at Captain Kirk's Personality." I really like these articles on the triad and the other regulars—keep 'em up! Apart from "A Private Little War," I had never seen *any* of the episodes on TV! But on Tuesday, 26 June at 6:40 p.m., GMT, Star Trek returned to BBC1 and they plan to show all the episodes! I have made a scrapbook to log each episode, with help from the *Star Trek Compendium* for the trivia and info on each episode.

And now to tomorrow. Thursday, 26 July. *Star Trek III: The Search for Spock* opens at Edinburgh's ABC Cinema. They are showing it tomorrow only *with STTMP* and *Wrath of Khan*, but I doubt I will be able to go. Oh, sure, it will be showing on its own from then on for several weeks. But those six and a half hours would be the most exhilarating and enjoyable of my life, if only . . . never mind.

*****We're thrilled that* two *letters from Scotland showed up in the same batch of* Roundtable *mail. We just had to run them both. We're only sorry that our friends in Great Britain and elsewhere overseas have such a difficult time obtaining our books. Be assured we're working on it. And let us hear from* *you, wherever you live! One of the wonderful things about this forum is that it allows anyone to participate, regardless of their location or circumstances, and brings us all closer together in a very meaningful way. —The Editors*****

Mindi Dorfman
Trotwood, Ohio

No matter how many times I try to convince myself, it is impossible for me to accept the fact that, in reality, Star Trek ended in 1969, when I was only one year old. But then again, that was reality. This is fantasy. Reality is saying that I discovered Star Trek long after it was technically "off the air." No matter. I still seem to be strangely drawn to the television whenever reruns come on. I still keep following the new movies, and I religiously collect all of the Star Trek books in print. This is what is keeping Star Trek alive. Not those who lived at the time of the TV show, but those of us who live in the new era, that of the Star Trek hobby, the fantasies, and the dreams.

My brother was a Trekkie first. He can still tell me about any of the shows that come on, but he claims to have outgrown the addiction. Even though he tries to live in the modern, normal world of television, he's still very much up to date on everything from the past and present of Star Trek, such as books and movies, and, of course, he knows his reruns. It's just one of those things that you can't grow out of . . . Once a Trekkie, always a Trekkie.

I think that is how most of the new Trekkies get hooked. They need to be introduced into the world of Star Trek. Not only to the physical mementos, but to the dreams behind it also.

What a way to begin!

If I had known at that time that I was going to live the rest of my life surrounding Star Trek, I probably would not have wanted to live!

But now my curiosity had been sparked. I had to see some more of this strange show. I watched every day for months, maybe even years, until it got to the point that I would kick my dog out of the room during Star Trek so that I could watch the show in privacy, and I would shut and lock the door so that I wouldn't be disturbed during "my" show. I used to pretend that I lived on the *Enterprise*, and my swingset in our backyard was the bridge. I started to buy all kinds of magazines so that I could cut out all of the Star Trek pictures. I even named my goldfish Kirk and Spock.

But that was at least ten years ago. Now I've matured past all that. Instead I center my days around my quarters/bedroom. I don't cut out *Enterprise* pictures from magazines anymore—I buy the posters. I've had six fish named Kirk and four named Spock. Furthermore, instead of *pretending* to be on the *Enterprise*, I now *fantasize* (there is a difference).

Speaking of fantasies . . .

There is that time in every Trekkie's life where it is no longer a "prime-time" dream show, but Star Trek becomes a "full-time fantasy" show. Let's face it, how many of us are there who refer to our homes as the *Enterprise*, and our cars are now called shuttlecraft?

It isn't entirely uncommon. It just seems to some that the *Enterprise* would be the perfect place to live. You'd be in the perfect place with the perfect friends. Sure, you'd face life-threatening situations every day, and would be out in the middle of the galaxy chasing stars around, but then again you'd have 450 friends all out there for the same reason. You would be away from poverty and from the city noises or country boredom. You would not have any concerns about overpopulation or about being laid up in bed for a month with the flu. Yeah, it really sounds good, but perfect? Well . . .

If Star Trek is so perfect, then why are there so many flaws? Even Mr. Spock isn't so perfect. His Vulcan nerve pinch didn't work on Gary Seven in "Assignment: Earth." Even in *Star Trek III: The Search for Spock*, with good ol' Spock himself, Leonard Nimoy, directing, there were flaws. To my knowledge, it was always the Romulans who flew a Bird of Prey ship, not the Klingons. And to strike another point, the Klingons must have had a heck of a time getting the cloaking device from the Romulans, because I thought they had that, too.

Oh well, so they made a little blunder. But even with the goof or blunders, it's still Star Trek, so that makes everything all right. So for now, I'll overlook the goofs and turn on the television and wait for Star Trek to come on. I'll be there when the five-year mission continues in its eighteenth year. But once again, that is reality. This is fantasy. . . .

Even when the adults claim to have outgrown Star Trek, as my brother did, there will always be someone to follow in their footsteps, as I did in his. As long as there are reruns, there will be Star Trek. As long as there are dreamers, fantasies, and believers, there *will* be Star Trek.

In fact, I know of someone now who will probably carry on the tradition of keeping Star Trek alive. She is a real trivia buff and can answer Star Trek questions at the drop of a hat. She asks me Star Trek questions, and she calls me on the telephone every night at six o'clock to remind me that "our" show is on.

She is my five-year-old niece.

It was said best at the end of *The Search for Spock*: "The Adventure Continues. . . ."

*****We suppose you've noticed that except for the passing reference, very little was said about* Star Trek III: The Search for Spock *in the preceding letters. Well, since we went to press last time so soon after the film's release, we've decided to extend this edition of the* Roundtable *to include a few selected comments and observations about* The Search for Spock.

Nothing, but nothing *in Star Trek history has brought more mail into the* Trek *offices than did the third Star Trek film,* The Search for Spock. *Not surprisingly, with this volume of mail, we found that opinions on the film and its events varied wildly. Never have we seen so much vehement disagreement among fans; if Harve Bennett and Leonard Nimoy set out to make a movie which would stir the thoughts and emotions of the fans, they've succeeded magnificently. As the number of letters was so large and each reader's opinions so heartfelt, we decided that the only equitable thing to do was to present excerpts from selected letters. Even so, we are able to present only a small percentage of them here. If your letter isn't among those excerpted, don't feel bad. We* did *read it and we appreciate the time and effort—and care—with which you wrote it. Thank you. —The Editors* *****

Elizabeth Lipka,
Conneaut, Ohio

The theme of friendship prevails throughout *The Search for Spock*. Leonard Nimoy does a beautiful job of expressing the friendship between characters. I believe that through the experience of Spock's death, Kirk begins to realize how much Spock means to him. I also feel that through this experience

Kirk has learned that the people closest to him are more important than his ship and career. McCoy finally admits to Spock that which we have known all along, that he really cares for Spock; we hear him admit that he has missed Spock and could not stand to lose him again.

The Search for Spock also develops a deeper friendship between the old crew and Kirk. When Kirk tells them that the mission will be a risky one, they respond by offering him their services and loyalty without questioning his judgment. Kirk also seems to now be able to let his emotions show. When he learns that his son has been killed he expresses his deep anger and grief right in front of the crew. I believe that the Kirk from the series would not have shown his deepest feelings to his crew as he does here.

Shirley Gibbons,
Titusville, Fla.

I felt each emotion as if I were standing with Kirk, one of his crew; which, in fact, I truly felt for the first time in this movie.

If critics don't recognize the brilliance, the sensitivity, the love and care which have gone into the making of *The Search for Spock*, they can all go take a flying leap!

This movie is what every Star Trek fan had hoped and prayed it would be. What could be more wonderful than having our beloved Mr. Spock back?

Norma Hawkins,
Islington, Ont., Canada

While some people claim that resurrecting Captain Spock is unfair to the viewer's emotions, I disagree. I am glad that Spock is alive. I rejoice that Spock lives because if he did not return to life I can picture Jim Kirk sickening with guilt and grief and ultimately going mad. I don't believe I could bear that. Spock is a very necessary character for personal interplay between Admiral Kirk and himself, as well as the other crew members. If Spock must die, then let it be when the whole crew is destroyed. They are family and you just don't break up a family that easily.

Allison Murray,
Potomac, Md.

Was anyone else as disappointed as I was? I'm not sure

what I expected, but to see Spock simply brought back to life wasn't it; it was just too easy. I truly believe when a character dies he should damn well stay that way. Why were the Klingons brought in at all? Kirk may be a genius, but the way he destroyed them was a bit simple. It never would have worked!

Many parts of *The Search for Spock* had surprising parallels to other movies. The Klingon's "dog thing" seemed surprisingly like one of Jabba's pets from *Return of the Jedi*; McCoy's trying to find transportation to the Genesis Planet was much like the famous bar scene from *Star Wars*; even McCoy's rescue was like Princess Leia's. Couldn't they write their own movie?

Wendy Worthington,
Huntingdon Valley, Pa.

Did you share my awe and wonder and delight? And what are we to say to all these religious overtones? I had expected reverence from the director, but all the allusions, as we were brought from Genesis to Armageddon, were an unexpected bonus. After all, *The Search for Spock* brought us a son sacrificed that another might live . . . an empty "tomb" in the morning . . . even a resurrection made possible through the "house of David." (And I had always heard a rumor that the lost thirteenth tribe of Israel was called Vulcan. . . .)

I was especially delighted to see so much *humor*, arising rightly from characters and their responses to situations. And I was thrilled to see so much of those old familiar blue eyes. What a lovely twist on the long-standing feud, for circumstances to place it squarely within the good doctor's head!

I had a lot of little quibbles, from casting (why was Kirstie Alley busy elsewhere when they needed her on Genesis?) to editing. (Discretion in treating violence is one thing, but that's Kirk's *son* being knifed in the back, for heavens sake! If he must die for his sins of creation, then let me *see* it! I blinked the first time and never believed he was dead at all!) The final scenes were rather too drawn-out without being filled in with enough meat (jeez, I know we're on Vulcan, but these guys are only *repressing* their passions—they *do have* them), and where was Amanda during all of this? (Yes, I know Vonda McIntyre explained it in the book, but *somebody* had to.)

Linda Walden,
Louisville, Ky.

They finally got down to confronting the major reason for the show's success—the interaction between the major and supporting characters. It is in this that most of us see ourselves.

I have also heard that people are disgruntled that the *Enterprise* has been destroyed. This is utter rubbish, for there have been many *Enterprises* (not the least of which was the space shuttle). The *Enterprise* is an idea, a concept. It lives and breathes with men, not cold hard steel. It is that spirit to which a lot of Trekkers cling, not some old destroyed mass of metal and wire, computer chips and warp nacelles. It is this spirit which will allow it to go on.

As for the crew, in addition to all of the good they've done on their unauthorized mission, they brought about the capture of an intact Klingon ship, and an intact Klingon officer. If there is a court-martial, how would they classify Spock? Starfleet status *deceased*? You've got to admit that a court-martial would be quite an interesting thing to see in the next movie, and I have heard that they are considering it. At any rate, I do not think the Vulcans will allow any severe punishment of the famous five.

I hope they don't ignore Maltz, by the way. One gets the idea that he is something of an anomaly in the Klingon Empire. Where Kruge and Torg typically saw power, Maltz seemed more impressed with the positive aspects of the Genesis Device. You really get the idea he wanted to be a proper Klingon, but that he wasn't exactly the bloodthirsty type. I can imagine him sitting in the brig contemplating his situation. In many ways, I kind of liked him. He almost seemed hurt when Kirk said he lied about killing him. Maybe he was wrong about not deserving to live.

Ellis Cambre,
Gretna, La.

I can't believe it! She's gone! NCC 1701 scuttled by her crew's own hand! Not destroyed in glorious battle with all flags flying and all phasers blazing, but burned up in the atmosphere of a dying planet. She was a good ship and deserved better than this!

Oh, I am quite sure that somewhere down the line is an NX 2001 or an *Enterprise II*, or some such successor. But it won't be the same corridors that the crew gets tossed around. It won't be the ship of the Tribbles that did battle with the Klingons and Romulans so many times and returned home bloodied sometimes, but always undefeated and unbowed. How can we have "continuing voyages of the Starship *Enterprise*" when it is not *the* Starship *Enterprise*? All sailors can tell you each ship has a personality, a magic all its own. They killed NCC 1701 and we all lost something special.

Joseph Portelli,
Taylor, Miss.

It isn't a secret that the producers of *The Search for Spock* did not like the *Enterprise*, so in order to rid themselves of a problem, a cheap and totally unwarranted solution was written. Harve Bennett doesn't seem to realize that the very foundation of Star Trek rests on four pillars: Kirk, Spock, McCoy, and the most subtle of all, the *Enterprise*. True, pure, unadulterated Star Trek *must* have these four pillars.

The destruction of the *Enterprise* was absolutely unnecessary. In the real world, the *Enterprise* is only a model used in special effects, so it didn't have to be eliminated or replaced because of contractual disputes, à la Kirstie Alley's Saavik. In the Star Trek universe, Kirk's actions leading up to this act are totally out of character. The *real* Jim Kirk would not have lost his ship with only a halfhearted battle. The *real* Jim Kirk would have found another way out of this "no-win scenario." How many times before had he regained control of the *Enterprise* after seemingly losing her?

The real danger from this, however, lies with the small yet vocal group of blind or complacent fans who will do their utmost to rationalize, in any possible way, a justification for the destruction of the *Enterprise* simply because it occurred in a "bona fide Star Trek" movie. This is unacceptable—we must speak out against this or else future films will become pseudo-Star Trek posing as real Star Trek. We must not allow Hollywood marketing experts to destroy piece by piece something so treasured.

As the Star Trek movies get farther and farther away from the series, there must of course be logical changes in the ST universe—but everything has a limit. There comes a time when we must stand up and protest. Now is the time. A treasured piece of Americana has been lost. Real Star Trek without the *Enterprise* is like the Lone Ranger without Silver.

Jim Dawson,
St. Augustine, Fla.

This time I wasn't dazzled by a crossfire of lasers or an explosion of incredible magnitude . . . I was deeply (yes, deeply!) touched by the love that these men have for each other! I mean, I *really* felt it! Then it hit me . . . Star Trek isn't about lasers, planets, and aliens. It's about friendship . . . *love*!

Renita Lane,
Jackson, Miss.

I have just seen *The Search for Spock* and finished reading the novelization by Vonda McIntyre. I enjoyed both, but there were two scenes in the novel that I felt should have been in the movie.

The first of these scenes is the one in which Uhura requests political asylum from the Vulcan embassy. This is certainly a dramatic scene and I feel a necessary one. I have a friend who saw the movie with me and she was puzzled about Uhura's sudden appearance on Vulcan when she had been last seen on Earth.

I also felt that Amanda should have had some kind of brief appearance. Her absence left a slightly lopsided feeling to that part of the movie.

Jane Land,
Larchmont, Pa.

Gene Roddenberry has said that he thinks *The Search for Spock* is the best of the three movies, and he may be right. Certainly the feel of it is very authentic. There are so many details which connect this movie to the whole Star Trek universe. For the first time it is clear that the person in charge was intimately familiar with Star Trek.

Kirk's ability to sacrifice his ship when it became tragically necessary is a real indication of how much he has grown and matured. There was a time when he seemed to need the *Enterprise*, not simply because he is an excellent and inspiring commander, but as a prop for his ego. This is no longer true, and as Kirk's character has deepened, so has William Shatner's performance. At times in the past I have found them both irritating, but not now.

It should also be noted that in five minutes on camera at the end of the movie Leonard Nimoy made the audience remember why we wanted Spock back in the first place. When he looked at his old friends and shipmates and raised that characteristic eyebrow, it made everything that had happened seem worth it.

Kenneth King,
Houston, Tex.

I am pleased with the movie, but do not love it as I did *Star Trek II: The Wrath of Khan*. *Wrath of Khan* was loaded with action and adventure, while *The Search for Spock* dealt with the deep friendship and love between her crew, and just how far they would go to help one of their own. Friendships like those in the movie are very rare, even today. This friendship and love for one another is one of the many things that have kept Star Trek alive for all these years.

The acting in *The Search for Spock* was the best I have ever seen from the regular cast. I do feel, however, that DeForest Kelley stole the movie away from the other actors. His brilliant acting made this movie seem better than it really was. The two I was not happy with or convinced by were Robin Curtis and Christopher Lloyd. Curtis's Lieutenant Saavik seemed too emotional, and when she tried to be witty she came across as being very sarcastic. Lloyd did look good as a Klingon commander, but it takes more than looking good. To me he did not project "being evil" as he should have. You or I could look evil in Klingon makeup, but one has to *act* really evil, not just look evil.

I would much rather see the *Enterprise* be destroyed, taking a few Klingons out with her, than be cut apart to be sold as scrap metal. I really did like the science/research ship that David and Saavik were on. It looked a lot better than the new *U.S.S. Excelsior*, which looked more like a beached whale than the most advanced starship of its time. Its bridge looked awfully cheap when compared to that of the *Enterprise*. It looked more like someone had thrown it together in his garage than a product of Starfleet.

Hilarie Grey,
Los Angeles, Cal.

I thoroughly enjoyed the film, which was excellently crafted, but one void still remained: Kirstie Alley's absence. Whereas the part of Saavik seemed almost second nature to Alley, it was completely lost in the efforts of newcomer Robin Curtis. Saavik is the perfect role for Alley because of her childhood obsession to play Spock's daughter. The part of Saavik, his beloved pupil, is damn close. While watching the movie, I could visualize Kirstie Alley in every scene, saying each line with the Vulcan poignancy lacking in Robin Curtis's performance. For me, Kirstie Alley is the only "real" Saavik, my personal heroine and Trekkie role model. I implore the producer to rehire Kirstie for any further Star Trek films. Just looking at the screen chemistry between her and Leonard Nimoy is justification enough.

Michael Clifford,
Scottsdale, Ariz.

I loved it! Things always seem to work out for Kirk, don't they? He says in his log at the beginning of the film that since Spock's death he feels he has left a part of himself behind, a spiritual part. I know how he feels. The only difference is he gets another chance at getting it back. And he takes it. I found it ironic that McCoy is holding Spock's *katra*. The *katra* of a Vulcan is like the soul of a human, to be trusted with only the few people a Vulcan can count on to set it free. I would've bet a million that it would have been Kirk, as did everyone.

Laurie Lu Leonard

My brother told me he'd seen a small ad on the back of a comic book, in one corner. There was to be a third Star Trek movie! I could hardly believe it at first. Then I began to see the ads myself, and finally my local paper printed the date it would open. It was real! I cried with joy when I found out! Finally, it came. It was a dream come true, and five months of waiting were finally over!

The early show was completely sold out, even though I got to the theater two hours ahead of time. The lines were three blocks long. As soon as they let the lines for the early show in, I got in the line already forming for the second show. I was on the edge of my seat all the way through it. It was fantastic! They had brought Spock back from the dead, and let the *Enterprise* die with dignity, in the service of her duty, rather than toss her in the scrap heap as a derelict. Of course, we all felt a tightening in our stomachs at the loss of the great lady who served to carry our favorite crew to "where no man has gone before."

Of course, I couldn't be satisfied seeing it only once, oh no. I had to see it again and again and again! I saw it twenty six times! (Now please don't think I'm crazy, I couldn't help myself.) I even memorized all the dialogue in *The Search for Spock*.

*****Well, that's all we have room for in this volume, gang. We hope you enjoyed the letters and the extra comments about* The Search for Spock. *And be sure to let us know what you think of our new policy of answering mail and making editorial comments here in the Roundtable. We'll be looking for* your *letter very soon! —The Editors*****

OUT OF THE WOMB

by Joyce Tullock

A double dose of Joyce Tullock this time around, fans. Featuring two articles by the same writer in the same collection is something we seldom do, but Joyce's two contributions were so different in tone and viewpoint that we decided to bend the rules this time.

Here is Joyce in a somewhat more philosophical mood, musing upon the events which led to Star Trek's formation, and also upon those things contained in its format, characters, and stories which make Star Trek so important to us. We think you may find yourself somewhat surprised by some of the things she says, but will—as we did—ultimately find yourself agreeing with her.

Of all the things that have been said about Star Trek, both in articles by the fans and by those creative minds behind the making of the series, nothing has ever really accurately "nailed down" a convincing explanation about what makes Star Trek so special to so many people. And to add to the frustration, we can't even try to explain it all by examining the makeup of the modern American mind; Star Trek's appeal has no national or international boundaries. It has a devoted following throughout the world.

But it's highly likely that one word *does* more or less sum it all up. It's a word that perhaps has come, in our troubled, very threatened twentieth century, to be more important than all other words in all other languages. Star Trek—and I admit that this may be a very personal, subjective view—has come to represent simple, human "hope."

The concept of hope for the future is Star Trek's focal

164

point. No matter *what* your personal preferences about the series may be, it's the one thing that binds every single Star Trek episode to all others, every single fan to all others. All the episodes, all the movies, have that feeling of optimism in common, no matter how they may have succeeded or failed artistically. Whether it was scientifically unacceptable, as was "Spock's Brain," or insulting in its supremely boring pseudointellectualism, as was "Let That Be Your Last Battlefield," every Star Trek episode has a grain of hope, a "spark" of future.

Let's relax for a moment, and go with the feeling that tiny spark gives us. Like Blake the poet, let's cast aside for a moment the crippling restriction of definition—and take a mind-journey through Star Trek as we "feel" it in our guts. Maybe we'll discover something. If we can't explain Star Trek, then why not try to at least evaluate what it *does* for us?

Let's remember. . . .

The 1960s were not good times, really. But they were powerful times, healthier than the "me-oriented" times that followed, some say. Historians the world over tend to agree that with the tragic death of President John F. Kennedy, the world went into a kind of shock. And when it came out of that shock, it had changed. Hardnosed, unhappy with "the establishment," angry. Rudely awakened. Humanity became so turbulent, in fact, that it might well be likened to a newborn child, screaming in confused anger at that first, unexplained slap on the bottom.

But it was not screaming blindly. Activist groups sprang up around the planet in protest of racism, war, human greed, and political and religious imprisonment of the mind. And there were those—labeled at the time as fanatics, but now recognized as prophets—who warned that man's environment, his very home, the planet Earth, was in *grave* danger.

And as luck would have it, the great meeting place of humanity in those days (perhaps more than in the present?) was the new, all-powerful institution known as network television. TV had only recently come into its own. It was still young and eager to try new, daring ideas. Network television wasn't yet successful enough to be ruled by the stodgy-minded businessmen who are strangling it today. And it was a marketplace. It is to our good fortune that in those days gone by, the concept of a *future* wherein all men could live and work together in peace was a very commercial idea. Very salable. It was also a time when controversial ideas thrived on the video tube, as if the industry wanted to cast off all memories of the repressive McCarthy blacklist era. So it was a time when all things joined together to work creatively for a little while, as if television came out of some dark age for a too brief moment, to give its audience a gift of hope.

And in that brief, shining moment, a world of marvelous wonder, kindness, mystery, and excitement came to be. The gentle genius of a man named Gene Roddenberry (remember him?) and the tough, farsighted likes of Lucille Ball, caused it to happen that this so-called "*Wagon Train* to the stars" should be given a chance.

Out of the turmoil of the sixties, then, came our beloved *Enterprise*, with her crew of so many different races, with her ideals of the reverence for difference, for adventure and human progress. For hope.

The *Enterprise* became a meeting place for and of the many. Not only aboard the ship herself, but throughout the world. If people all over the television viewing world had nothing else in common, they knew and cared about Kirk, Spock, McCoy, Scotty, and their fellow crewmen.

The men and women of the *Enterprise* were, according to Roddenberry's own description, simple heroes. Flawed human beings who were nevertheless idealists. Real, believable people, who, though filled with the usual imperfections, showed great promise. Maybe it's the fact that they *are* imperfect—from Kirk on down—that makes them live still, and makes them continually valuable. They illustrate that even the stumbling human race has a chance at something akin to greatness.

Look at Kirk. His idealism is legendary, but so are his imperfections. If it were not so, he would not be an interesting character to an intelligent, enlightened public (especially to the public of the late sixties and early seventies). And while he has regretfully grown to be a superhero in the *minds* of many fans, he did not start out that way. (Many Kirk fans disapprove violently of the flawed Kirk they see in the first two movies, maintaining that it is not in the true character of Kirk to make a mistake or treat any of his crewmen poorly. I suggest that it is not Kirk who has changed, but his fans. Perhaps they need to look at some of the episodes yet one more time.) But Kirk's character certainly *does* suffer the most from the stifling kind of media sickness which today demands that heroes be perfect. For example, some of McCoy's best lines were cut from *Star Trek: The Motion Picture*, simply because someone thought he was being too hard on

Kirk. (As if the good admiral should ever have to be babied!) And in *Star Trek II: The Wrath of Khan* we are quite clearly supposed to believe that Kirk's having cheated on a test as a cadet was an act of genius (he got a commendation for original thinking). Hardly believable—since Kirk's reprogramming of the computer for the *Kobayashi Maru* test indicated abrupt failure. The test was designed to examine a potential officer's behavior when confronting a "no-win situation." Any officer who so naively refused to believe that there is such a thing would certainly never have been sent into space, where the chances of death are infinite. Kirk quite frankly and refreshingly *failed* the *Kobayashi Maru* test. He had to take it three times! And like all good, reliable testing methods, it did bring to light what may be his fatal flaw.

Kirk was, and is, a spoiled little boy. A poor loser. A man who continually seeks to have things *his* way. And thank goodness for that, as it makes him a character worth the viewing. It makes him believable and it allows even the most non-hero-worshiping fan to enjoy him, to relate to him. It surrounds him with a kind of sympathetic melancholy. After all, the things Kirk "wants" are usually very good, very desirable, whether it be the love of a beautiful woman, or peace and brotherhood for all intelligent life forms. We are all pulling for him, as we pull for ourselves, hoping that he, our own representative of drive and ambition, will one day cheat the fates. He *is* an imperfect man, a selfish one at times, who longs for progress for himself and his fellows. He dares, the defiant Prometheus still, to hope for a better way. A better time. And he fervently believes that he, a simple human being, is worthy of greater glory.

Jim Kirk carries his religion of hope to the farthest limits, like some noble, imperfect Arthurian knight on his lonely pilgrimage. He is always aspiring to those things which lesser, more practical men would blindly accept as being beyond their grasp. He is always hoping.

And, of course, one of Kirk's most valuable prizes early on in the series is the attainment of that which others would have thought to be unattainable—the friendship of Spock the Vulcan.

From the outset Kirk refused to see this alien as others must have seen him: cold, isolated, humorless, uncaring in matters of the human condition. Kirk's sensitivity and determined belief in Spock's ability to feel deeply led an entire viewing audience on a subtle but recognizable journey through human understanding and awareness. He demonstrated the

human capacity to put love above tradition. He did not understand Spock's ways, but he cared for him. In the racially
unsettled times of the sixties, the Kirk of the television series
took racial difference as a matter of course. And by the very
fact of his seeming ignorance of "difference" he made an
entire world a little bit ashamed.

In fact, the whole crew of the Starship *Enterprise* appears
to be quite naive about problems which were (and are) major
questions of our own century. They are, after all, beings from
the future whose forefathers have pretty much overcome those
stumbling blocks to progress: racism, greed, political oppression, religious self-deception, and war. They still have the
negative feelings, of course, such as fear, hatred, jealousy—
but they have taken a step, they have admitted to those
feelings unashamedly, as a part of the human creature. *Today, I will not kill.*

So the mankind of Kirk's time certainly has taken a step
further than the mankind of today. Star Trek does indeed
paint an optimistic picture.

To the average viewer of the sixties, though, it was not
Kirk who captured the imagination as much as it was that
strange, almost mystical sidekick; the one from the planet
Vulcan. The one with the ears.

Spock was young in those days, proud of his Vulcan
heritage, open to the acceptance of difference in others. In his
grand loneliness, he was a symbol to a viewing audience
which was hungry for some kind of greater understanding
between people, races and nations. He began in Star Trek as a
very isolated individual who, despite his own fear and inhibitions, grew to be part of the family that became Kirk/Spock/
McCoy. He became loved. And to some, perhaps, he was
even a messenger of peace, a promise of how it *could* be, if
only people would cease being afraid to care.

Of every man and woman aboard the Starship *Enterprise*,
Spock is the most pure of heart and deed. The ascetic, who,
with his superior strength and intelligence, is a prototype of
what man might become. As Kirk's idealism gives us hope,
so Spock's sheer fineness of bearing offers promise of what
man can become if only he would learn to cherish his intellect
and keep his emotional self in check. There's no need to go
into detail about his willingness to care for others, despite his
insistence that he does not indulge in emotions. He has
offered to give his life for Kirk and ship many times (and

finally does), and his depth of feeling for the very emotional Dr. McCoy is legend.

The subtle irony of Spock and McCoy's deeply felt, needles-and-pins friendship brings a poignancy to Star Trek unmatched in filmed science fiction. Of the many relationships in Star Trek, theirs is the most relevant, the most complicated, and the most potentially beautiful. It demonstrates the ability of intelligent beings to overcome vast differences for the sake of simple friendship. Unlike the Kirk/Spock friendship, which developed quite smoothly, the friendship between McCoy and Spock has to overcome tremendous obstacles. And that makes it all the more profound. In the McCoy/Spock friendship we see a very real, very "sixties activist" statement about man's need to find love where he might once have seen only hatred, prejudice and distrust.

McCoy, after all, represents twentieth-century man, in all his idealistic glory, in all his flawed sadness. He comes complete with a fine complexity of attributes and shortcomings. Spock is his emotional negative and, at times, his ideological one. Whether it be thanks to Roddenberry or Nimoy and Kelley, Spock's and McCoy's "contrary" personalities gradually developed into a sophisticated and mathematically precise juxtaposition of character traits. Their relationship and the interactions it involves can be examined on so many levels that it tempts one to say it may be the single most complex aspect of the Star Trek phenomenon.

Chances are, though, that the profound symbolism of this relationship came about because of the mood of the times during which it was created. It's a case of writers, actors, and directors working together, sometimes unconsciously perhaps, to explore their own interpretation of the questions and ideals of the day. And while Nimoy once brushed off the McCoy/Spock relationship as "Doc Adams and Festus," his great fondness for it is apparent whenever the two seem to interact. His Mr. Spock spars with Kelley's McCoy with a subtle sharpness and sensitivity that say, "These men are enjoying this . . . and they feel that they are doing something special." As if to underscore the point, Nimoy, as director of *Star Trek III*, put forth a great effort to see to it that McCoy's feelings about Spock are given more than a passing glance. All the more to add to that special Star Trek "spark."

Whether or not the McCoy/Spock feud and resulting friendship was a conscious effort of Kelley and Nimoy, there is no doubt that it held much relevance for the audience of the racially unsettled sixties. It offered something beautiful, something hopeful. It still does.

But the hope Star Trek symbolized when it first aired goes beyond the question of racism. World peace was always a major theme, as we see in episodes like "The Savage Curtain," "Day of the Dove," and "A Private Little War," to name just a few. All such episodes at least attempted to show the futility of war and violence. "A Private Little War" succeeded a bit more, perhaps, simply because it did not end "happily ever after." Every once in a while, in those days, a TV show managed to get by without a "Hollywood ending."

In "A Private Little War," Kirk is quite realistically left to make a decision of war or peace. He chooses war. It's a case of limited warfare versus peaceful oppression. The Klingons in this story have provided the village dwellers of the planet Neural with primitive firearms, seeing to it that they use the weapons to bully the hill people. The only way Kirk can help his friends, the hill people, and thus maintain the planet's already disturbed status quo is to provide them with equal, but not greater, firepower. Kirk and McCoy argue bitterly over this point, McCoy, as the pacifist, raging against the uselessness and waste of a war that cannot be won. Kirk here represents the established political-militaristic attitude, refusing to believe that an oppressed people should be denied the right to fight back. The painful, almost unacceptable truth is that both men are right in what they say. There is no "easy out" for Kirk the decision-maker in this episode; even the *Kobayashi Maru* has not prepared him.

"A Private Little War" was one of Star Trek's boldest antiwar statements, and remembering the time period in which it was aired, we can only think that its contents were intended to be a statement about the Vietnam situation—the "no win" war. While there is no clear-cut answer to the McCoy/Kirk debate, it's interesting to note that Kirk's militaristic view won out—the hill people were provided with Federation-made firearms. Diplomacy with the Klingons was not even discussed as a possible solution. It is a clear parallel with the East-West world struggles of our time.

It would seem that there is very little "hope" in this episode at all, except for the fact that it was clearly intended to make people *think*.

But that is to be expected. Science fiction is the literature of ideas. And, remembering the mood of the sixties—Star Trek's womb—it is perfectly reasonable to expect to find in the series many ideas which are often controversial, conflicting, even confusing. *If* we want to consider Star Trek to be science fiction, then we *must* be able to approach it from many varying, sometimes uncomfortable angles. We must be ready to admit that we can't agree or even always understand all the questions that are put to us. You don't go away from reading a true science fiction novel and say, "Oh, I understood that *perfectly*." Not from a good one, anyway. It is the nature of science fiction to try to force the audience's mind to stretch, and if it does not do so, then chances are it has failed to some extent.

The "feel" of Star Trek, then, involves the idea of science fiction as it was intended to be—controversial, intellectually complex, traditionally opposed to organized religion, with an emphasis on the ideals of free thought. It is not simply a matter of space-age gadgets and liberal morals. Some very fine science fiction has very little gimmickry and postulates surprisingly conservative ideals. It is a matter of human discovery, of changing perspective "at will" in a mind-bending attempt to understand the not yet experienced. To give the feelings, ideas and lifestyles of others a chance.

Science fiction is often accused of being a literary genre which attempts to "replace" religion. Nonsense. Science fiction is simply the one literary means by which we may imagine beyond the known limits—beyond the "mind-forged manacles" of our traditional, habit-filled, almost superstitious world view.

Science fiction is an imaginary means of being free, for the *sake* of being free, so that we may step back for a moment from the world that controls us and "look around."

And that is the mood, the "feel" Star Trek captures at its best. It takes us a step or two beyond ourselves. For a moment or two, it yanks us from the comfort of our cradlelike, self-defined world. It makes us the tiniest bit bolder, daring enough to think about things which might otherwise be considered "forbidden fruit." At its height, it allows us to see our universe from a very alien perspective. It allows us to imagine other universes, other ways of being.

The ability to change perspective, even for a short time, is certainly a basic key to human understanding. We all know the old American Indian saying about walking a mile in another man's moccasins—as basic a concept as it is, it is also a far-reaching one. And it is what anyone does when he identifies with the futuristic characters of Star Trek.

And in those episodes where Star Trek is working hard at being science fiction, it *is* taking us on a journey beyond our traditional human perceptions. We stand "without" so that we may "see" within.

There are moments when the "feel" of genuine science fiction is attained: "City on the Edge of Forever," "The Menagerie," "The Tholian Web," "The Corbomite Maneuver," to name some—not necessarily the best. And in *Star Trek: The Motion Picture*, we find a sort of elegant summing up of what the "idea" aspect of Star Trek has been all along. We see Gene Roddenberry's grand hope for mankind culminate in the birth of a god-child. Those who feel threatened by what this fine piece of science fiction suggests label it "the dehumanization of man" and thereby dismiss the important questions it raises about man's perspective on himself and his future. But the V'Ger experience isn't dehumanizing at all. It is a story about possibilities, about man's potential for growth beyond his most daring dreams. It's a venture into another perspective. The very truest and most daring kind of human adventure. It reminds us that as long as there is someone willing to journey beyond the edge of the known, there is hope.

Star Trek is—as Mr. Spock might be inclined to say—a series about "possibilities." And it deals with every subject under the sun; racism, war, religion, industrial development and the problems it presents to man, sex, equality, overpopulation, time travel, pollution. The list is virtually endless. It shows us many viewpoints (including the opinions and prejudices of the people involved in making the series); sometimes we agree with it, sometimes we do not. But we always *think* about it.

So, at the bottom of it all is the fact that we experience a "feeling" that is good and positive in Star Trek. There is the challenge to try. A desire to know the unknown. There is hope. Even at Spock's death, we understand the flash of puzzlement in McCoy's eyes when he utters the words "He's really not dead." And we indulge ourselves in the tiniest hint we see there, remembering that when man's mind works with his spirit—as it does so often with the combination of McCoy, Spock and Kirk—there *are* always possibilities.

Who knows, maybe Kirk's attitude about the no-win situation will one day be vindicated.

It's no joke. As the crew of the *Enterprise* is always ready to remind us, wherever there is open-mindedness and human affection, there is hope. There is the opportunity to reach beyond our present self-defined limits. Instead of greed and the war it always brings, there can be positive growth and peace. Instead of hatred and prejudice, there can be love. Instead of death, there can be life.

It's Star Trek's simple promise of the future. It prods us: "See who you are? See what you can do?" In a thousand different ways, Star Trek appeals to the audience's hope for the future. It reminds us of our ability to change perspective—so that we might feel the other man's sorrow, so that we might take part in his joy. And as we identify with Kirk, Spock, and McCoy, we are enchanted by the great affection they share for one another. We love the fact that they love one another. We find a kind of solace in seeing how they believe in one another, as imperfect, but exceedingly worthwhile, beings.

Love, self-worth, the potential for limitless growth—these are all part of the Star Trek experience. When added up, their sum equals one mighty "yes!" to us all, by daring us to believe in ourselves. Can there be any greater hope than that?

THE THREE-FOOT PIT AND OTHER STORIES

by Ingrid Cross

Thinking about writing some fan fiction? Or are you even thinking about taking the plunge and publishing your own fanzine? If so, then you'll find that Ingrid's article contains invaluable advice and information, presented with humor and insight into the irrepressible urges which drive fans to write and publish. We only wish it had arrived eleven years ago when we first started to publish Trek. *We would have been saved a lot of headaches and mistakes!*

Captain Kirk, Mr Spock, Dr. McCoy, and Scotty beam down to a planet which is rich in dilithium crystals. They hope to establish trading relations with the natives. Negotiations go well, a treaty is signed, and everlasting friendship is proclaimed. The natives offer their planet for shore leave. Everyone is happy.

Then wouldn't you know it. When it's time to leave orbit, Kirk makes a terrible discovery: *McCoy is missing!* Panic ensues! Search parties are organized! After an exhaustive combing of the planet, they are called away on another mission. Kirk reluctantly (indeed, even tearfully) abandons the search.

In the meantime, the good doctor has managed to fall into a pit. (Never mind how he did it. Let's assume he's a klutz.) He has no food or water (this is desert terrain—for some reason he's decided to take shore leave in an area with all the attractions of the Mojave) . . . and he's dying a slow, tortured death—hallucinations and all.

Meanwhile, back on the *Enterprise*, Kirk and Company decide to go back to the planet (a hunch, perhaps?), defy

Fleet orders, and resume the search for their missing comrade. Of course, they find him in the proverbial nick of time. End of story. Happy ending all around. As the Big E warps out, life is hunky-dory. Friendships have proved the test of Starfleet, McCoy's emaciated body is filling out quite nicely, and Spock admits his undying affection for McCoy.

What major flaw exists in this story?

One and one only: Dr. Leonard McCoy was trapped in a three-foot pit.

I admit I wrote that story, nearly fourteen years ago. And I have been grateful ever since that at the time "The Three-Foot Pit" (as a friend aptly named it recently) was written, I didn't know fanzines existed, and that story ended up in a desk drawer and later the trash basket. My budding career as a fan writer might have ended abruptly if someone else had read that story. His laughter alone would have driven me to drink.

For that matter, I didn't realize there were other Star Trek fans "out there," bitten by the same bug: the driving need to write further adventures of the *Enterprise* crew. Through the years, I found these other fans, expanded my interests in Star Trek through fandom . . . and discovered the wonderful world of fanzines.

A quick note of explanation: Fanzines are fan-written magazines containing fiction, poetry, articles, and original artwork covering almost every facet of Star Trek imaginable. Fanzines are an underground counterculture of sorts, providing an outlet for writers, editors, and readers who constantly demand more and more material about their heroes. It's a good thing they exist, too—Paramount and Pocket Books could not possibly provide us with material fast enough to satisfy our appetites.

Fanzines are nonprofit by nature and by force. By force because Paramount Studios holds copyrights on the Star Trek properties and it's illegal to make a profit from their property. They are aware of fanzines and have let them continue because they are good publicity. And zines are nonprofit by nature because production—assembling them, printing them, mailing them—gets downright expensive.

I evolved (some would probably say "devolved," but let's not quibble) from a reader of these fanzines to a writer for them and, finally, into an editor of several. As an editor of *Odyssey*, an amateur fan press, for the past seven years, I've learned more about the Star Trek characters than I ever hoped to. I've seen writers expand the major characters (Kirk and Spock) into something bigger than life. Writers have also taken the other characters (most notably McCoy and Scotty) and fleshed them out, given them more to do than all the episodes and the three movies combined. These writers have created an open universe, a place where the crew of the *Enterprise* have become friends . . . known quantities. The characters have come alive on a page, have grown up. And the writers and artists have given thousands of people the chance to experience life through someone else's eyes. At their best, they provide a look at reality through fiction.

That is the most important thing a writer can do. Not only do writers of fan fiction supply their readers with an escape from reality—something we all need to remain sane—they have shown us what can be done when the imagination is stretched. A great deal of successful writing involves *presentation*.

Writing is a craft and it is a discipline. Putting a blank piece of paper into a typewriter and producing a story (or poem or article or whatever) takes talent, work, and courage. We'll take the talent for granted (for the moment, we'll assume talent is a "given"), and the courage will have to be accepted as truth by nonwriters.

Writing is, far and above anything else, *work*. Frustrating, difficult, tyrannical, and very seldom financially rewarding work. If you doubt it, listen in when writers get together and start complaining. They are driven people, and special rest homes should be built to accommodate them. Listening to writers go on about how plots don't seem to work out right, or how they feel compelled to sit at the typewriter and work even when they hate it . . . it all makes the eavesdropper wonder why they do it in the first place. It's because they're hooked, that's why. So if you're bitten by the bug, don't say so in public. They might commit *you*.

There are similarities between fan writing and professional writing, but the writer who works for fanzines has an advantage or two. First of all, he or she can be flexible, even with set characters and fixed patterns established during the past nineteen years of the Star Trek phenomenon. It's easier to talk about moral issues, for example, in the pages of a fanzine than it is in a piece submitted to *The New Yorker*. Secondly, there is an established audience hungering for anything about the Star Trek characters. This audience is also already divided into specialized segments—Kirk fans, Spock fans, action lovers, poetry buffs, etc.—so you can tailor your story to whichever of them you wish. Likewise, any story you wish to tell in any of these areas will find a ready audience. Thirdly, because the rules are sometimes freer in fanzines and the requirements not quite as stringent, the chances of being published are much greater than in the pro market, giving a writer the chance to polish his or her skills in front of an audience.

But fan fiction (amateur by nature, since writers are not paid, except in contributor's copies) and pro fiction (where the writer is paid and gets a professional byline) *are* similar in many ways. The rules are the same for both—though these rules are often fractured, overlooked, or simply thrown out the window by inexperienced writers.

Most Star Trek writers agree that realistic characterization is the most important of these rules. When you're writing about characters created by someone else, you must, above all, be true to the original. You are interpreting here, not creating. Don't restructure them to fit your needs.

Characterization is an important part of a story line. Spock's character was not created as emotional or lovesick. Spock is and should remain a Vulcan . . . a creature driven by the need to see his world through logic. As he frequently tells his captain, logic dictates his actions . . . not his gonads or the phase of the moon or any emotions that authors try to force upon him. Spock, as we see in the episodes and later in the films, does not make decisions based on irrational or whimsical emotions, the way we humans do.

This can also be called the "believability factor" that Gene Roddenberry fought for so vehemently. Spock simply does not fall for a woman the way Kirk does. If he *did* feel attracted to a female, he would not use the same approach.

If you do want to create your own characters, by all means go for it! There's ample opportunity in the ever-present Star Trek alien. Literally thousands of stories have been written in fan fiction, and 99 percent of them contain aliens. Unfortunately, most of them are your basic WASP (white, Anglo-Saxon, Protestant); this is a result of limited imagination. (And a fault seen in *Star Trek II: The Wrath of Khan*.) After all, the odds of meeting up with an alien from Zanzibar

7 who looks like an Earthling and eats hot dogs are rather astronomical.

(I won't swear to it, but I'd lay good odds that the natives of Planet X in my "three-foot pit" story were WASPs. There's something to be said for writing what you *know* . . . but that can be carried to extremes when writing about the outer reaches of our galaxy.)

Another rule involves the sensible *expansion* of the Star Trek characters we know. For example, if you're dealing with people who are in a quasi-military organization like Starfleet, have them act accordingly. In "The Three-Foot Pit," Dr. McCoy wanders off into the desert and no one knows where he went. All right, maybe it's *plausible*, but is it realistic? A seasoned Fleet officer would make sure someone knew how to contact him. Especially if he's the chief medical officer of a ship. What if someone needed him? That one flaw could destroy the story because it's not very believable and is a distraction for the reader.

It's equally unbelievable that Kirk can sidestep Fleet orders *constantly* and never get hauled on the carpet for some of those decisions he makes. I'll accept the idea that limited contact with the Fleet enables Kirk's character to be flexible and gives plots handy outs. But after nineteen years of "easy outs," the device is old.

Research, too, is necessary. Star Trek is supposed to be science fiction; the fiction should be based on science. Scientific gaffes were found throughout the series and movies, visible even to a viewer without a sophisticated background in science. (In *Star Trek III: The Search for Spock*, for example, I find it difficult to believe that the *Enterprise* could warp out so close to that repair station . . . and not leave debris scattered in its path.) In the infamous pit story, the *Enterprise*'s sensors—a well-established mechanism—should have located a lifeform in an area with no one around for miles and miles. When the science falls short, so does the story.

Research plays an important role in stories dealing with historical dates. In a time-travel story, for example, where Kirk, Spock, and McCoy go back to the late thirties in America, we know what that time was like. Don't have a character contract pneumonia and not receive medical treatment. There *were* hospitals in that time, and people cared enough to help the sick. A writer ends up the fool when he ignores the facts for the sake of his plot.

Plot devices are an easy out, and a sign of laziness. Popular plot devices in Star Trek fan fiction are: the Guardian of Forever; convenient *pon farr* for a certain Vulcan; the transporter; and having a character "act now and neglect to think later." The transporter was a necessary evil of the series, but in fan writing, it's a cliché waiting to happen.

There are many types of stories in fanzines, and many variations on a theme. There are "get-'ems," wherein Kirk/Spock/McCoy are killed, tortured, abused, and/or emotionally tampered with for the sake of emotional satisfaction for the writer or reader. Some stories are "Mary Sues"; they maneuver one of our heroes into a situation where another character—usually a woman with *unbelievable* talents and qualities—has to get the hero out of trouble. They then inevitably fall in love. (There are good Mary Sue stories, of course, and fun ones as well. These stories are difficult to write, but rewarding to read. I'm just surprised that in my story there wasn't someone bearing a remarkable resemblance to myself single-handedly hauling the doctor out of that pit. Everything else went into it . . . why didn't I include some vicarious thrills as well?)

There are action-adventure stories, love stories, stories with a moral, alternate-universe stories, stories dealing with the Friendship, stories about alien civilizations. Then there are Three-Foot Pit stories, but we already know about *that* kind, right?

In short, there are endless possibilities . . . an infinite number of situations that we can write about, numerous universes to create and revel in. Those possibilities are exciting for the reader, writer, and editor, and that's why fanzines continue to spring up all over the world. That's why we continue to feed our addiction with new tales of intrigue and adventure.

The problem, of course, is to avoid writing the same story someone else has written at least twice before. That's where the individual imagination comes into play. Three writers can start off with the same idea and end up with nine or more presentations of that one idea. The writer can spin himself or herself into a universe where no one has ever been before or create fresh situations . . . but it takes work. A lot of work involving characterization, research, and presentation of another sort.

Let's assume that you, as a writer, have completed a story

that avoids all the problems we've discussed. You hold in your hands a stack of paper that tells the *ultimate* story of the *Enterprise* crew in a new way. The story is interesting, free of time-worn plot devices, and completely researched. You are *done* with this story.

No, you're not. You might have a fantastic story line, your characters could be completely right, the dialogue is believable. But more than likely that stack of paper is *not quite* ready to be packed off to an editor.

Let's go back to my horrendous story as a case in point. If I remember correctly (and my memory is cruelly correct about this story), it was handwritten on lined notebook paper and looked terrible. Its major problem was that it was a first draft.

First drafts are just that: a draft that rolls out of the mind in rough form.

A story needs revisions to toughen it up or tone it down. It can take three times as long to revise a story as it took to write it. A well-written story is so finely tuned that it draws the reader into it and makes him forget that he's reading at all. A writer should make the reader *experience* that story.

What does revising entail? When you go back to the story and work on the second draft (or third, or fourth, and so on), you should be looking for several things. Are there holes in the plot, places where something doesn't quite work? Smooth it out; take another approach; clean up the problem. Does the dialogue sound right? Do your characters seem to be "on the mark"? If not, try writing a scene from another angle to get a better "feel." Have you described everything adequately? Does the story come *alive* to someone who doesn't know it as well as you do? Have you conveyed your ideas clearly? When you revise, keep in mind that the reader will not know what you're talking about if you write in "shorthand." Describe scenes adequately, but don't overdo it; don't give them more than they actually need.

If you find that there are a lot of holes in your story and you can't seem to fix the problem, throw that first draft away and start again. A first draft accomplishes one major purpose: It gets the story told, no matter how roughly, so that you can tackle it again and refine it. A first draft allows you to start over and correct yourself . . . before a reader gets ahold of it and (via a letter) does it for you.

When the revisions are complete, make sure the story is

polished. Check your grammar. Check your spelling. You hope your editor has a rudimentary sense of both punctuation and spelling, but don't count on it. Editors are just as likely as you are to overlook things. They are human beings, not dictionaries in the flesh, so take the time to look up words you're not sure of, words that seem "strange" to you. For example, "torcher" should spell trouble to the writer as well as to the character being "torchered." An editor will probably pick up on that . . . but don't take it for granted.

Make sure your manuscript looks good. Nothing turns an editor off faster than a handwritten or single-spaced manuscript. The former shows poor manners and amateurishness— editors are not pharmacists, by profession forced to put up with illegible scrawls—and the latter shows a lack of understanding of how the editing process works. An editor cannot make notations for editing purposes in a single-spaced manuscript . . . and editors *always* feel they must do *something* to a story, no matter how minor. Humor them. Give them the space to make their cryptic remarks.

(A cryptic remark from the editor editing this article: Single-spaced typing can sometimes be just as difficult to read as handwriting . . . especially if the typewriter keys were not clean.)

Accepted form in both professional markets and fan circles is to type and double-space a manuscript on white, standard-size (8 ½ X 11) paper, leaving adequate (at least one inch) margins on each side, and the top and bottom of the paper.

And *please* number pages and put your name and the title of the story on each one! Your editor could be a klutz who drops your story as she pulls it out of the envelope and then simply cannot figure out which page goes where. Pages should be paper-clipped together (*not* stapled or bradded), but if they do become separated, your information on each page will see that they get back together safely.

Take the time to choose a good title. There is an abundance of title stealing in fandom, by the way. Shakespeare is a great one to borrow from . . . no one knows whether it's because he's dead (and can't sue) or because he was a great writer. You can borrow if you like, but it's worth your while to sweat one out on your own. (Sometimes good titles are harder to come by than good plots!) A title should be original, and should jump off the table of contents, demanding to be read first.

Okay. *Now* your manuscript is ready to go, right? Well, not quite yet.

"The Three-Foot Pit" might have been interesting to me or to my friends (kind, tactful people that they are), but the editor of *Romulan Love Tales* would have sent it back. The story did not fit that market.

Know the market. Two publications available in fandom will help: *Universal Translator* (200 W. 79th St., #14H, New York, NY 10024) and *Datazine* (Post Office Box 19413, Denver, CO 80219). Both list currently available fanzines for sale and zines that are looking for material. The descriptions of the zines will give you a clue as to what material they print. Odyssey Press, for example, is likely to be begging for McCoy stories. *Contact* will be looking for Kirk and Spock. *Galactic Discourse* accepts general Star Trek stories.

Include a self-addressed envelope big enough to hold your manuscript (with sufficient postage attached) just in case it doesn't fit the needs of the zine. Some writers also include a self-addressed, stamped #10 envelope, so an editor can reply to the submission. (This shows confidence in your work . . . tells the editor you expect him to accept the story. Even if he doesn't, he'll be impressed by your belief in your work.) It also helps the editor out financially.

Now. You've sent out the manuscript and are waiting for the reply. It doesn't hurt to start another story while you're waiting.

Now, about that wait. Fan editors are not independently wealthy. If they were, they might not be editors. (That's a theory no one has ever tested, since fandom has yet to produce a wealthy fanzine editor.) Editors have jobs in the "real" or "mundane" world; they are secretaries, computer programmers, biologists. Fanzines are a hobby for them . . . time spent on zine editing and production is carved from busy schedules. Editors spend maybe 10 percent of their waking hours on their hobby. That could mean a delay in receiving an answer about your story. Editors by nature have a lot of correspondence to handle, especially if they enjoy any sort of extensive readership. They try to respond to a submission within three weeks . . . but sometimes, it's a little longer.

If you feel you've waited long enough to hear about your submission (Let's say you sent the story about Easter and it's now Christmas), write to the editor and politely ask what's going on. You have the right to do so.

From the time of your submission, one of two things will happen. Your story could be accepted, or . . .

One day you'll find a large envelope in your mailbox. It's addressed to you—in your own handwriting.

The story has been rejected.

Don't panic! Don't go on a drinking binge or give up on writing. No one likes rejection—that's basic to human nature— but sometimes it happens. The majority of editors don't *like* to reject manuscripts, but at times they have to bite the bullet and do so. There are several reasons for this. Someone else might have written a similar story and it was accepted first; your story might not be exactly right for that zine, or the editor might not agree with the ideas in your story (which isn't a reflection on you personally, just a matter of differing tastes).

So don't pout after getting a rejection letter. Just turn around and send it out to someone else. There are many fanzines out there and plenty of chances to "sell" someone on your story.

If you get a letter of acceptance, congratulations! Next step: maybe a little editing (from minor word changes to possibly reworking the plot). If you do have an editor who wants changes, again, don't panic! You have the right to see those changes and comment on them before the story is published. If you don't agree with the editor, say so. Take this chance to say what you feel. Better to do it now than be miserable when you see the story in print.

Expect a delay in seeing your work in the finished zine. Producing a fanzine in one's free time is difficult at best. An editor works with several writers, assigns artwork for the stories, answers mail, and hassles with printers. That's why you might have to wait several months (maybe longer) for your copy of the zine. Have patience. They have not forgotten about you.

There are advantages to writing for amateur fanzines. For one thing, it's a fun way to enjoy Star Trek and spout your views at the same time. And it's a great way to learn about writing and the creative process. A lot of talented fan writers use Star Trek zines as a practice ground with an eye toward going professional.

So there you have it: Protocol, in a way, for writing Star Trek fan fiction. There are a lot of editors out there waiting to get a manuscript in the mail. Send that story to them and have the reward of seeing your name in print and reaching out to other fans around the world.

But please. *Do not* use "The Three-Foot Pit." It's been done already. And I reserve the right to be embarrassed by it for quite some time to come.

IN SEARCH OF SPOCK: A PSYCHOANALYTIC INQUIRY

by Harvey R. Greenberg

Want a good laugh? Close your eyes and picture Spock lying on a psychiatrist's couch. Yet the longer you keep that image in your head, the less funny it becomes. Spock undoubtedly has problems, so why shouldn't he (or any of the Enterprise crew) seek professional help? And how is it that we know this character so well that we can understand and emphathize with his problems?

Few characters in fiction have been so finely drawn as those in Star Trek; we know their strengths, weaknesses, foibles, and inconsistencies perhaps even better than our own. The greater part of this information was naturally developed during the course of the series and in the films, although fan writings have done much in the way of examination and explanation.

Working from such information, Dr. Harvey Greenberg took a clinical look at Mr. Spock and his world. What did he discover? Read on. . . .

Star Trek was launched by the National Broadcasting Company during the fall season of 1966. The series immediately received an enthusiastic reception from science fiction readers. It offered the pleasures of the best speculative literature: plausible characters in a plausible future, searching out new life forms throughout the galaxy. A second season followed, but then ratings wobbled and rumors of cancellation spread. At the eleventh hour, Star Trek was rescued by an incredible grass-roots write-in campaign. It did not survive its third season, mostly because of its inexplicable unpopularity with NBC executives.

During its later airings, episodes were moved from 7:30 p.m. on Monday evenings to Fridays at 10:00 p.m., a sure "kiss of death" slot. Network pundits thus demonstrated a perverse disregard for many of Star Trek's staunchest advocates—adolescents and preteenagers. But when Star Trek went into syndication, canny local station managers screened it between 5:00 and 7:00 p.m., prime time for the adolescent viewer, including flocks of youngsters who had never seen the series before. (Late-adolescent college students were hooked—or rehooked—by post-midnight showings.) David Gerrold writes in *The World of Star Trek* that "it was the same thrill of discovery that the first generation of 'trekkies' had experienced only three years before, and it was happening all over again. . . ."

Week after week, Star Trek still continues to savage every kind of competition across America. Its incredible popularity reaches throughout the world, and even beyond the Iron Curtain. It has generated three successful feature films, innumerable novels, and "fanzines." At national conventions, Star Trek actors receive the veneration ordinarily accorded rock idols and Hollywood superstars. Scraps purloined from outtakes are hawked at galactic prices, while over five million copies of *Enterprise* blueprints have been sold.

This article focuses on the character universally nominated as a major source of Star Trek's enduring appeal: Mr. Spock, the elfin-eared science officer of the *Enterprise*. To date, Spock's psyche has been plumbed most extensively by Karin Blair in *Meaning in Star Trek*. She views him from a Jungian perspective as an archetypal hybrid, a healing mediator between clashing polarities. She believes Spock has a particular impact on female fans because identification enables them to contact their "animus-selves." Lichtenberg et al. (*Star Trek Lives!*) write from a similar feminist viewpoint.

My theories about Spock and Star Trek derive from my work as an adolescent psychotherapist, as well as from a passion for speculative fiction and cinema that reaches back to my own teens. For two decades, adolescent clients, children of friends, and two sons have told me why they found Spock compelling. Their observations lead me to conclude that he embodies the central virtues and dilemmas of puberty. His noble, flawed figure recapitulates in outer space many a Terran youngster's search for a viable identity. I will also show that the series entire, as a late-1960s creation, is informed by a curious political torsion, an "adolescent" wrenching between conservative (even prejudicial) values and libertarian ideals.

Beyond the following brief outline, the reader will require at least a nodding acquaintance with Star Trek's milieu. Star Trek postulates that by the twenty-third century, mankind will conquer its earthbound evils, explore the solar system, and make first contacts with other civilizations of the galaxy. A loosely knit "United Federation of Planets" is formed to promote amity, trade, and exchange of scientific data. Starfleet Command comprises the Federation's military and exploratory arm. The reach of Starfleet's authority is epitomized by its starship class vessels. The *U.S.S. (United Space Ship) Enterprise* possesses awesome weaponry and research capacities; its almost completely human crew is balanced according to the democratic principles demonstrators marched for in the 1960s. (Other starships are crewed by aliens from their own home planets, supposedly in aid of greater efficiency. Note the "back of the bus" table of organization.)

Vulcan and the Vulcans

Spock's role was relatively minor in early Star Trek episodes. His background was never presented systematically, but was sketched in as interest grew. Although some guidelines existed, it was left to the writers to interpret Spock's persona as each saw fit. The result was an inconsistent mélange, a fascinating quick study of popular myth in the making.

Spock hails from Vulcan, a deep-red planet in a far-off solar system with a hot, harsh environment similar to that of Mars. While some episodes suggest that the Vulcans originated there, one implies that Vulcan was seeded by vastly intelligent beings from outside the galaxy (shades of *2001*); they probably conducted similar applied anthropology on Earth, the planets of what was to become the Klingon and Romulan empires, and the other "M-type" worlds with humanoid life, explored by the *Enterprise* during her five-year mission.

Vulcans are slender, attractive, with upswept eyebrows, a chloritic complexion, and large elfin ears; stronger than humans, they also possess more acute senses and limited telepathic ability. Their sexuality and aggression are intimately wedded. Every seven years, the adult Vulcan male goes into "rut"; he must then return to his home territory, mate, or die. Any impediment—particularly by another male—arouses murderous rage. Between cycles, both sexes seem to eschew copulation, cherishing "mind melding" instead.

The ancient Vulcans were a virulently militaristic race. Several times they forged mighty empires, only to nearly annihilate themselves through civil war. Finally, the philosopher Surak persuaded them to renounce anger and be guided by reason alone. Down through the millennia, their conscious suppression of aggression somehow evolved into repression of every affect (emotional mood). In *Civilization and Its Discontents*, Freud likened acculturation to the imposition of an obsessional state. He was not sanguine about its ultimate success, believing that the collective superego would ultimately be unable to restrain aggression. While our world seems daily to fulfill his bleak vision, the Vulcans have fared better; their sublimations have held due to the steely Vulcan will or some other fortunate accident of alien metapsychology.

Contemporary Vulcan mores include altruism, industry, and stringent observation of the proprieties, particularly personal privacy. The Vulcans are respected throughout the Federation for their achievements in art, science, and diplomacy. They have also become an intensely spiritual people. Although women hold high political and religious office, the father still rules the Vulcan home. With its valorization of the obsessional virtues and the patriarchal family, Vulcan bears an uncanny resemblance to Victorian England, happily without the latter's undercurrent of hypocrisy and vice.

The excesses of the rut cycle have long been mitigated by arranged mindlock between prepubescent children. When the Vulcan youth goes into definitive heat after several nonfatal cycles, he is quickly married to his childhood intended. (Vulcan women apparently are not affected.) Thereafter, Vulcans are monogamous to a fault. Both sexes put the highest premium on an enduring partnership and stable family life.

Spock's History

Spock is the only offspring of a rare interspecies marriage. His father, Sarek, descends from one of the most illustrious Vulcan families; he is a noted astrophysicist and statesman like his father before him. He is about a hundred years old (late middle age) and cuts an austere yet charismatic figure, the very personification of Vulcan *gravitas*. Spock's mother, Amanda, is an Earthwoman. By profession a teacher, she met Sarek while he was assigned to the Vulcan embassy on Terra.

We do not know how he managed to elude child betrothal and win her hand. She was not welcomed easily into his family; the Vulcans, despite conscious disavowal of prejudice, harbor an unconscious sense of superiority verging on xenophobia. Eventually her own considerable diplomatic powers prevailed. She and Sarek have remained devotedly together for forty years.

Although Vulcan in appearance, Spock was taunted throughout his childhood because of his mixed birth; possibly he betrayed too much affect on the playground. At length, he resolved to become more Vulcan than the Vulcans in suppressing emotion.

(Vulcan emotiveness receives the widest interpretation from Star Trek's writers. In some scripts, the Vulcans appear to have an inborn absence of affect—subtly implying that the ancient teachings engendered genetic modifications. Other episodes suggest that Vulcans learn to suppress feelings at some unspecified point in their development. Spock's hazing by his classmates seems to indicate that Vulcan children indulge in irrational abuse as readily as their human counterparts.)

At the appropriate time, Spock was affianced to T'Pring, the daughter of an equally noble family. His academic career was brilliant. Sarek hoped his son would follow in his footsteps on Vulcan. Instead, Spock enrolled in officer candidate training with Starfleet Command. His decision was as hurtful to his father as his childhood withdrawal of affection was to his mother. Consequently, Sarek and Spock became virtual strangers.

After graduation, Spock entered active duty and served aboard starships with brief respites (including one painful visit home). As the series opens, he has lived aboard *Enterprise* for fifteen years. He is regarded highly throughout Starfleet, and has become something of a legend on Vulcan. During his first decade, he was Captain Christopher Pike's science officer. Following Pike's transfer, he continued in the same capacity under Captain James Kirk until the death of Gary Mitchell, Kirk's exec and close friend. Spock then accepted Kirk's offer to Mitchell's post in addition to his regular duties. He inherited the mantle of Mitchell's affection for Kirk as well.

Spock's Adolescent Qualities and Conflicts (or Keeping the Lid on the Id)

Joe, a fifteen-year-old client, affectionately calls Spock a "reformed nerd," and thinks of himself as grossly unreformed. He entered therapy because of depression, which began after his first "girlfriend" (1.5 dates) threw him over for the class jock. Joe's teachers rate him a genius in math and computer science, like his idol. He's been a rabid Trekkie since he was eleven. His parents, more modestly endowed in brains and ambition, find him pretty much of a mystery. His orderliness and nitpicking drive them to distraction. Behind his weisenheimer facade, he is painfully shy, fearful of aggression. He frequently provokes his peers with brash displays of intellect, then morbidly anticipates attack or rejection.

It is easy to see why compulsive overachievers like Joe admire Spock, but less cerebral youngsters identify with the sublimatory, obsessional cast of his defenses, too. For Spock's battle to control his passions accurately reflects the consuming struggle of the early adolescent to master biological turmoil and integrate a radically new body image. The transforming body of the adolescent is mirrored in Spock's physique, with its incredible strength and adaptability, its uncanny blend of the familiar and strange. His ears are the most visible signets of change, lovely, unsettling phallic metaphors. He owns the appealing grace and awkwardness of many adolescents before they have settled comfortably into their expanded dimensions. (Frankenstein's movie monster, whom I have elsewhere analyzed as the incarnation of his master's disavowed adolescent self, shows a more exaggerated stiffness.)

Spock's ancestors nearly perished because their intemperate aggressiveness was melded to a savage reproductive cycle. Their ancient barbarism resonates with the adolescent's worst fears of unleashed aggression and sexuality. But centuries of logical praxis have all but eliminated the clamor of instinct from Vulcan puberty. The rut cycle's disruptions have been all but neutralized by encrusted ritual. Compared with the stormy course of Terran adolescence, an orderly ripening marks the Vulcan child's maturation. In humans, the downside risk of an uneventful pubertal progress can be an unquestioning attitude toward the status quo in adulthood. Vulcans do not seem to view this resolution amiss.

Thus, hybrids like Spock are possibly Vulcan's only true adolescents; they are understandably rare. Throughout childhood, Spock's emotive human half rendered him an object of scorn and distrust to his fellows and himself. Besides displaying detestable weakness, he could be forced into angry retaliation, just as serious a threat to Vulcan self-esteem. Within Spock's bosom was resurrected the murderous potential of the entire Vulcan past. Even more than his peers, Spock prevailed through denial, suppression, repression, reaction formation, intellectualization, and sublimation. The adolescent ego summons these defensive strategies to tame and redirect rebellious instinct—putting the lid on the id, so to speak.

Spock's endearing attributes bloom in the adolescent, but are inevitably alloyed with a large dose of narcissism and insensitivity. Spock's "adolescent" virtues, his loyalty, altruism, and idealism, are purely manifested, defying external incitement or intrapsychic muddle. Where lesser men would lust or rage, he calmly saves the day, offering a helpful example to his colleagues and to viewers. The following example is but one of many.

In "Balance of Terror," the *Enterprise* is attacked by a vessel crewed by Romulans, a race which had battled the Federation to a truce a century before without making visual contact. Now on viewscreen, they appear Vulcan, leading Spock to theorize Romulus was a colony that lost touch with the mother culture millennia ago and kept its warlike ways. Lieutenant Stiles, whose family was slaughtered in the old conflict, sneeringly insinuates that Spock is a spy, a summary offense to Vulcan probity. In the climactic engagement, Stiles is overcome by a coolant leak and cannot respond when Kirk orders him to engage the phaser banks. At mortal risk, Spock fires the weapons and drags Stiles to safety. After the Romulans are destroyed, Stiles apologizes. Spock demurs; he could hardly be offended since Stile's behavior was so patently "illogical."

Exasperated parents of youngsters like Joe will readily recognize Spock's maddening exactitude; fellow crewmembers find it equally aggravating, especially when he insists on announcing their imminent destruction to the nanosecond. But adolescents know that Spock's nerdy precision is the less adaptive side of his "cool," making him fallible and even more endearing. Joe figures if Spock can act like a wimp and still come off as a hero in the end, perhaps he has a shot, too.

Were Spock always in control of his emotions, he would simply be too perfect for teenagers to identify with. During several of Star Trek's most popular episodes, emotional upheaval fractures Spock's cool facade. Through typical dream-factory rationales, his dyscontrol is never seen to arise from brittle defenses, but from some outside agency; often, it afflicts humans even more painfully, legitimizing Spock's "breakdown."

In "The Naked Time," the *Enterprise* is infected by a virus that causes loss of inhibitions. Spock suffers exquisite torment from the eruption of his feelings, which is cured by Kirk forcibly confronting him with his duty, and by his empathy with the captain's unmasked loneliness. "This Side of Paradise" has the settlers of Omicron Ceti III expose the crew to spores that transform them into placid pod-people and Spock into a goofy romantic. Kirk discovers that violent emotions reverse the pod's effects. He hurls racist epithets at Spock, provoking a vicious attack that returns the horrified Vulcan to his senses.

Eros, not Mars, rules such transformations. When Spock's psychic redoubts go down, tenderness rather than aggression emerges from his human half, albeit transiently. Lelia Kalomi, a beautiful botanist who had once wooed him unsuccessfully, deploys the spores of Omicron Ceti III to win his heart. The virus of "Naked Time" turns sober Nurse Chapel into a vamp; Spock is profoundly shaken when she reveals longings for him, and for the first time acknowledges the psychic scars caused by his hybrid birth. He becomes so ashamed that he locks himself away from his companions like a mortified teenager. When he recovers, his love for Chapel vanishes. Poignantly, hers endures.

"Amok Time" (*vide infra*) is the only episode where the agency that unleashes Spock's affect originates within him, provoking violence rather than midsummer madness. Here, of course, Spock's savagery is clearly intrinsic to the Vulcan rut cycle, no part of the tender humanity which, according to Star Trek's unconscious agenda, constitutes his "genuine" core. Adolescents may thus sympathize with his unruliness, while maintaining comfortable ego distance.

Spock as Adolescent Mediator

Every adolescent is a hybrid, a fascinating blend of what has been and what is yet to come. Adolescence regularly spurs inquiry into the status of the status quo. Hence, teenagers admire Spock's ability to confront novel situations with a fresh outlook, unencumbered by preconception. Confronted with inexplicable phenomena, the very rationality called up in the service of Spock's repressions paradoxically opens the world to his lucid understanding. When his shipmates are revolted by the appearance of alien life or baffled by the customs of some distant race, Spock's unbiased perception prevails. Kirk also has excellent intuition about extraterrestrials, but Spock's native alienation and telepathic power give him an intuitive edge Kirk prizes.

In "The Devil in the Dark," the pergium miners of Janus VI are being incinerated by a monster in their tunnels. Cornered, it resembles a mobile slag heap. Nevertheless, Spock guesses it is sentient and stops its extermination. His mind meld shows that the creature is a mother "Horta," a gentle being with a silicon biochemistry, capable of liquefying rock. It killed when its eggs were destroyed during the excavations. The angry miners are mollified. Through Spock, they apologize and contract a symbiotic arrangement: The newly hatched Horta will fulfill their biological imperative by digging for the costly pergium while the humans grow rich.

"The Way to Eden" is of particular interest because Spock mediates between the crew and a group of human youths revolting against the arid mechanization of twenty-third-century life. From a hijacked, crippled vessel, the *Enterprise* rescues an unlikely assortment of dropouts and bohemians who are seeking a bucolic existence on the mythical planet of Eden. Their leader, the brilliant renegade Dr. Sevrin, is unmasked as a charismatic paranoid who blames technology because he carries a potentially fatal germ. He steals the shuttlecraft and flies his acolytes to Eden, where the lush soil proves highly toxic. With their paradise exposed as a poisonous delusion, the young people quietly return to the *Enterprise* and home (Sevrin's bacteria would have killed them if Eden's environment did not). Sevrin defiantly bites into a fruit and dies.

The episode's apparent "liberated" text conceals a rightish critique of 1960s counterculture. Sevrin is a Leary-like narcissist, his project fueled not by revolutionary ardor, but by narrow resentment over his health. Spock's receptivity to the dissidents is balanced by a subtle conservatism, ambiguously deployed here (and elsewhere) to defend the established order. Although he sympathizes with the "space hippies," he never joins them; nor is he happy to have been the the agency that brought them to their fatal Eden. One must live in the real world, the text seems to say, not in the fool's or knave's paradise of Sevrin's cracked ambition—a conclusion sadly echoing the facile advice heaped upon "political" youth by their parents, their government, and, all too often, their therapists.

(One notes that, without explanation, the Terran Sevrin bears huge scalloped ears, emphasizing his negative doubling of Spock, his intriguing *sequestration* of Spock's potential disruptiveness throughout the episode. Exiled from humanity much like Spock, Sevrin plays Mephistophelean fomenter of adolescent revolt, the harbinger of chaos instead of the healing mediator.)

Spock and McCoy: Bridging the Galactic Generation Gap

Embattled adults rarely accept adolescent re-vision gracefully. The perennial struggle across the generations is nicely captured in the prickly relationship between Spock and Dr. Leonard "Bones" McCoy, the *Enterprise*'s cantankerous senior surgeon. McCoy's exasperation with Spock is a staple of Star Trek's humor. McCoy frequently seethes with indignation over Spock's bloodless *modus operandi*. When he demands that Spock forsake the head for the heart, one may be sure that Spock's irritating precision will escalate. McCoy's congenial humanism is balanced by a chronic rigidity of disposition. He is an inherent conservative, not always in the best sense of the word; under pressure, he often invokes unhelpful "commonsense" explanations for uncommon phenomena or "practical" solutions that are not daring enough to succeed. Thus, Spock's challenges to the quotidian incite him even more than the iciness of Vulcan logic.

Fired by the rationality McCoy deplores, Spock's imagination soars aloft while McCoy's limps behind. The two are natural foils: Spock plays adolescent *agent provocateur* to McCoy's stodgy parent. In Leonard Nimoy's reading, Spock is much more conscious of his provocation than a deadpan demeanor betrays, which is not lost on amused teenage viewers. The duo's rapprochement, frequently mediated by Kirk, proves to the adolescent that conflict between the generations can be fruitfullly resolved. Equally pleasing is the support each character finds in the other. Despite his bluster, McCoy genuinely values Spock's intellect and uncompromising honor, while Spock garners secret comfort from McCoy's tough-minded compassion. It is a testament of Spock's respect that he consigns his *katra*—the Vulcan immortal spirit—to McCoy's unconscious, shortly before sacrificing his life in *Star Trek II: The Wrath of Khan*.

Oedipus in Space

Humanity's ancient myths often portray the adolescent boy as hero/outcast, wrestling with a contested patrimony to forge his identity. Taken together, the two episodes "Amok Time" and "Journey to Babel" comprise a futuristic reinvention of this primal drama; its obvious Oedipal theme, the resolution of Spock's prolonged adolescent identity crisis, which largely stems from his struggle with his father and the repressive Vulcan tradition Sarek incarnates.

It is a clinical commonplace that a charismatic father like Sarek may engender intense competition in his son, the original object of which is the woman both love; *mutatis mutandis*, a father whose Oedipal problems remain unresolved (often a function of competitive anxiety toward his own father) may secretly tremble before the son's majority. In either case, the result is likely to be an escalation of the son's Oedipal conflict, with delays in psychological maturation and often far-reaching effects upon choices in love and work.

Oedipus was rescued from his father's reprisals by strangers and became a youthful wanderer. When we first meet Spock, he has long since quit the scene of Sarek's wrath to live as an exile in Starfleet. He seems to have reintegrated well within his new "family." His talents are widely recognized; first Captain Pike's support, then Captain Kirk's warmth appear to have supplanted Sarek's dissatisfaction (McCoy remains an ambivalent surrogate in his chronic criticism—Sarek's nearest human replicant).

But, in fact, Spock is profoundly unhappy. He has never been comfortable in Terran company, even with Kirk. He has shunned the limelight, denied himself promotion, and excluded the love of women. He has especially avoided home because he dreads confronting Sarek's displeasure and the yoke of Vulcan custom. In "Amok Time," he can elude his instincts and their social consequences no longer; if he does not mate with T'Pring, his childhood betrothed, he will surely die. To save him, Kirk flagrantly disobeys orders and reroutes to Vulcan.

During Spock's absence, T'Pring has turned to Stonn, a thoroughly unprepossessing type she no doubt selected because he is more pliable material. Vulcan law dictates that if she refuses the contracted marriage, her fiancé must battle a male of her choice to the death. She becomes the winner's chattel. When Kirk and McCoy beam down with Spock, the wily T'Pring chooses the captain to fight Spock rather than Stonn. Kirk only discovers the lethal implications of the challenge after accepting it as a favor to his distressed friend.

According to T'Pring's devious logic, if Spock triumphs he will gladly put her aside. In the unlikely event Kirk prevails, he will just as surely refuse the dubious honor of her hand. Either way, she gets the negligible Stonn. The subsequent "marriage-or-death" ceremony fuses wedding with adolescent *rite de passage*. The combat unfolds in the ambiance of an Achaean dream. The setting is spare and surreal: bare rocks against angry red horizon, hieratic costumes culled from a Martha Graham Atrean ballet. The Oedipal thrust of the proceedings is underscored by a piece of simultaneous negation/affirmation. Sarek does not attend and, instead of a fellow Vulcan, Spock contends with an obvious father surrogate. The absence of Sarek—indeed, of any relative—highlights the triangulation between Kirk, Spock, and T'Pring (Stonn is such a nonentity that he fades into the rocks).

(Although the lack of kin is probably due to a writer's oversight, one may speculate from what is known of the Vulcans that family members are excluded because it would be exceptionally painful for them to watch combat should it occur, and no less mortifying for the bridegroom later. It is also not unlikely that a couple would be married quickly and privately, reserving a large public wedding for a later time when the groom, safely out of heat, could behave with proper Vulcan decorum.)

After being thoroughly mauled, Kirk is pronounced dead by McCoy. Spock rejects T'Pring—true to her scenario—and beams back to the ship with Kirk's corpse, which miraculously revives. McCoy reveals that a stimulant he gave Kirk to buffer the Vulcan climate was actually a delayed-action depressant mimicking death. Spock's enormous joy at seeing his friend alive somehow acts as an antidote to the rut cycle's perturbations for the remainder of the series. He is liberated from the chemistry that would have killed for lack of a suitable sexual outlet, or had him dwindle down to a dutiful slave of Vulcan custom—death, either way.

(In *Star Trek III: The Search for Spock*, Spock's mindless body evolves rapidly on the Genesis Planet and undergoes several rut cycles. The beautiful Vulcan/Romulan Lieutenant

Saavik guides him through the ordeals. While they touch fingers ritually, it is left unclear whether they have mated or whether Spock will be afflicted anew with rut once his corpus and spirit have been rejoined.)

The latent patricidal motif of "Amok Time" emerges undisguised in "Journey to Babel." Sarek appears in the episode with Amanda for the first and only time. (He figures briefly without her in *The Search for Spock*.) In this episode, the *Enterprise* ferries Federation ambassadors to a conference considering admission of the mineral-rich Coridan system. An unusually tangled narrative has Sarek inadvertently fingered by Spock for a murder he did not commit; Sarek's collapse from a heart ailment during Kirk's interrogation; cardiac surgery by McCoy, requiring that Spock undergo dangerous marrow stimulation to provide blood for his father; a seriously wounded Kirk forced to quit the bridge while the ship is being attacked by the assassin's confederates (smugglers seeking to protect their interests on the Coridan planets); Spock halting the operation to assume command; Amanda furious with her son for putting his and her husband's life in jeopardy; Kirk's return, feigning good health, so that Spock can rejoin the surgery; the invader's defeat; and, finally, Spock's reconciliation with Sarek after McCoy's efforts succeed.

In this convoluted tale, sinister outsiders disrupt the Federation's adoption of a new "child," the Coridan system. The surface text echoes a deeper theme: the disruption of Spock's relationship with his father by the latter's implacable ire. Its "realistic" basis is Spock's disavowal of his heritage and Sarek's misgivings about Starfleet military aims. But the psychoanalyst intuits another wellspring of Sarek's hostility, an atavistic contradiction to millennia of Vulcan logic. Lest the following seem too anthropomorphic, let us remember that Vulcans were, after all, created out of the fantasies of Earthmen.

Ample clues indicate that Sarek's aggressive and erotic drives are fiercer than the average Vulcan's (or his controls more tenuous). His romance with an Earthwoman points to a singularly passionate disposition. As for his aggression, Spock states with chilling certainty: "If there were a reason, my father is quite capable of killing . . . logically . . . and efficiently. . . ."

Amanda speaks of her profound love for her son and her distress over Spock's torment by his playmates. Given the generosity of her nature, she undoubtedly comforted him by word and touch throughout his childhood, try as she may have to restrain herself. Her affection must have been enormously unsettling for Sarek, given Vulcan abstemiousness in physical matters. It is likely that Sarek's undemonstrativeness stimulated Spock's human mother's demonstrativeness. Here we have an atypical, needy Vulcan father who watched his wife lavish inordinate attention upon his son. This, I submit, kindled the flames of an ancient, deadly Oedipal rivalry.

Nota bene: Sarek's father was a "competitor" at least as illustrious as himself. It is legitimate to inquire if he might have been as disapproving. Exogamous object choice is a well-known resolution of Oedipal conflict; one assuages incestuous anxiety by marrying a partner of a different religion, class, or race—or, in Sarek's case, of a different species.

Of course, Sarek would have found murderous rivalry with his own child even more reprehensible than a human father in similar circumstances, the zenith of unreason. Despite rigorous repression, his unconscious jealousy escalated the normal austerity between Vulcan father and son. Sarek became an even more frightening and removed figure throughout Spock's childhood. It was then tragically inevitable that Spock should distance himself even further from Sarek during adolescence. Being semihuman, his Oedipal strivings were closer to consciousness, even more frightening than his father's; the means to control them were faultier. Terrified of his resurrected jealousy, dreading Sarek's imagined retaliation, ever hoping to preserve a vestige of his father's love, Spock executed the characteristic defensive maneuver of puberty: identification with the aggressor. He identified with Sarek's *aloofness*.

He had already turned away from Amanda during latency, forswearing the object of Oedipal competition, placating the internalized father, and demonstrating to his peers he could be as Spartan as the next Vulcan kid on the block. For further protection of father and embattled self, he quit Vulcan altogether. Spock repudiated Sarek's provenance to make common cause with the Terrans of Starfleet. The gesture was ambiguous. Oedipal combat, instead of being negated, was merely relocated to a different arena. Joining his mother's people was a potent signet of Spock's revolt against Vulcan patriarchy. It recapitulated the intense affiliation between Spock and Amanda which Sarek had earlier found so painful, and from which he had exiled himself.

Sarek dealt with his suppressed rage, savaged pride, ambivalent but genuine love for Spock the only way he knew—

with more culturally sanctioned withdrawal. The punishing quality of his stoic stance is grasped when, with barely a trace of disdain, Sarek acknowledges Spock's presence upon his arrival on the bridge. Amanda has endured Sarek's frosty despair for nearly two decades; that she still loves him is a testament to his virtues, his charisma, and quite possibly a schizoid thrust in her own disposition.

Spock outdoes his father's coldness with his own obsessional withdrawal during "Journey to Babel"; his behavior toward human and Vulcan alike is as mechanized as his computers. But rage will out: a plot replete with menaced fathers and their substitutes repeatedly implicates, then exonerates him of patricidal motive. His "artless" revelation of the Vulcan execution method used to murder one of the ambassadors and his appalling candor about Sarek's aggression put his father under suspicion. Kirk's interrogation of Sarek nearly induces a fatal cardiac seizure—once more, Spock nearly breaks his poor parent's heart! After undergoing perilous marrow stimulation, he abandons Sarek at the eleventh hour to supplant a gravely wounded Kirk, Sarek's surrogate. As in "Amok Time," his human friends rescue him from his racking between intolerable alternatives through guile, self-sacrifice, and medical art. Kirk disguises his wounds, allowing Spock to retire with honor, so McCoy can heal Sarek.

While Sarek and Spock never discuss their differences, they do reach a mild *rapprochement* by the episode's conclusion. The surface plot contrives to discharge their mutual rancor safely. Spock can pursue his career with a lighter heart, while Sarek returns to Vulcan with a mended one. But it is poignantly evident that Spock will never experience the communion with Sarek his humanity craves. Their antagonisms—and similarities—run too deep.

Spock and the Infernal Feminine

Spock's chronic isolation from his mother remains unchanged at the end of "Journey to Babel." While her feelings toward him have warmed again, he is, if anything, more glacial toward her. After she expresses pleasure to Kirk about seeing her husband and son reconciled, Spock says to his father: "Emotional, isn't she?"

Sarek: "She has always been that way."

Spock: "Indeed . . I have often wondered why you married her."

Sarek: "At the time, it seemed the logical thing to do."

Amanda smiles, consenting unwittingly to their derogation.

Spock has asked a summary question of his existence: Why her? Why the outsider, this labile creature with her unseemly emotions? Why not a good, cold Vulcan wife who would not trouble us with her tears, her smiles, her touch? Sarek's ironic answer implies he was so infatuated that he did not realize the trouble he was buying when he sought to warm his obsessional spirit at Amanda's hearth. For him, the reward has been worth the jangle.

Unfortunately, Spock's hybrid nature and the undefendedness of childhood rendered him far more vulnerable to the anxiety of her comforts. It is a reasonable speculation that Spock was chronically overstimulated by his mother through no fault of hers, *de rerum naturae*. The pleasure of her nurturing was always countered by the fear of flooding from tidal waves of unmastered affect. Consequently, he withdrew first from her, then from all women behind a schizoid carapace. In the adult Spock's psyche, Amanda's representation still remains deeply split between the Good and the Bad. His love for her is tainted not only with the fear of Oedipal reprisal, but with far weightier pre-Oedipal dread. In similar clinical cases, fantasies derived from this primal *angst* range from mere exploitation by the Bad Mother, to being engulfed, devoured by her.

"Amok Time" incarnates Amanda's Bad Mother persona both in the cold schemer T'Pring, and in T'Pau, the matriarchpriestess of the marriage-or-death ritual, who dominates a rut-maddened Spock and a diminished Kirk. But even women unambivalently devoted to Spock own a malevolent aspect. Their passive presence is fraught with peril or they actively pursue devious, hurtful means to win his heart. In either case, the toll exacted by their intimacy is unendurable. To cite only one example, the spores released by Leila Kalomi on Omicron Ceti III reduce him to a witless buffoon.

Spock's dilemma reinvents the misogyny of the early adolescent boy. Like Amanda, many contemporary mothers must endure contemptuous avoidance by the pubertal son who a few years before seemed the sweetest fellow imaginable. From the son's perspective, she has been transformed into the forbidden Oedipal object and the awful Bad Mother's signifier of childhood dependency. His scornful withdrawal rapidly extends to sisters, their friends, and the entire feminine tribe. Until his independence is more assured, he will probably take comfort in groups of like-minded misogynists.

Spock's ambivalence toward women further identifies him with Kirk and McCoy. They too have a penchant for ladies with dangerous tendencies. For McCoy, the Bad Mother's vampiric menace surfaces blatantly in "The Man Trap." An old flame of McCoy's, the archaeologist Nancy Crater, has been killed for the salt content of her body by an intelligent shape-shifter, the last survivor of its race. It joins her husband in a malignant symbiosis, sustaining the illusion of her presence in return for the salt of his body. When the *Enterprise* arrives at the Craters' dig, the creature preys upon the crew, dispatches Crater, and even assumes the moonstruck McCoy's identity. Finally cornered as Nancy, it is phasered down by the anguished doctor when it attacks Kirk. As it dies, it changes back to its true form, a loathsome thing of tentacles and suckers.

Kirk is more romantically inclined than Spock or McCoy, but his affairs come to no better end. Many temptations are strewn in his path, but his ruling passion for the *Enterprise* invariably triumphs.

Occasionally, Kirk's amours bear the Bad Mother's obvious harpy imprint; the worst of these is Dr. Janice Lester of "Turnabout Intruder," whose jilting by Kirk many years before precipitates fulminating paranoia. Delusionally certain his success has caused her lack of advancement, she engineers a punishment fit for his "crime" by switching their bodies.

Even Kirk's numerous wholesome loves, like Spock's, regularly threaten to deprive him of identity, life, or prestige, albeit through "circumstances" rather than malicious practice. In "Court-Martial," he stands wrongfully accused of manslaughter over the death of a fellow officer. Starfleet compels another old flame, the brilliant attorney Areel Shaw, to prosecute him.

Kirk's deepest affection of the series is stirred by a woman harboring titanic destructive potential for the entire human race in "The City on the Edge of Forever." Another tangled scenario sends Kirk, Spock, and McCoy back in time to Depression-era New York, where the captain becomes infatuated with a charismatic social worker, Edith Keeler. The episode concludes as Kirk stands by helplessly while she is killed by a truck. Were she to survive, she would lead a pacifist movement that would inadvertently enable Germany to win World War II, precipitating an Armageddon from which the future of the Federation could not evolve.

These are only a few of a disproportionate number of Star Trek episodes where the *Enterprise* is threatened by disruptive alien females, troublesome past or present lovers. The subsequent narrative recaptures the *Status quo ante* for the ship and, usually, one of our three heroes. At the end, the galactic trek is resumed—shades of Shane clopping off into the sunset or Rick Blaine and Inspector Louis Renault embarking on their journey to Brazzaville in *Casablanca*.

In such adventures, Star Trek's main protagonists are seen to share a common estrangement from women, as intense as their bonding with each other and their dedication to the missions that keep them far from Mother Earth. Spock's avoidance obviously springs from intrapsychic conflict; McCoy's is ascribed to the hurtful divorce which made him leave a lucrative private practice to enlist in Starfleet. Kirk's shrinking from commitment is chalked up to the exigencies of duty, a familiar pass of the cinematic commander. These are dramatic plausibilities, but also rationales for an overarching vision of the feminine as a seductive menace. The final fault for fleeing intimacy is never ascribed to masculine *angst* of being unmanned, humiliated, having one's ego absorbed in foul fusion, or merely being brought to ground or bored to death. Instead, it is *woman* who stands accused as prime disturber of the (male) peace.

In the Star Trek universe, one approaches woman with exceptional caution, frequently to contend with her for survival. Given the inevitability of her presence on a liberated vessel, one might try domesticating her; indeed, the *Enterprise's* female crew, unlike the legion of bumptious feminine intruders, are a generally placid lot, passively observing the action or servicing male endeavor. One might try doing without women altogether, like Spock. Whatever the *modus vivendi*, it is strongly implied that life would be easier and the work at hand would proceed more efficiently in trustworthy male company.

Similar figurations of adolescent misogyny, including the woman-hating companionability of the male pubertal gang, pervade film genres enjoyed by adolescents of all ages—the Saturday serials of my youth, private-eye capers, Westerns, horror and science fiction cinema, sundry epics of the road, the air, the sea, the jungle or mining camp. The masterbuilders of the adventures are "men's men" like Hawkes, Huston, and Walsh. Siegel and Peckinpah are their direct inheritors; recently the mantle has passed to Milius, Schroeder, Scorsese, Coppola, Lucas, Spielberg, Kotcheff, Eastwood, and Stallone.

The scenarios of these luminaries and others less worthy repeatedly summon up the same conservative, patriarchal ethos: a lonely hero or male group undertakes dangerous military or professional challenges, uncovers sinister plots, faces down a multitude of evils with exemplary valor and skill. Woman may be the occulted villain of the piece—the spider at the center of the web entangling the private eye, the symbiotic menace improbably toothed and clawed in weird cinema. In the "task-oriented" adventure film, she is kept essentially peripheral to the action as the hero's adoring girlfriend, the group's den mother, or raucous mascot. At best, she gains entry into the charmed circle by proving herself a diminished buddy. In another variation of the theme, a worthy female enemy is won over by the hero's character or sexuality—*viz.* the bondage of Pussy Galore in *Goldfinger*.

Star Trek evolves out of these "macho" genres into a decade of turbulent social and political change. The sexism, racism, and "rightism" of its antecedents do not usually jar within their social context or filmic text. However, the collision of genre conservatism with the jaunty liberalism of Star Trek's day does generate textual "uneasiness." Star Trek's illiberalisms often mix poorly with the overall progressive thrust of many episodes. One analogizes to the adolescent's struggle between outworn parental values and newer adaptive possibilities.

The internal wrenching with each Star Trek adventure varies, I suspect, according to the ideological bent of the individual writer. Scripts like "The Way to Eden" are virtual conservative apologias. In others, the influence of rightish or prejudicial tendencies is negligible. "Devil in the Dark," for instance, portrays a repellent alien who possesses strong sympathetic qualities once Terran xenophobia can be transcended.

Star Trek's sexism and misogyny constitute its most thoroughly reactionary problem, an egregious example of which is Shatner's hysterical portrayal of the feminized Kirk/Janet Lester in "Turnabout Intruder." Nevertheless, a few competent and attractive women do appear. The Romulan commander of "The Enterprise Incident," whom Spock stolidly romances during the rather unsavory theft of her ship's cloaking device, is quite admirable. (Beyond a shared ancestry, the two have much in common, are obviously drawn to each other, and would make excellent partners were it not for the fact that she is also the Federation's avowed enemy.) *Star Trek II: The Wrath of Khan* and *Star Trek III: The Search for Spock*, produced after a generation of advances in women's rights, contain several unambivalently likable, capable female characters: Dr. Carol Marcus, another former love of Kirk's who mothers his illegitimate child as well as the Genesis Project, and Lieutenant Saavik, the feisty Vulcan navigator.

Spock in the Spirit

Tales of exploration like Star Trek have always delighted adolescents. The teenager's thirst for new outer horizons often is matched by an inner quest for meaning. Beyond wondering what vocational path to follow or which friends to choose on life's journey, many youngsters ponder the agency which set them on the road and the fate awaiting them at its terminus. Star Trek rarely inquires after the Big Questions; no chaplain services the *Enterprise*. While Kirk occasionally waxes eloquent about the insatiable curiosity that drives man to the stars, his rhetoric, deconstructed, reads as a materialistic panegyric to the American Pioneering Spirit. Only Spock seems to hunger after ontological truth. In his search resides the final locus of adolescent identification I will address.

Spock's spirituality is firmly grounded in his heritage. Vulcan mysticism is a fascinating enigma to the Federation's other races. Though we know little of their beliefs, there appears to be much Zen in the Vulcans. They perceive unceasing change as a central aspect of existence. According to Spock, the universe's "infinite diversity in infinite combinations" is an abiding focus of their daily meditation. Their impressive achievements in art and science may be taken as a continuous realization of their contemplation. They have the kind of massive speculative intelligence that inclines one to seek a transcendent figure in the elegant tracery of mathematical logic. Under obscure circumstances, their *katra*—a psychic organ akin to an immortal soul—can be reincarnated.

Suffering may spur a spiritual vocation as decisively as one's own theological or intellectual antecedents. The void created by Spock's estrangement from parents, home, and self have intensified the normative anguish of adolescent alienation. His exile, the inherent spirituality of his temperament and race, all impart a special religious quality to his quest for a new belonging. Human companions and Starfleet duties cannot afford a final resting place for his perturbed soul; these are necessary but provisional attachments in the phenomenal realm. Like Terran mystics of East and West, Spock pursues a union more profound, with an ineffable ground of immanent reality.

Spock's philosophical and spiritual beliefs were to have been a major focus of Star Trek's canceled fourth season. Instead, they were developed in *Star Trek: The Motion Picture*, and to a lesser extent in *The Search for Spock*.

In *Star Trek: The Motion Picture*, Spock has retired to Vulcan for several years. Rigorous mental discipline prepares him for the supreme Vulcan test of *Kolinahr*—shedding all emotions. But he fails at the last moment: His human feelings are stirred by telepathic contact with a vastly intelligent entity sweeping through deep space. Sensing its purpose may be linked to his quest, he rejoins the *Enterprise*.

The entity, which calls itself V'Ger, is a megalithic living computer, crafted by a machine race from an ancient NASA Voyager satellite which fell through a black hole on the other side of the galaxy. The machine beings programmed it to wander the universe, learn all it could, then return to its "Creator" and yield up its data. After three centuries, V'Ger now travels back to its Terran origins. Unfortunately, it has conceived that the Creator is a mightier machine, and humans mere "carbon-based" infestations interfering with its mission. Hence, it destroys every living thing on its path back to Earth, until it receives the Enterprise's messages of friendship. Then it swallows the starship whole.

Spock's nearly fatal mind meld reveals that despite its awesome technology, V'Ger is an empty vessel, incapable of understanding the simplest emotion of friendship. "In all this magnificence, V'Ger finds no awe, no delight . . . no meaning . . . no answers." A short time later, Kirk discovers his friend on the bridge, a single tear coursing down his cheek, the only time Spock cries while in full possession of his faculties. "I weep for V'Ger as I would a brother," he tells the captain. "As I was when I came aboard, so is V'Ger now, empty, incomplete, searching. Logic and knowledge are not enough . . . each of us, at some time in our lives, turns to someone, a father, a brother, a God, and asks, why am I here? What was I meant to be? V'Ger hopes to touch its Creator, to find its answers. . . ."

(This crucial scene was inexcusably cut when *Star Trek:*

The Motion Picture was first shown; it was later restored in the televised and videotape versions.)

To study the crew, V'Ger vaporizes Ilia, a beautiful Deltan officer, and resurrects her as an android probe. Captain Will Decker, Kirk's protégé, had loved her when she was alive and now awakens the affection embedded in the Ilia-android's circuitry. As V'Ger enters Earth orbit, Kirk and his officers are taken to V'Ger's core, where the ancient satellite is enshrined. It is ready to transmit its enormous store of data but does not respond to the old NASA trigger code. Spock finds the antennae leads have been fused so that it can only be triggered manually: V'Ger wants the Creator's personal touch. Decker hurls himself forward to complete the code, embraces the Ilia-android, and both are engulfed in swirling plasmas of light. The entire V'Ger complex dissolves, leaving ship and crew unharmed. Afterward, Spock elects to remain onboard— "My task on Vulcan is completed."

The film's conclusion implies that V'Ger has discovered the meaning it sought through the infusion of human love; analogously, Spock will find the meaning of his existence by allowing himself access to his own tender feelings. Such materialist/humanist texts commonly assert that the heterosexual union is as much an intimation of the Divine as any being can reasonably expect. Since numerous conflicts bar him from woman's love, Spock must settle for the sublimations of male friendship.

An alternate reading rescues him from the bathos Spock occasionally seems to provoke in his narrators. It hinges upon a single question: Why, having come so far in his quest, does not *Spock* complete the trigger code and merge with V'Ger? Is he so surprised that he lets Decker slip under his guard? Hardly, for his reflexes are quicker than a human's. And even if Decker does catch him off balance, he is still powerful enough to push him away from V'Ger's control panel. Danger cannot stay his hand, for he repeatedly rushes against orders into the very teeth of death. I submit that his decision springs from a flash of altruism and insight. Mystic union cannot easily be prefigured by woman's affection for Spock given his chronic schizoid position. Furthermore, he knows Decker still loves Ilia, whatever her form. Nor can enlightenment come through fusion with V'Ger. All his life, Spock has been tormented by obsessional self-manipulation. He says, in effect, that even with its awesome power V'Ger still bears a peculiar taint of cog and wheels for him; it cannot possess this deadened connotation for Decker.

V'Ger, therefore, represents a tantalizing but rejected expedient, of which there are many along the seeker's path. Spock must employ less artificial means. Other Vulcans may dwell comfortably at home while they shed the constraints of ego desire and dualistic thought. His *Kolinahr* lies elsewhere, in far-off galaxies, in selfless service to the Federation with Kirk and McCoy at his side, in continued meditation on the eternally unchanging, unchanged source of his divided self. Through these expedients may he touch and be reborn into that profound emptiness that engenders, moment by moment, the universe's "infinite diversity in infinite combinations."

Personal death holds no qualms for this seeker. The ultimate ace of adolescent altruism—laying down his life for his friends in *Star Trek II: The Wrath of Khan*—is merely another minute metamorphosis in the ceaseless ebb and flow of creation. We shall leave him now, incompletely resurrected at the end of *The Search for Spock*. Unlike television's recycled heroes, Spock has served as a durable ideal for adolescents of all ages during the past twenty years. There is every reason to believe he will continue in the same capacity for generations to come.

It is utterly unimaginable that any actor other than Leonard Nimoy could play Spock. In the Star Trek pilot, Spock seemed like a gangly teenager. Nimoy grew palpably into the role to convey Spock's lucid intelligence, somber dignity, quirkiness, and wit. Offstage, Nimoy persistently refuses exploitation of Spock for commercial gain. He has avoided becoming permanently identified with his avatar, pursuing a remarkable variety of unrelated roles and work in other fields. One likes to think that Spock would have found him admirably "in character" on every score.

Harvey Roy Greenberg, M.D., is in private practice of psychiatry and psychoanalysis in New York City. He is also associate clinical professor of psychiatry at Albert Einstein Medical College. He has published frequently on both adolescence and cinema. The author expresses his appreciation to Mr. Alan Pakalns for furnishing invaluable research data.

ABOUT THE EDITORS

Although largely unknown to readers not involved in Star Trek fandom before the publication of *The Best of Trek #1*, WALTER IRWIN and G. B. LOVE have been actively editing and publishing magazines for many years. Before they teamed up to create TREK® in 1975. Irwin worked in newspapers, advertising, and free-lance writing, while Love published *The Rocket's Blast—Comiccollector* from 1960 to 1974, as well as hundreds of other magazines, books, and collectables. Both together and separately, they are currently planning several new books and magazines, as well as continuing to publish TREK.